CRITICAL P

"It is very rare that a coming of age novel transcends its inherent limitations and attains the complex emotional resonance of adult fiction. *Dragon Chica* does this with great aplomb. The book explores with subtlety and depth the mature, universal issues of identity and connection, but it also retains its direct appeal to younger readers.

"May-lee Chai has performed a remarkable act of literary magic."

—Robert Olen Butler, Pulitzer Prize-winning author
of *A Good Scent from a Strange Mountain*

"Eleven-year-old Nea has seen the very worst this world has to offer – from civil war in Cambodia, to the rice fields of the Khmer Rouge, to the bullying hallways of American public school. Thankfully, her heart and imagination bloom wide enough to let her continue longing for the best. As she grows into a woman, Nea navigates her difficult life with clear-eyed and courageous idealism. May-lee Chai has written a brilliant and important coming-of-age story about a young refugee who refuses to give up her search for that promised refuge.

"*Dragon Chica* is an important and deliciously readable novel that will hold you in thrall; you won't be able to look away from these pages, even as your eyes fill up with tears."

—Nina de Gramont, author of *Every Little Thing
in the World* and *Gossip of the Starlings*

"From the killing fields of Cambodia to a Chinese restaurant in the middle of the cornfields of Nebraska, *Dragon Chica* takes the reader deep into a compelling story about two sisters and the secret histories that surround them."

—Marie Myung-Ok Lee, author of *Somebody's Daughter*

"Powerful, witty and profound, *Dragon Chica* introduces readers to a new kind of American heroine."

—Alicia Erian, author of *Towelhead*

ALSO BY MAY-LEE CHAI

Hapa Girl: A Memoir
Glamorous Asians: Short Stories and Essays
China A to Z (co-authored with Winberg Chai)
The Girl from Purple Mountain (co-authored with Winberg Chai)
My Lucky Face: A Novel

Translation
The Autobiography of Ba Jin

DRAGON Chica

DRAGON
Chica

a novel by

MAY-LEE CHAI

GEMMA

Boston

First published by GemmaMedia in 2011.

GemmaMedia
230 Commercial Street
Boston, MA 02109 USA
www.gemmamedia.com

Printed in the United States of America

15 14 13 12 11   1 2 3 4 5

978-1-934848-48-7

Library of Congress Cataloging-in-Publication Data

Chai, May-Lee.
Dragon chica : a novel / by May-lee Chai.
     p. cm.
Summary: "Funny, bittersweet story of a Cambodian-Chinese refugee teenager coming of age in the American Midwest"--Provided by publisher.
  ISBN 978-1-934848-48-7
1. Refugees--United States--Fiction. 2. Cambodians--United States--Fiction. 3. Teenage girls--Fiction. 4. Adolescence--Fiction. 5. Maturation (Psychology)--Fiction. 6. Middle West--Fiction. I. Title.
  PS3553.H2423D73 2010
  813'.54--dc22
                              2010035196

CONTENTS

DRAGON
Chica

CHAPTER 1

The Shelf-Life of Miracles

"Hurry up, Sourdi!" I hollered to my older sister. I was packing the spring rolls Ma had made before she left for work that morning so that we could sell them to the pilgrims lining up to see the apparition of the Virgin Mary on the freezer case at Mrs. Lê's QuikMart. "If the taco trucks find out about the pilgrims, we are hella screwed!"

"You said a dirty word! You said a dirty word!" My little brother, Sam, started jumping up and down excitedly on the sofa bed that I hadn't bothered to fold up since it was Saturday and Ma had to work all day and wouldn't know. Plus, I was busy wrapping the spring rolls in Saran Wrap so they wouldn't leak through the paper bags and ruin my T-shirt again.

"Shuddup, squirt. You're not allowed to jump on the bed," I snapped. "Come over here and help if you're not gonna watch cartoons."

"I'm watching cartoons," he said and sat back down on the bed next to my younger sisters, the twins, Navy and Maly.

I finished packing the two grocery bags full of spring rolls when Sourdi made her entrance, emerging finally from our apartment's lone bathroom. She'd reached the age where she liked to lock herself in there to do her eyes and cover her pimples with Clearasil—though I could still see them under the Cover Girl—and make movie star faces in the mirror. I know what she did, because she used to let me stay in the bathroom with her when she put on her makeup. But this summer, when I was eleven and she turned fifteen, she locked me out, too.

"'Bout time," I said.

She ignored my sour mood. "Come on," she said, picking up one of the paper bags. "Y'all behave while we're gone, you hear me?"

"I'm in charge, I'm in charge!" Sam shouted, jumping again.

"Sourdi's in charge," I snapped. "Anything goes wrong while we're gone, we'll tell Ma." Then I grabbed my own sack and ran out the door after Sourdi.

It was a typical hot summer day as we headed over to the QuikMart, four and a half blocks from our apartment. We only had the one dinky air conditioner in the window that didn't work so good and two fans, so it actually felt better to be outside, although the asphalt was melting beneath our flip flops when we crossed the street. I turned to look over my shoulder to see if we'd left footprints, but Sourdi was impatient now, and tugged on my arm.

"Who's the slow poke now?" she said.

"It's just cuz you like Mrs. Lê's stupid son, Than," I said, and Sourdi pulled my hair, hard, so I stopped teasing her.

Then I could see them. Already snaking around the corner, two blocks from the QuikMart, all the Pilgrims come to see the Virgin, and my heart beat faster in my chest as I calculated how much more we could charge everyone, and I wished Ma had made more spring rolls. Sourdi ran ahead to get the Pepsis from Mrs. Lê. (She gave us a deal; she'd started charging admission so she was okay if we made a profit too. Maybe she figured if the people were fed and hydrated, they'd keep coming.) The Pilgrims were snaking down the sidewalk in an uneven line, some sipping from Icees and cans of Tab and thermoses of hot black tea, others just panting in the hot sunlight. Mostly the Pilgrims were older, people who had begun to fray around the edges, chipped teeth, thinning hair, liver spots, but there were a few families, women with squalling babies, and crippled people. A very few were just young, like the pair of round-faced nuns from India, their foreheads bright with sweat, smiling like happy Buddhas, who had arrived one Thursday and reappeared in line every day for a week. They remembered us, their bright black eyes lighting up and their tiny white teeth flashing in smiles as they waved me over, ready to buy their lunch. It was strange. They would wait in line all day, and then, just as it was their turn to go inside and see the miraculous appearance of the Holy Mother, they would give up their place and move to the very back. I asked Mrs. Lê about the mystery of it once, and she whispered almost in awe that it must be a form of penance. I nodded then sagely, even though I didn't know what that meant.

"Spring rolls! Fresh spring rolls!" I called out, and a couple of old people pushing a listless looking young man in a wheelchair waved to me.

It was amazing how much you could charge people for simple spring rolls when they were hungry and hot and desperate enough to wait for hours in the sun to see a shadow on some permafrost on a freezer case. I would've said that was the real miracle. If anyone had asked me.

We made three hundred forty-seven bucks that day. So we treated ourselves to a six-pack of soda and a box of rocket pops for the kids waiting for us at home. We figured Ma wouldn't mind if we spent a little of the money, since we were flush.

"She's gonna be so happy," I said to Sourdi as we walked home, sucking on our own popsicles. Mine was Green Apple, Sourdi's Grape Surprise.

"Who will?"

"Ma! Who do you think?" I stuck my green tongue out at her, wiggling it for effect.

She returned the favor, flashing her purple tongue at me.

Sourdi was always dreamy after talking with Than, although they didn't really talk that much. Mostly I talked to Mrs. Lê as she counted her money for the day while her husband restocked the shelves. Sourdi and Than stood there looking at each other like deaf mutes, until Than got up his nerve to say something dumb, like "Did you see that guy on 'The Price Is Right?' Man, what a freak! He thought the whitewalls retailed for three ninety-five! Three ninety-five for all four! Man, that's lame! Those were Firestone, man. Major tread." And Sourdi giggled, like he was so witty.

I had made gagging sounds then, but if she heard, Sourdi never let on.

Now as we crossed the street, the wind finally coming up, whipping loose plastic bags down the sidewalk, flinging them into the tree branches and on tops of fire hydrants, I tried to get Sourdi to stop thinking about Than.

"If Ma makes more," I said, "I bet we could sell double tomorrow. It's Sunday. All the church people will be coming in the vans, even from the 'burbs. You think we could make a thousand dollars maybe?" I tried to imagine what that would feel like in my hand. A thousand whole dollars.

"I dunno," Sourdi said, licking her popsicle daintily. "They bring potluck."

That was true. I hadn't thought of that. The church groups were organized in a way that the ordinary Pilgrims, who were just desperate and poor mostly, weren't.

"Still. I think we could sell more than today," I said. "It's like the crowds are just growing. Mrs. Lê said when her husband opened this morning at six, there were people camped out on the sidewalk. Word's spreading. They're thinking of staying open twenty-four hours like the Hinky Dinky in Dallas."

Heat lightning flashed in the distance.

"It's going to storm tonight," Sourdi said, as though she weren't listening to me at all. "Good. It's so hot. I can't sleep lately."

Then the first drops of rain hit the top of my head like pricks from an acupuncturist's needle. I held my left hand out. Thick raindrops pooled in my palm. "Look!" I tried to show Sourdi, when, all at once, the clouds like a flock of angry hens dropped hail the size of eggs upon our heads. "Ow!"

"Run!" Sourdi shouted.

I stuck my popsicle in my mouth, grabbed Sourdi's hand, and ran as fast as I could in my flip flops.

That night the storm raged for six hours. Ma came home from work drenched to the skin, just before the hail started falling again. The brown bag of leftovers she'd brought us for dinner had disintegrated in the rain, and she clutched the styrofoam containers to her chest.

"Here, Ma, let me help you." Sourdi jumped up from the sofa where we were seated, watching TV.

The weatherman interrupted "The A-Team" to show a Doppler radar image of an angry mass of red approaching like a marauding army. The thunder boomed. The lights flickered, and then the electricity cut out.

We ate by candlelight. The stove was electric, so we couldn't heat up the food, but it didn't matter. The kids were upset. The thunder reminded Sam of the sound of bombs falling. Once he started crying, the twins followed suit, and there was no consoling them. Ma held the twins, and Sourdi tried singing a lullaby for Sam. Still, he cried.

Sirens wailed, and I jumped up onto the sofa to peer out the window to see if I could see flames, a building burning up, a twister bearing down, but there was only a blur of lights as the fire trucks rushed down the street. Then, nothing but water pounding against the glass and the bright flashes of lightning.

Finally, the rain no longer drummed at the glass but calmed to a mere patter. Thunder growled in the distance, a hungry animal moving far away, and lightning forked infrequently. Sam stopped crying. I fluffed the pillows on the sofa bed so that he and the twins could curl up and fall asleep, and Sourdi went to the mattress in the corner that she and I shared and slept as well.

Only Ma and I remained awake in the pale blue light that seeped inside the apartment in the hour before dawn.

She used to say that was the only trait we shared in common, our insomnia.

Ma sat in the kitchen, before the humming air conditioner, and lit up a cigarette.

"I have such wonderful memories," Ma sighed. "When I was a little girl, before I was married, it was the best, most wonderful time of my life." Ma's night voice was dreamy, sensual. She only spoke to me in this voice when everyone else was fast asleep. It wasn't at all like her morning voice, her business voice, the loud voice she used for talking with the outside world. It was a spoiled child's voice, and it emerged from the very pit of her heart.

"I was very protected. My father would have done anything for me. I was his favorite." Ma smiled, remembering. Then she described how every night before she went to bed, her father would go to her room and methodically kill every insect he found. Cockroaches and mosquitoes, brown spiders and black, centipedes and scorpions, and all the ants, biting, flying, stinging, black ants, red ants, fire ants. He also killed the gentle bugs, beetles and crickets, even though they were supposed to bring good luck. He killed them all because she disliked them so.

Ma drew on her cigarette then exhaled a long sigh of smoke that curdled in the pale light of dawn as it slipped into our apartment.

"I pity you," Ma said to me. "You'll never have memories like that."

"I have good memories, Ma."

"No." Ma shook her head sadly. "I'm sorry." She added, tiredly, her voice beginning to fray at the edges, "It's already too late for you."

Then she patted me on the back. "You should go to bed. Go to sleep."

"I'm not tired."

"Go to sleep anyway. I have to get up soon." Then she stood up, stretched her back, and left me to go to her room. We only had the two rooms—her bedroom, our outer room with the kitchenette—and the bathroom, so I knew she didn't want to talk anymore.

I wished then that I knew how to talk sweet like Sourdi, in a soft voice that didn't make my mother irritable. Then I could get her to tell me what was bothering her. But I only knew how to speak in my one voice, and everything I tried to say seemed to make my mother sadder.

I went to bed then, lying down by Sourdi on the mattress without even bothering to change into my pajamas. I wasn't tired at all, and I knew I'd never be able to sleep, not with the refrigerator humming back to life, and the fans whirring, and Sam and the twins grunting and kicking and farting in their sleep. But when I opened my eyes again, the sun was shining bright as new nickels throughout the apartment, Sourdi was already locked in the bathroom, and Sam and the twins were watching TV. A Western, it seemed like, from the sound of the gunfire and the whooping cries of the movie Indians.

Because I overslept, we had a late start getting off with the spring rolls Ma had left for us to sell. I wondered how Ma always found time for everything. She could work all day, make us dinner, go to bed, and never forget to get up in time to make the extra spring rolls before leaving for work again. She never seemed to need an alarm.

"Do you think Ma takes drugs?" I asked Sourdi as we walked to the QuikMart.

"What?" Sourdi appeared genuinely shocked. "Are you crazy?"

"They showed us this movie in school. This kid takes drugs, and, in the beginning, he has a lot of energy, and he thinks he's a superhero. He never needs to sleep, so he can play superfly basketball and skateboard like a punk, and he can do his homework faster than the calculator. But then he gets all skinny and he has dark circles all around his eyes, and he thinks he can fly. He jumps out a window like Superman and dies."

"That's stupid," Sourdi said. "They just show you that so you won't take drugs."

"But Savannah Lee said there really were drugs that made you stay awake all the time. Her dad's a trucker, and she says her dad used to take them, but he got addicted, then he got in an accident, and now he's in prison. But they really worked for a while. You don't need to sleep for months."

"Savannah's a liar." But Sourdi chewed her lip, so I knew she was worried and thinking.

"Should we look in her purse 'for signs'?" I asked. Because that's exactly what the mother in the movie in school said. She didn't say what "the signs" were, but after she searched in her son's backpack, she looked straight into the camera and started to cry. Everyone else in class started laughing then, and I laughed, too, like I knew what it was all about, but I didn't really know.

"Don't talk so much, Nea. I have a headache."

Then Sourdi squared her shoulders and walked a little faster, so I was left in her wake, dodging the puddles and broken branches and trash that were strewn about the sidewalk after the storm.

I was so distracted by our conversation, by Sourdi's moodiness, by my own worries, that I didn't notice until we were practically at the door of the QuikMart that the Pilgrims were gone. Only their trash—the Pepsi cans and the wadded-up candywrappers and the empty chip bags and spent flash cubes—lay in a line extending behind us all the way to the gutter.

We ran inside the QuikMart where Mrs. Lê was sitting behind the counter looking desperate. She didn't even see us come in at first, so intent was she on shouting at her husband in Vietnamese. He was banging on something with a pipe while her son, Than, was busy trying to spray the freezer case with a plant waterer, trying to grow the miracle frost back. Apparently it had all melted during the storm when the electricity was cut off; all the permafrost was gone now, and with it, the Virgin Mary's face.

"I'm so sorry," Sourdi said.

"Maybe she'll come back," Mrs. Lê sniffed. "I put a mass card inside. And my grandmother's rosary."

Sourdi nodded politely.

"You girls, see if there's any popsicles you want. Just take them. Take them all. No good to me now."

"Cool! Thanks!" I ran to the freezer cases, and mostly everything was melted, but in the very bottom of one case, there were some Eskimo Pies, Strawberry Shortcake Good Humor Bars, and even a box of RocketPops that weren't too bad. They'd been in the very corner, frozen together. They were sticky, and half-way melted, but half-way good still. So I gathered them up. They were free, after all.

"Do you want some spring rolls?" I offered Mrs. Lê a bag.

She didn't answer but reached inside and pulled out a spring roll, and without looking, unwrapped it and popped it into her mouth whole, her cheeks bulging dramatically as she chewed and chewed. Then she did the same with the next spring roll, and the next. Finally, she began to cry, large messy mascara-laced tears that bounced down her cheeks in an endless stream.

Her husband and son were working on the freezer case, oblivious to her pain, as they banged away from behind with monkey wrenches and ratchets, louder and louder.

Sourdi and I waved good-bye quickly to Mrs. Lê and hurried home. Something about her despair seemed contagious.

That evening, Ma returned with more money than usual. She'd been paid, plus two weeks. We all knew what that meant: she'd been laid off.

But it was good news, Ma explained. She'd had a dream three nights in a row. Even though she'd tried to stop sleeping, if she even so much as dozed off, the dream came back to her. It was time to move again, she said.

Sometimes Ma had visions in her sleep and then she had to wait to understand what they meant, but this time Ma said she knew immediately. This neighborhood was not right for us anymore.

She'd had dreams like this in the past. Once in our first year in America, when we lived in the mustard-colored trailer our sponsors at the First Baptist Church rented for us, some of our neighbors got into a fight, and the police came to break it up. At first it had been the same as every night, the same kind of argument, with bottles breaking and a baby shrieking. Then a gunshot rang out. My sisters and brother and I clambered to the windows to see better, standing on the edge of the sofa bed, but Ma made us come down and move away from the glass.

She herself stood in the doorway, however, watching, her arms folded over her chest, her lips pressed together tightly, until the police finally came, their sirens wailing unhappily. Standing before the screen, Ma didn't move. She was bathed in the light from the police cars. The red light made her face look angry and the blue light sad.

She stood there watching as the police dragged the man and the woman away, both still shouting, and then drove off. Long after the police had left and the rest of our neighbors had gone back into their trailers, Ma continued to stand in the open door, her arms crossed over her chest, staring into the dark.

The next morning, Ma looked older. It was as though those red and blue lights had penetrated to her bones and changed her face. Sourdi said Ma was merely tired, it was only the shadows under her eyes, but I saw the way Ma's mouth turned downwards at the corners, the way her skin pulled away from her bones.

Ma announced over breakfast that she'd had a dream that we should move to the city. The Refugee Services Coordinator was going to help her find a job. He was supposed to be a good guy, a nice guy, a hero who'd escaped Cambodia by swimming to Thailand before the Khmer Rouge took over. That's how he'd lost his arm, he said. A shark bit it off.

When he and Ma first started dating, he liked to brag like that all the time.

I never believed him.

He had a name, but Sourdi and I called him "One Arm" behind his back.

One Arm liked to dress flashy, in a nice suit, even on a hot day, his hair perfect, heavily pomaded and slicked over the top of his head so that you couldn't see the bald spot, see that he was really a lot older than he pretended to be. At first glance, most people almost didn't notice the missing arm either, because he pinned up the extra sleeve onto his shoulder as if it were really just a scarf; he dressed with such aplomb.

Ma used to say that he had "élan." When he lied about something, but in a charming way, she called it "esprit." Later, when she was angry at him, she called it something else, but in the beginning he really enchanted her. I think she liked best of all his beautiful movie-star smile, all those white teeth. Ma's teeth were brown and some were missing. Gum disease, the Red Cross dentist had said, very common. But One Arm had never had to live in a work camp, eating gruel. He'd escaped.

One Arm worked for Refugee Services in Dallas and used to drive to our small town, some three hours west, periodically to check on us. After he got to know Ma, he started coming out more often.

Ma prepared special food just for One Arm. She let him eat first and made us wait until he was done, because our kitchen table was too small for all seven of us to squeeze around. She smiled when he spoke and listened without interrupting as he complained about all the hard work he did visiting all the other refugees. Ma nodded, and said, "You work so hard, it's not fair to you." She was lying because we all knew One Arm liked this job. People were grateful to him and always cooked him fancy dishes and treated him with respect, more respect than he would have had back home in Cambodia before the war. I could tell by the way he spoke that he had not been an educated man—he had a funny provincial accent, plus, he spat his bones out on the table. Whereas Ma always spoke beautifully, with a Phnom Penh accent, her grammar perfect, and she never spat.

Sometimes while we were living out in the sticks, Ma would burst into laughter for no apparent reason. She'd be standing in the kitchen, her arms elbow-deep in suds in the sink. Or she'd be hanging out the laundry to dry on the line that ran from the corner of our trailer to the neighbor's pecan tree, our underwear flapping in the wind with a sound like hands clapping, and Ma would bow, graciously receiving her applause, and then she'd laugh. Hysterically. Until she hiccupped and tears ran from her eyes, and still she laughed on and on.

We all joined in, giggling around her, touching the hem of her shirt, her arm, her thigh. We couldn't keep our hands off her when she was happy. It was as though we thought the feeling were contagious, something we could catch and pass among us as we had chicken pox and pink eye and bronchitis, one after the other, after we first started school.

But sometimes Ma sat in the kitchen with her head in her hands and refused to speak at all. She sat completely still, as though she'd been turned to ice.

And then my sisters and brother and I sat around her forlornly on the linoleum like a circle of stones.

One Arm did eventually find Ma a new job working in a Chinese restaurant in East Dallas.

He also stole all the money she'd saved from working as a maid, the job our sponsors had found for her at the Motel 6. I said then that we should call the cops, but Ma said we couldn't afford to call attention to ourselves. She said One Arm promised to pay her back; he was basically a good man but he gambled. She said he'd pay her back when his luck returned.

I didn't think One Arm was gonna pay her back, but I didn't say anything then.

I obeyed my mother in those days.

The next time we moved, Ma had had a dream about the war. In the dream, it was just as it had been in real life. She was walking through a minefield, the twins in her arms and Sam riding on her back. They were so thin in those days, they didn't weigh much. Ma was thin too, though, so we had to walk very slowly.

We only traveled at night, so the soldiers wouldn't see us and shoot us for trying to escape. But it made it hard to see, not just the mines— sometimes no one could see them, and you just died or you didn't—but we couldn't even see the stars. Clouds covered the moon, and we didn't know which direction to go. If we were headed east or west, south or north. If we were doubling back through the jungle or heading toward Thailand.

Ma made us all lie down once when the moon was hidden behind thick clouds. Lie down just where we had been standing so we wouldn't trip a mine and die. I remember lying down next to Sourdi, who fell asleep almost immediately. She had to carry me on her back most of the time, so she was very tired. I felt her breath on my neck.

A giant snake slithered by. It stopped, and I realized it must have seen the whites of my eyes. (I didn't know snakes could sense the heat of my body.) I didn't dare blink then. I hoped the snake would think my eyes were just stones, or bones, or glass, or metal. Something it wouldn't want to eat. Debris that lay in the fields everywhere, signs leftover from battles or bombings or soldiers laying mines so the people couldn't escape.

My eyes grew dry as dust. I wanted to blink. I almost didn't care if the snake bit me, or squeezed me to death, but finally the snake extended its forked tongue, touching a stone in its path, then quickly it slithered away, farther and farther, slinking in S shapes into the dark jungle behind us.

Then I heard my mother whisper.

"Are you awake?"

"Yes, Ma."

"Don't move. There's a bomb hidden in the dirt."

"I know, Ma."

"I can see this one," Ma said. "There's an arm bone beside it. So there must have been two bombs. But the person only stepped on the one. The explosion exposed the second bomb. Lying here, I can see it."

"I won't move, Ma."

"I fell asleep," Ma whispered. "I dreamed we were walking in the wrong direction."

"Are we, Ma? I saw a snake. It went behind us."

"Yes, that's right. We're going the wrong way. In my dream, I realized at the last second, but before we could turn around, I stepped on the bomb. Then I woke up." My mother's voice was parched, a raspy sound, the same sound when she cried without tears.

"It's okay, Ma. You didn't step on the bomb. It's good you had that dream."

"I know," she said.

And then slowly she got back onto her feet. She woke Sam and the twins, ordered Sam to hold onto her back. Then she picked the twins up, having wrapped them in cloth slings so she could carry them.

I woke Sourdi, and we turned around and walked in the opposite direction. Like the snake.

That's how we didn't die. Ma's dreams kept us alive.

Later, Sourdi would claim she was the one who was awake, she was the one whispering to Ma, and that she'd told me this story later. I only thought I remembered. But Sourdi never mentioned the snake. That's how I know this is my memory, not hers.

After the storm that destroyed the apparition of the Virgin Mary, Ma didn't tell me what her dream was that convinced her that we needed to move again.

"Where are we going, Ma?" I asked.

"I don't know yet," she said. "But we should start packing."

CHAPTER 2

The Letter

A week or so after the storm, the next part of our miracle arrived with the junk mail—Lillian Vernon catalogs, coupon flyers for various grocery stores—and the bills, which Ma was ignoring since we'd be moving soon anyway. We almost threw it away, but when Sourdi was clearing the table for dinner, she discovered the letter. The envelope was battered, torn along one edge. The Red Cross had sent it first to our sponsors at the Baptist Church in our old town, and the Baptists had forwarded it to our former address in East Dallas before the post office had sent it along to our latest apartment.

At first I thought it might be from One Arm, although I couldn't imagine why he was writing through the Red Cross. Maybe he'd been sent back to Cambodia, I thought. Maybe he was sending Ma back the money he'd stolen from her, but I was wrong.

"You should open it," I suggested slyly to Sourdi, who was holding the envelope up to the light so that she could just see the outlines of the letter folded inside.

"It's for Ma."

"It might be important. We might have to call her at work." (She'd found a temporary job in another restaurant while we waited to find out where she wanted us to move.)

"You open it." Sourdi pushed it across the tabletop at me like a dare. I snatched the envelope up, and I was ready to rip it open, truly I was, but the paper seemed so fragile, the neat handwriting on the front so precise, like something ancient discovered in a tomb or a time capsule, something that might disintegrate if exposed to air. I examined the envelope instead. Whoever had written the address had also decorated the envelope with vines and curlicues, little dots, like leaves dancing across the pale blue paper.

"That's Khmer. You don't remember, do you?"

"What?" I had no idea what she was talking about.

"It's how we used to write." Sourdi took the letter from me and put it on top of the refrigerator where the little kids couldn't get at it.

I didn't correct her. It was the way *she* used to write. Never me. I never learned.

When Ma came home that evening, she was surprised that we all looked up the moment she came in the door. I turned off the television. We waited while Sourdi grabbed the letter off the refrigerator and held it out to Ma.

"This came for you."

Ma reached for the fragile, airmail envelope with the spidery handwriting on it. Then she withdrew her hand quickly as though the letter were a snake that could bite. She sat down heavily in her chair, staring. Sourdi put the letter on the table before her.

"What is it, Ma?" Sourdi looked frightened, her dark eyes narrowing. Because she was afraid, the rest of us felt afraid, too.

Now we clustered around the table, pressing close to Ma.

She told us to back off, to give her room to breathe. We were suffocating her, we were like animals, she said. Like animals in a cage, pushing against each other out of fear until the animal in the very center would have the life squeezed out of it.

We backed away. Ma took a deep breath and ripped open the fragile airmail envelope.

"Golldang! Golldang!" Ma said in English. Then she began to cry. She held the letter in one hand and covered her face with the other as her shoulders shook.

"What happened?" Sourdi tried to read the letter even as Ma flapped it through the air. She grabbed hold of an edge and bobbed up and down, trying to keep the page smooth as Ma continued to wave her hand. Sourdi could recognize a few words in Khmer, but not enough to read the letter. "Tell us, Ma!" she begged.

But for several minutes, forever, all Ma could say was "Golldang!" in English, over and over, like the chorus of a song.

"Golldang" was our all-purpose exclamation word. We had heard it so often that we learned to use it the way other people might say "Oh!" It could mean anything. The letter might say we had won a million dollars, or it might be telling us that we'd failed in the U.S. and were being sent back to the refugee camp in Thailand or even back to Cambodia. Who could tell?

Finally, Sourdi began to cry in frustration, biting her trembling lips, sniffing her runny nose, as fat tears rolled down her cheeks. Then Navy and Maly and Sam cried, to see Sourdi crying. I wanted to slap all of them. I stamped my foot on the linoleum. "I'm going to call the police!" I shouted in English.

Then Ma uncovered her face and looked at me quizzically. She clicked her tongue against the roof of her mouth. "Don't shout," she said. "Did I teach my girls to shout like this?"

I hung my head.

Ma wiped her nose on a paper napkin, then sighed. She spread the letter out on the tabletop, smoothing it flat with the palm of her hand. Then Ma told us that everything was going to be all right. We were saved, she said. It was a miracle. She smiled.

It had been a long time since I'd seen Ma smile like this, with her whole face, even her eyes.

Seeing her smile made my entire body feel light.

The letter was from a man named Chhouen Suoheang. My Uncle. The man married to my mother's oldest sister. The letter meant that we had family, alive and living in the United States, in a place called Nebraska, in fact. We looked it up on the map in my social studies book, and yes, it was there, a real state, part of the United States. A miracle.

"Oh, this letter is so old. They'll think we're dead. They'll think we're lost forever."

"Maybe it's a lie," Sourdi suggested, chewing on her nails. "Maybe they're imposters."

"Don't talk nonsense. Give me some paper." Ma sat down at the kitchen table as Sourdi carefully tore a sheet of paper from her notebook (Language Arts).

Her tongue pressed against her teeth, Ma broke the lead on her first pencil from pushing too hard. She switched to a Bic pen, but each time she placed it against the paper, the sheet ripped, again and again, line after line. Ma's hands shook as she tore a new sheet from Sourdi's notebook. She smoothed it against the table top, licking her lips, as she held the pen over the page. While we stood in a ring around her, holding our breath, she put the pen to the paper very lightly and wrote:

"Dearest Older Sister, dear Older Brother . . ." she wrote politely, repeating the words as she traced their outlines in her most beautiful cursive.

She didn't tell them that Pa was dead, or about all the jobs she'd had, about the shooting we'd witnessed or how all her money had been stolen. She wrote only happy news. Grateful words. Loving phrases.

Ma finished her letter, said a prayer to the Buddha, then sealed it.

"I can mail it for you, Ma," Sourdi said, frowning still.

"I'll mail it tomorrow before I go to work," Ma said, her tone so casual, it made my stomach hurt with fear. She talked of the letter as though it were a bill. As though it were nothing special. But I could see in her face that she was as anxious and scared as Sourdi.

I bit all my fingernails off until even my thumbs were bleeding.

That night, I lay beside Sourdi on our mattress and whispered so we wouldn't wake Ma.

"Do you remember them? Uncle and Auntie?"

"You don't remember them at all?" Sourdi squinted at me in the dark.

"How could I remember them? I was too young."

Sourdi licked her lips. "I remember them all right."

She said Uncle had been a prosperous man, an engineer who had worked for the government. He and Auntie had lived in a large house with three stories and many servants in central Phnom Penh, the capital city. He'd had a car and a driver and his children had rooms filled with toys. Auntie had worn nothing but silk dresses and high heels, just like the foreign ladies whose husbands were diplomats or businessmen or else drug lords in the city.

"What were our cousins like? How old are they now? Will we meet them?" I asked, but Sourdi remembered other things.

She said Uncle's boss was implicated in a plot to overthrow the president, Lon Nol, who was very paranoid. Lon Nol was suspicious of everyone in his own government. He understood how subordinates could turn on you. He himself had come to power after he'd staged a plot to overthrow the last chief of state, Prince Sihanouk. Now Lon Nol had Uncle's boss arrested. Soldiers escorted him from his office, guns to his back. No one expected to see him alive again.

Sourdi said a neighbor had come riding back home on his Vespa just to tell Ma and Auntie what had happened. They all had assumed Uncle would be arrested, too, maybe not immediately, but sooner rather than later. Ma and Auntie went to the temple to pray. They didn't trust anyone, not even the servants, so Sourdi had babysat all the children.

But fortunately, Uncle hadn't gone to the office that day. Maybe he'd been feeling under the weather. Maybe it had been Auntie who was not feeling well. She was often sick, Sourdi said, mysterious ailments that kept her bedridden for weeks on end. Anyway, something had delayed Uncle so that he was not at the office to see the soldiers drag his boss away, upending file cabinets and desks, destroying typewriters and terrifying the secretaries, because the soldiers had no real idea how to investigate a crime—they only knew how to terrify the accused. Uncle heard about it later from a friend who had heard from someone who was there but who had been too lowly to be arrested at the time. When Ma and Auntie returned from the temple, Uncle was already with Sourdi, saying goodbye to the children. He said he had to leave that night before the soldiers came for him, too.

"Where did he go? To America?"

Sourdi shook her head. "I always thought he went to Thailand. Or maybe Singapore. He had cousins there. I overheard Ma and Auntie talking once. But he was already gone when the Khmer Rouge came. Ma said he'd always been a lucky man. Some people have luck, some people don't."

I nodded then as though I understood. I had more questions, but Sourdi wanted to sleep and turned away from me. Lying in the dark, listening to the jangling fan, the humming fridge, I closed my eyes and tried to imagine my grand, rich, wonderful uncle. He was tall, I decided. And handsome, like a Hong Kong movie star. When he arrived in East Dallas for us, I figured he'd come with a suitcase full of silk dresses just our sizes, and new Barbies, because I had wanted a new Barbie ever since Sam set my last one on fire, and I would recognize him immediately. "Uncle, you've come back!" I'd cry out, placing my palms together before my face in a gesture called the *sompeah*, like the old people did in the Buddhist temple we visited once when Ma didn't have to work one weekend.

In the weeks that passed after we had received the letter, I waited eagerly for Uncle to arrive at our apartment in a gleaming black Mercedes, his gloved chauffeur at the wheel, just as Sourdi had described. But a full month passed and our savior uncle was still just a name on an envelope, a filmy sheet of spidery handwriting, hardly more real than a memory or a dream.

And then, the next part of our miracle.

Another envelope arrived. The same spidery handwriting looping across the paper. Ma's hands shook so much that she handed the envelope to Sourdi, who opened it carefully, with the edge of a knife inserted just beneath the fold. She sliced the paper delicately as tissue. Then my sister placed the letter on the table before Ma, who held her fluttering hands pressed tightly together in her lap.

"We received your letter," Ma read aloud. "We received your letter," she repeated. She put her hands across her eyes as though there were nothing more to read. "We received your letter."

Ma spoke so quickly as she read aloud in Khmer, I could barely follow. Sourdi had to translate. (I didn't want to admit, I was forgetting words, or maybe Ma was speaking words I'd never learned.) In addition to Uncle, Ma's oldest sister—her only living sister, our only living Auntie—was in Nebraska now, she and her husband. They'd just opened a Chinese restaurant that spring. They were well.

Ma laughed then, laughed until she cried and then started laughing all over again.

"A Chinese restaurant is like a bank," Ma said, waving the letter in the air like a winning lottery ticket. "My father used to say that. 'If you work in a restaurant, you're just a teller, but if you own the restaurant, you own the bank.'"

"Did your father own a restaurant?" I asked.

"Of course not! My father was a teacher. You don't remember your own grandfather." Ma shook her head, but with the miracle letter in her hand, it was hard for her to remain angry, even at me. "My father's father owned a restaurant," Ma said, and then she laughed some more.

"Back home," Ma said, meaning in Phnom Penh, before the war, "all the families who owned the big Chinese restaurants were wealthy. They could afford to send their children to school in France. The men had enough money to keep several wives, and even the first wives had lovers. It's true. I saw them with my own eyes."

"You saw their lovers?" I asked, wide-eyed.

"No. I saw their restaurants. And they were always busy, night and day. They made so much money, there were guards at every door." Ma sighed, thinking about the past. And I sighed, too, pretending to remember.

"Do they want to see us?" asked Sourdi, eyes wide.

"Of course they do! We're family."

"All of us? Or just, you know, some of us?"

Ma scowled. "All of us. We're all the same family. That's all that matters. Family is family."

Ma wrote another letter and another and another, and each time a reply came back, letter after letter after letter, miracle after miracle after miracle. There were a few phone calls, too, although they cost too much and weren't as useful, because Ma had a tendency to cry at the sound of her oldest sister's voice. She'd cry until she couldn't speak, her voice turned hoarse, and once when I pressed my ear close to the receiver, I could hear a voice at the other end, crying hoarsely as well, without saying any words. Then after this kind of exchange for many weeks, the last and best part of our miracle occurred.

Uncle wrote, saying that he spoke for himself and his wife both, and they were asking us to come to join them in Nebraska, in business paradise, where there were no gangs and where hard work was rewarded. He said that family was family and should stick together. Would we come to help run the Family Business?

Ma didn't hesitate before agreeing. She understood quite well that there was no point waiting around for our miracle to turn sour, to melt in a thunderstorm and break our hearts. It was time for us to move. She'd known. She'd dreamed everything.

And so we packed up our apartment, Ma said good-bye to her boss at the restaurant where she gutted fish and chickens, and we stuffed everything we owned into Hefty bags and plastic milk crates we found

behind the 7-Eleven. We climbed into Ma's dusty dented Ford that used
to belong to One Arm and headed north to Nebraska.

We left quickly, not because we were naive or simple or foolhardy,
any of these things people might want to accuse us of being, but rather
because we understood about miracles all right, how their shelf life was
as long as a butterfly's summer.

CHAPTER 3

Last Chance, Nebraska

The highway stretched before us like the long, narrow blade of a knife. The sky touched the earth in every direction, empty even of clouds, as blank as a sheet of paper. The air was too hot for color. Sourdi hummed along with the radio for hours, and then after a while she stopped. I couldn't remember when exactly; at some point, I realized she was silent, that was all.

For hours there were no towns, no buildings visible from the highway save the occasional abandoned barn, faded and derelict. Just the dark earth, the corn and wheat and soybeans just beginning to grow, a thick green carpet swaying in the wind. In the distance, hidden behind a knot of trees, I imagined there were farmhouses, people, dogs, but on the highway, this was only a guess.

Sourdi and Ma sat in the front seat, the television and the tape player balanced between them. My younger brother and sisters stretched out in the back, leaning against me, kicking, scratching, farting. They'd fussed nonstop for sixteen hours straight before they, too, at last had fallen into a deep slumber. Hefty bags of clothes lay on the floor. My feet rested on top of a crate of dishes, pushing my knees up uncomfortably into my chest. It hadn't seemed as though we owned many things when they were spread about the apartment, but now with everything we owned packed into the car, it seemed we had too much.

Heat waves shimmered above the highway, forming imaginary lakes, pools of cool blue water that disappeared just as our tires would have splashed across the banks. If I squinted, the jade fields on either side of the highway appeared like water, spreading all around us, to the very edges of the flat earth, green as the ocean before a storm, simmering.

Then it seemed as though we were driving across a narrow bridge, trying to cross the entire ocean before the weather turned and the green waves began to lap at the sides of the road, reaching higher, swirling around our tires, sweeping us away. The sea was like that, deceptive. It could hide its anger until it was too late. I didn't know yet about the fields.

I turned away from the window and stared at the back of my mother's head, observing the way her short black hair curled away from her sweaty brown neck. I couldn't see her face in the rear-view mirror, couldn't tell if she looked sad or determined or excited still, if she was squinting behind her dime-store sunglasses, suspiciously surveying this flat empty land, or if she had a faraway look in her eyes, as she imagined our miraculous future in Business Paradise, the Family Reunited, our Saviors stalwart and kind.

Her hands gripped the steering wheel tightly, her knuckles glowing yellow through her skin. She held the steering wheel as though she thought it might try to jerk free of her hands and take us in another direction.

"Tell us about Auntie again, Ma," I asked from the back seat. "Tell us how rich she was."

"My sister, ha!" Ma laughed, a sound like a bark escaping from her throat. "She lived her life as though she were living in a book." Ma shook her head. "She always had to have the best."

Then she told us all the arrogant, impractical, glamorous things her oldest sister had done: the marriage party that had lasted three days, the three-story house with servants on every floor, the shiny black car and the man who wore white gloves just to drive it, the French accent Auntie had adopted even though she couldn't speak a word, the high heels, the makeup, the perfume imported from Paris.

"I said to her, 'Why do you need to smell like that? As soon as you walk on the sidewalk, you'll smell like everyone else, like food, like sweat, like this city. Why waste your money? Who'll notice the difference?' And my sister said to me, 'I'll know the difference, that's who! I'll know.'" Ma clicked her tongue against her teeth. "My sister was crazy."

For Chinese New Year, Uncle paid a man to come to the house and light strings of red firecrackers outside the door while another man played on a horn and a third man beat two cymbals together to drive away evil spirits. Uncle didn't believe in evil spirits—he was an educated man—but he'd wanted his children to see the traditional Chinese celebration.

In those days, before the Khmer Rouge won the civil war, all the different ethnic groups—the Chinese, the Vietnamese, the Cham Muslims, Cambodians from north and south, the French, anyone—could intermingle in the cities. Many intermarried. Only when the Communists took over did this kind of mixing become taboo, and a mixed background became an almost certain death sentence. We had to lie then. Pretend we weren't mixed people, weren't what the Communists called "new people" because they considered us alien to traditional culture, even though Chinese had been in Cambodia for more than five hundred years, and Cambodian culture had always been mixed.

Ma had married a non-Chinese. Maybe that's what saved us. Maybe nothing but dumb luck saved us.

Before Ma was married, she used to go to her eldest sister's house for the New Year to receive her red envelope, and she'd seen the firecracker man and the musicians at work. She'd pressed her ears closed with her fingers, but still the sound like thunder exploding from a tin drum found its way into her skull. Afterwards the red paper wrappers lay on the sidewalk in pointed mounds, tall as her waist. Three old women with bamboo brooms had had to sweep the street for half a day to clear the red away.

Ma said her sister had spoiled all her children. They behaved like members of the royal family. If they ran about the house and broke something or did something wrong at school or caused any kind of problem at all, the servants were punished instead of them. Once, when Ma had let Sourdi go over to their house to play, the daughter had pulled Sourdi's hair and made her cry, but it was the maid whom Auntie criticized. "You can't even watch two little girls?" she'd said, and the maid had bowed her head and apologized.

"My sister," Ma sighed, "she really knew how to live."

"We're all going to stay, aren't we, Ma? All of us?" Sourdi asked.

"That's what the letter said. *All* of us."

Sourdi leaned her head on her arm, letting the wind whip her hair about her head like the tail of a kite in a storm. She didn't hum anymore.

"Do you remember Uncle and Auntie, Nea?" Ma asked.

"Me? No."

"Not one bit? You don't remember anything I told you?"

"Why would I remember them? Sourdi was the one who played over in their house, you said." I must have let my voice slip a bit. Sounded irritable instead of respectful. It was hot in the car; the road was so long; I hadn't meant to, but I couldn't help myself. Anyway, Ma looked annoyed then. I'd spoiled her happy mood.

Now she fell into a long silence that she refused to break, and I took to staring out the window again at the endless jade fields and the steely blue sky and the waves of shimmering heat rising above the asphalt.

CHAPTER 4

The Ghost in the Window

We took the first exit for the town where Auntie and Uncle were supposed to be living, but it took us three passes through this village before we could find any Chinese restaurant.

The business district was not quite four blocks long, marked by a J.C. Penney at one end and a hardware store at the other. In the middle, there were the Blue Bunny ice cream parlor, a five and dime, a funeral home, a sandwich shop, a fabric store, a photography studio, and seven bars. The post office was on one side of Main Street and the police station on the other. There were also two grocery stores, a Piggly Wiggly and a Tom & Bud's, at opposite ends of town. A couple service stations were sprinkled conveniently in between. Next to the J.C. Penney was a vacant building that, we learned later, had once been a very successful John Deere outlet, but since the farm economy had taken a turn for the worse, it had closed shop and its wares consolidated into the main showroom in Yankton, a larger town of ten thousand about thirty miles northeast across the South Dakota border. A branch of the Missouri river ran along the eastern edge of town, which was consequently known as a flood plain. On the drier, western border were the local grain elevator and a few stores that sold farm implements, Purina feeds, and veterinary supplies.

We found the restaurant finally on the far northwest corner of town, practically on the border of the town limits, just off the last exit on the state highway, near a Super 8 and a laundromat. Someone had painted the squat building a bright red; it stood out like a firecracker against the deep green of the cornfields. A lighted sign proclaimed "The Silver Palace." It was the tallest pole in the parking lot and would become, we soon discovered, a magnet for lightning strikes. There was also a bright yellow plastic banner across the front of the building. It caught the wind and flapped ferociously, although in rare moments when the wind subsided we could just make out the words "Grand Opening."

As we stood in the parking lot after our long ride in our cramped car, our boxes pressing against our knees, I stared at the Palace and tried to imagine that it looked like the Family Business that would save us all, that would send me to college and rescue Ma from night shifts gutting chickens, the kind of Chinese restaurant that needed guards to protect all the money hidden inside.

I couldn't tell how Ma felt, whether she was still excited or if her silence meant that she was worried, or even panicked, by the emptiness of the sky above us and the flat fields around us, whether she wondered as I did where all the people were, and who were the customers, when it seemed as though we were the only living people left on earth. I looked up at Sourdi, who was standing between me and Ma, to see if I could read the answer in my sister's face, but she looked merely sweaty and tired from the long drive. She was rubbing her eyes with one hand.

"I'll wake the kids up," Sourdi said.

"Let them sleep," Ma said. "They wake up, they start yelling all over again." She smiled then, and I knew she was in a good mood. Maybe she'd realized we'd made a wrong turn. Maybe she just wanted to go in and ask directions so that we could find our real family's restaurant. Ma surveyed the Palace, a hand over her eyes to shield them from the sun beating down from the cloudless sky.

"It's beautiful," Ma said finally, and for a second I thought she was joking, but it wasn't like her to be sarcastic.

"Mmm-hmm." Sourdi nodded. "Our own restaurant." She craned her neck to read the grand opening sign again.

"It's not ours," I pointed out quickly.

"Auntie's then. And Uncle's." Sourdi scowled. "It's *our* family's. That means all of us. Right, Ma?"

Before Ma could answer, an old man came running out the front door. He waved his hands in the air excitedly, and Ma gasped. Then she ran towards him. They met on the sidewalk, Ma covering her mouth with her hand, shaking her head, as the old man put a hand on her elbow. He smiled, revealing all the holes in his mouth where his teeth should have been. They spoke so fast, I couldn't understand a word they said. Ma was crying. She wiped the tears away quickly on the back of her hand, again and again, the gesture like a cat cleaning its whiskers.

I wondered who this old man was. Maybe a servant. Maybe a worker our rich aunt and uncle had hired to help them run their business. He was wearing a long-sleeved cotton shirt despite the heat and tan cotton pants with handprints in flour along the thighs. Because of all the missing teeth, even when he smiled, his face appeared to be grimacing, as though he'd been in a fight. His hair was mostly gone, and what was left was gray. His skin was cracked and lined.

Ma pointed in our direction, and the old man turned toward us. He smiled again, his skin pulling back from his mouth.

"Don't just stand there," Ma said. "Come say hello to your uncle."

I couldn't move. I stood rooted in place, hoping there'd been a mistake, that Ma had misspoken, or was only polite. He was not really Uncle, but just a man she was calling an uncle. I grabbed hold of Sourdi's hand beside me, and she squeezed my hand back tightly.

Then the man who was certainly not Uncle came to us.

"You look just like my wife," he said to me. "I mean, when she was younger. When she was your age."

I looked at my feet.

"Oh, no," Ma said, politely. "She's much too tall. It's all this American food she eats." Ma shook her head. "She's going to be tall as a boy."

"So beautiful," he said, turning to Sourdi. "You've become a young lady since I last saw you."

Sourdi blushed.

"But where are the others?" He turned to Ma, confused.

"They're still sleeping." Sourdi pointed to the car, and the old man nodded.

"Go wake them," Ma said.

"No, let the little ones sleep. I'll just take a look for myself." He ran over to the car. We watched from the sidewalk as he peered inside the dusty windows.

"Do you remember your uncle now?" Ma asked us.

"I think so," Sourdi began, but I interrupted: "It's not him, Ma. It's not."

Ma frowned at me. "What are you talking about?"

"It's a mistake. He's not really Uncle."

"Don't talk crazy," she whispered. Then she pinched my ear between her finger and thumb as though I were still a small child, as though a little pain could make me see things her way.

Then the old man came back toward us, and Ma dropped her hand from my ear and smiled sweetly.

"Let me show you inside," the old man said, and he opened the door for Ma. Sourdi followed them obediently, but I hung back on the sidewalk. I wasn't going to follow this Pretender, this charlatan, this man who was certainly not our rich, savior Uncle. Auntie who always had to have the best would not have married such an old man. Why couldn't Ma see?

It was too hot in the car so I paced on the sidewalk. To my left, the soybean and cornfields were marching up to the state highway, a sea of green as far as I could see. To my right, the large empty parking lot, with the Super 8 at one end and the laundromat behind it. A paper bag blew across the asphalt, then caught on a light pole, flapping furiously like a pinned butterfly.

I turned back to examine the Palace, this place Ma insisted upon claiming as our own. There was a long bank of windows in the front, facing the highway and the fields. Someone had taped a hand-lettered sign in the door: "Chinese and Cambodian Cuisine." The windows had been recently washed. They reflected the fields and the road and my squinting face.

I noticed there was a window in the attic above the restaurant, with the curtains drawn. Then the curtains moved, and I saw a face staring out at me. It was a strange, terrible face, split in two, dark on one side, light on the other. A face like the half moon. A ghost's face. Before I could gasp, the curtains fell shut, and the face disappeared.

Suddenly a shadow passed across the asphalt, moving my way. A cloud of white hovered in the sky, rising over the Palace roof, coming closer, growing larger, casting a shadow over me like a net. The cloud began to descend, behind the Palace. I followed the sidewalk around the building just in time to see the cloud disintegrate into a hundred seagulls. I covered my head and darted behind the metal dumpster, but the birds were not interested in me.

The gulls circled over the trash, swooping and diving, the wind filled with their mewling and cawing. They fought over bits of chicken flesh, their feathers flying like snowflakes. They stole bones from each other's beaks, tore mushrooms in two, pecked at empty cans, and still more birds appeared, bobbing in the sky, crying loudly.

"Hey!" a voice called to me.

Another old man, skinny as a wishbone, stood on the back steps of the Palace. He was wearing a long apron stained with blood over his clothes and held a trash bag in one veiny hand, a cigarette in the other. He smiled at me, revealing a mouth of long, nicotine-stained teeth. "You the niece?" he asked in an accented English.

I shook my head.

"I'm the cook." He nodded, smiling, and then tossed the trash bag into the dumpster, where it split open. The frenzied seagulls began to fight amongst themselves, their wings beating rapidly, feathers flying into the air, their cries rising above the wind. "They always wait for me," the cook said, jabbing a crooked thumb at the gulls. "Don't be scared."

"I'm not!" I said.

He laughed then, his eyes disappearing into the folds of his skin. "Welcome," he said. Then turned and went back inside the Palace.

"I'm not staying here," I called after him, but the screen door slammed shut.

I turned to watch the birds squabbling over the garbage. One large gull, its wingspan nearly twice as wide as the others', flew towards me, a long bone in its beak. It seemed to hang suspended in the air, perfectly buoyed by the wind, bobbing gently up and down. It peered directly at me then winked one yellow eye.

In a few minutes, the feeding frenzy was over. The flock rose and quickly disappeared into the clear sky.

I stood in the parking lot, frozen, staring up after them until the white cloud of their bodies was a mere speck above the horizon.

The wind blew an empty can of baby corn across the asphalt.

"I've been waiting for you," a voice said behind me.

I jumped and turned. A figure was approaching, walking around the side of the Palace, an old woman with a terrible face, one side dark, one side pale, a long purple scar like a serpent running from her cheek to her throat.

It was the ghost from the window.

Her snaky hair writhed in the wind. She raised one withered hand, palm upwards, and took a step towards me.

I shrieked and took off running. I ran around the other side of the Palace, as fast as I could. I was going to run to our car and lock myself inside with the little kids, but when I rounded the front of the Palace, I found the ghost was headed my way, standing between me and the car. I had no choice but to run inside the Palace itself.

The old man who was not Uncle was seated at a table with Ma and Sourdi, drinking tea. They looked up in surprise as I ran inside, my face red from the heat, breathing hard.

"Look out!" I shouted. "She's coming!"

Then all at once, Ma stood up from her stool, her eyes widening. She put her hand to her throat, as though she could not breathe.

I turned and saw that the ghost had followed me inside. Before I could say anything, Ma rushed past me and grabbed the old woman by the arms. "My God!"

"Little Sister," the ghost said.

"All these years, I thought you were dead," Ma said. "I never thought I'd see you in this life again."

Ma put her arm around Auntie's back, Auntie put her head against Ma's shoulder. They stood like this for some time.

CHAPTER 5

A Million Shades of Black

Auntie apologized that she had not been able to greet her sister properly, explaining that she'd been resting upstairs. There was a little apartment there. Originally she and Uncle had thought about renting it out for extra income, but then Auntie had found it useful for her bad days, when she felt too tired to work, when her head hurt, when she grew dizzy, when her heart stopped beating.

"Your heart," Ma gasped.

Auntie shook her head.

"You should wake me," she said to the old man who was now un-questionably Uncle. She scowled. "This is my sister!" She took Ma's hand in hers as they sat together in a booth. "My baby sister!"

"Your face," Ma cooed, stroking Auntie's darkened flesh, where her skin had been burnt, the waxy pale side where the scar tissue had formed and the raised purple scar that ran down her cheek to her throat. "Your beautiful face," Ma whispered.

Auntie unbuttoned the cuff of her blouse and slowly rolled the cloth up her arm to her elbow, revealing the skin beneath, the crisscross of scars, her flesh patterned like the weave of an elaborate basket.

Ma cried to see her arm. She shook her head, back and forth, back and forth.

"The Red Cross doctor, he said to me, 'What a lucky woman! It's a miracle! You kept the arm with cuts like that!' He said I was lucky because he didn't see what happened to my son. What happened to my baby." Auntie shook her head as though she could dislodge the memory, tip it out the side of her head like water.

Ma stroked the inside of Auntie's arm, her fingers fluttering above the skin, touching down here and there, like nervous moths hovering around the flame of a candle.

They sat in a back booth, while Uncle brought them tea, and Auntie told us how she'd walked through a mine field, carrying her youngest son in her arms, her middle boy following behind her. The oldest son was sent away to a work camp at the beginning of the war, and she never saw him again.

Auntie waited too long to leave with her sons, she said. The soldiers watched her night and day. She should have left sooner, but she was afraid. Too many people like her, city people, had been beaten to death before her eyes. Auntie was afraid. She tried to work in the fields, she tried to obey, but then a woman she knew, a woman who had a run a restaurant in Phnom Penh, fell while planting rice and broke her ankle, and the soldiers then convened a meeting, forcing everyone in the village to watch as they beat the woman to death with shovels. An example, they said, of what happened to lazy city people who didn't know how to plant rice.

Auntie ran away with her sons that night, while the soldiers slept. But by now she was too weak. She was too tired from the work, the worry, the fear, the lack of food. She should have carried both boys. She should have carried them the whole way, she said, but she couldn't think. She made the older boy walk. How old was he when she thought he was old enough to walk by himself? Was he seven? Eight? But he was so thin. In her memories he seemed even younger. She should have carried them both, she told us, over and over, shaking her head. She should have found a way.

"We were walking in the fields, in the dead fields where nothing grew anymore. The fields with bones. We were walking in the night. I was afraid. The moon was bright this night, the kind of night where soldiers can see who is running away. I carried my youngest son but made the older boy walk behind me. I hadn't slept for weeks. Then my boy saw something. Something shining in the moonlight. 'Look!' he calls to me, and his hand slips from mine, like water, and he is running away from me, he is running towards the shiny metal thing. What does a boy know? He was so close. I should have run after him, but I was afraid and then I heard the click, like bone against bone. The click, and then the bomb. I fell to the ground. I found his head but not his body. He was so close when the bomb went off beneath him, my face was cut by the metal, my arm was burned. What a lucky woman, the doctor said. So lucky."

Auntie wanted to lie there forever. She wanted to lie down on the ground and die but her youngest son was still alive. When the bomb exploded, and knocked her to the ground, she fell over the youngest son's body, and he was not hurt. Maybe she should have died then, Auntie would think later. Maybe it would have been better. But she got up and started walking.

She left her eight-year-old son's body on the ground, in pieces, and walked away. She carried her youngest son in her arms. He was three years old, but so light, like a baby. At the time his lightness didn't frighten her; instead she was grateful because she needed to carry him the whole way. He had a fever. She could feel the heat against her skin, like fire. At first he cried and she was scared the soldiers would hear them. After he stopped crying, she was relieved.

She was carrying his body when she reached the border. She thought, We are saved! She thought, I have done something right. I have saved my youngest son. She thought the doctors could do something. Auntie had great faith in Western doctors. But they took his body away and wouldn't give it back to her. And then the doctor looked at her face and he told her what a lucky woman she was to be alive. What a miracle it was.

She didn't kill herself then because she didn't know what had happened to her husband or to her oldest son or her daughter. Not that she would ever be any use to them. She understood that. She said she was a failure as a mother. "I stayed alive so that I could tell my husband if I ever saw him again how his children died. I am not a mother. I am not anything."

Ma held Auntie's hands as they sat in the back of the Palace, the sun falling lower in the sky, the sky growing darker, shadows slipping from the fields and seeping into town, inching across the parking lot, surrounding the Palace like an inky tide.

I squatted on the floor by Sourdi, listening, my arms around my ankles, my forehead resting on my knees.

After Auntie finished speaking, Ma was quiet for some time. All I could hear was the soup stock bubbling on the stove and the electric fans whirring back and forth in the kitchen, circulating the scent of garlic and mint and our sweat.

When Ma finally spoke, she did not tell Auntie the story of her own escape, of our escape, or of my father's death. Instead she took hold of her older sister's elbow with one hand so tightly that her knuckles shone pearl-white through her skin, as she said over and over, "Your oldest son, he must be alive, he must be alive, he must be alive."

Ma didn't mention the daughter. I took that to mean she figured she had died or been married off to a soldier at a young age, which was almost the same as dead. That used to happen, young girls married off to strange men who took them to different work camps and their families never saw them again. We left the village the soldiers had assigned us to before that could happen to Sourdi. I squeezed my sister's hand, grateful she'd not been married off to a soldier.

Uncle stayed in the kitchen, entertaining the little kids the whole time Auntie talked to Ma. He had them sit around the prep table on stools, rolling silverware tightly into the white cloth dinner napkins. After an hour, they grew bored, and he sent them outside to the parking lot to play. When I crept to the door to see what he was doing, I saw him sitting with his head in his hands, before a huge mound of napkin rolls, staring at them as though they were a pile of broken bones.

That night, in the house that Auntie and Uncle rented on the out-skirts of town, I could not sleep as I lay next to Sourdi on the floor of our bedroom. The wind blew so fiercely through the open windows, with a sound like a woman wailing. The floorboards creaked, the pipes in the walls hissed, the whole house seemed to sway.

The house was big and tall with many rooms that Auntie and Uncle had planned to rent out, but now that we were here, they were ours. I had never been in a house so large. I thought of my mother lying alone in her bedroom downstairs. "Do you think Ma's lonely?" I asked Sourdi, but my sister didn't answer me, and instead rolled onto her side, pulling her pillow over her head.

The fields around the house sounded like the ocean, the way the wind swept through the corn, with a shush-shush sound, like the surf creeping up the beach. When I closed my eyes, I could hear the waves lapping at the edges of the room, where the darkness touched the hem of my sheet.

When the moon had risen just high enough to escape the branches of the box elder tree in the middle of the lawn, the bedroom filled with a clear, white light. I got up then and waded through the moonlight to the window. I could see the cornfields illuminated as though by flame. The fields flickered with a million shifting shades of black as the corn rippled in the wind. As far as I could see, the earth was moving, swaying, rocking. I felt as though I were in the hold of a large ship, adrift in the middle of the sea, waves stretching darkly to the horizon.

"Sourdi," I whispered, but my sister had fallen asleep.

CHAPTER 6

Father Dream

That night, I dreamed that our father died.

His breathing was labored, whistling from his lungs, phlegmy and thick. He had been breathing like that for days, and then in the middle of the night, he spat the last of his breath from his body.

I alone was awake, lying beside Sourdi on our bedrolls on the floor. We were living in the village, in the house on wooden stilts, beside the brown river. I listened intently, waiting for Pa's next breath. His breathing had slowed, taken on a watery sound. Because I was hungry, I could stay awake all night. Sourdi slept soundly because she had to work in the fields with the older girls and the women. I watched the water buffalo with the other little children; we were not old enough to plant rice or to dig holes or to carry heavy loads. Not yet, but soon.

I lay awake, wishing Pa would breathe again. I had grown accustomed to the raspy sound. It broke the stillness of the long black night. Without it, my ears sought out other sounds, the snorting of the pig that lived beneath the house, the footsteps of the soldiers who stood guard all night in the village, the distant cry of a monkey. Such noises made my heart beat faster, made me think of the dead spirits that roamed through the fields at night, looking to cause harm. The dead were restless, the old woman who lived next to us had explained, because they had died unhappy deaths. No one had prayed for their souls, offered incense at the pagoda, hired monks to chant at their bedsides. They died alone and afraid. They could not be reborn yet; their souls had lost their way to the underworld without the prayers to guide them. They had lost their bodies and were looking for new ones. If you didn't look out, she said, they might snatch yours!

When the old woman talked like this, I wanted to clap my hands over my ears and close my eyes tight, to hide from the terrible things she talked about. But we weren't allowed to do such things, hide from evil spirits, because the soldiers said it was wrong, it was not true. At least, the older soldiers said this; the young ones were just as scared of spirits as we were, but they were not allowed to contradict the leaders.

In my dream, the old woman was sitting next to me, the night our father died. She was squatting just outside my mosquito net, her white eyes open and staring blankly in the dark. She was humming, a low animal-like song, singing our father's soul to sleep.

I wanted to reach out and touch her. I wanted to make her stop. But my limbs felt heavy, immobile. I lay on the bedroll, watching her, wishing Sourdi would wake up, but Sourdi slept on and on, and the old woman began to sing louder.

She was the oldest woman in the village. Her hair was mostly silver and was so thin in places, you could see her brown, shiny scalp. Her few remaining teeth were stained red-black from chewing betel, and her eyes were cloudy gray, not black like eyes were supposed to be. Some of the boys called her "Witch" but not me, not to her wizened face anyway. Ma said I had to be kind to the old woman. Ma made me bring her cups of water during the day, when it was hottest and the other women were still in the field. The Witch was too old to do such work so she did laundry for the others, sitting on the edge of the river, beating clothes against the rocks there.

When I brought her some of the water Ma boiled and kept in a pot in our house, she'd drink it, wiping her mouth on the back of her hand, then she'd smile at me with her red-black teeth.

The Witch had come to our house a few days before Pa died. Ma had wanted her to listen to his chest. The Witch said the spirits that controlled his head were out of balance. She said we needed to gather a special kind of bark from the trees in the forest and to boil it into a tea for Pa to drink. But Ma had not been able to leave the camp that night or the next. On the third night, Ma had disappeared for several hours, when everyone else was asleep and I lay awake, listening. She had returned just as the sun was rising, the pig was waking and the soldiers began to walk in twos and threes once again after settling down for the night. The soldiers were not supposed to sleep at night, but sometimes they did. If I pressed my ear to the cracks in the floor, I could hear their snores. Ma returned to her bedroll next to Pa's, pulling her mosquito net closed. She was pretending to sleep, so that the others would think she had lain there just like that all night long, but I could hear her breaths, too fast and shallow. I lay still, and she did not know that I had seen her return.

That morning, Ma boiled the bark tea for Pa, and the whole house smelled like rotting fungus and river water, the tea created such thick clouds. Ma was afraid the soldiers would smell it and then they would guess that she had left the village in the night, ventured past the fields and into the forest, where we were forbidden to walk. But the wind was strong and it blew the steam across the river, where the scent was lost among the odors of the fish and the mud and the reeds.

Pa couldn't drink the tea, however, even though Sourdi held his head while Ma poured the liquid down his throat. He coughed and choked and then vomited the green liquid back up onto his chest. Ma cried then. I saw her wipe her tears on the back of her hand quickly, drying her face just as fast as her tears could flow, so that when she left to work in the field, the soldiers would not see that she had cried.

In my dream, I was watching the Witch sing Pa's soul to sleep when he stopped breathing.

All at once, the wind returned, rushing through the reeds beside the river, causing silver fish to leap from the waves. I heard them splashing. I hoped the wind would carry Pa's soul far away from our village, away from the soldiers, someplace safe.

Because the wind had returned, the Witch stopped her song. Instead she threw her head back and howled like an animal. Her mouth fell open, wide as a python's about to devour its prey.

I woke up screaming.

Sourdi put her arms around me, telling me it was just a dream, just a nightmare, I should go back to sleep.

We were lying on the air mattress in our new bedroom in Auntie and Uncle's big house.

I cried. The wind rushing through the cornfields outside sounded like the witch's singing.

"I can't breathe," I whispered to Sourdi. "There's no air."

Sourdi told me to ssssh. She made her voice soft and low, she blew against my neck, she turned into the wind that used to blow through the open windows of the house on wooden stilts by the brown river in the village where we lived during the war.

She made her voice softer still, until it was a song, a song about a shepherd boy and a weaving girl who lived among the stars in the sky. They were in love but they lived too far away, separated by galaxies, so they could see each other only once a year. It was a sad song, but not a frightening song, not a witch's song, but a young woman's love song.

Sourdi's voice grew softer, just a tickle of breath on my skin, and I could almost sleep again.

"Ssssh," she whispered, "it's just a dream, just a dream." Her voice disappeared into my ear.

My eyelids grew too heavy, they shut across my eyes, and I was almost asleep again.

"Just a dream..."

I smiled, sleepy-like, just for her. But she was wrong. It was a memory.

CHAPTER 7

First Days in the Silver Palace

The Palace was beautiful. The six booths were covered in cherry red vinyl, a framed print of Angkor Wat in silhouette hung on the wall, a pink plastic chrysanthemum sprang from a bud vase on every table. Someone had even filled the vases with water to make the flowers seem more real. At the far end of the dining room, in the corner, was a little shrine with a pitched roof and curved eaves. A ceramic God of Wealth was seated within, behind a tiny urn for incense and a plate of miniature plastic peaches. The shrine plugged into the wall, and two red candles on either side of the pagoda glowed.

The spigots of the soda dispenser shone as did the table tops, the window glass, the tile floor. Everything was sparkling clean, brand new, ready for action.

"You should have seen it when we first arrived," Uncle said, shaking his head. "Dirt everywhere. A big hole here." He pointed to the ceiling. "Like a bomb had gone off. And the floors! Water everywhere."

Our first day of work in the Family Business, while we waited with excitement for our customers, Uncle told us happy stories. The cook, for example. The cook wasn't just some old Chinese guy down on his luck, willing to work anywhere, he was a bona fide chef, top tier. Back in the day—several decades earlier—he'd had his own restaurant that was so renowned, people lined up for hours just to peer in the windows at the other people eating inside. Reservations had to be made months in advance, and even then that wasn't always early enough. In his youth, Uncle said, our Palace's chef had apprenticed in a Shanghai gangster's favorite restaurant in Phnom Penh. Oh, the extravagant banquets he'd prepared then! Hardened criminals rubbed elbows with ex-Kuomintang government officials, gun molls sat mere feet from fur-clad *Tai Tai's* with their foreign businessmen husbands. A French priest had condemned the restaurant's signature dish—a ginger-infused mitten crab clay pot stew— as sinful because its vapors encouraged the mixing of the races.

I squinted through the smoke in the kitchen at the skinny man, who sat in his undershirt on a stool, a cigarette dangling from his lips, while he flipped through his Chinese newspapers, ignoring the soup pot bubbling on the stove. I could almost imagine the young culinary prodigy Uncle was describing.

Uncle said he considered himself a lucky man to have found such a chef through the classified ads in Houston. A very lucky man indeed.

The cook was well-versed in the five major flavors— hot, sour, sweet, salty, bitter—and the eight regional styles. He could prepare snacks as well as banquet foods, meat dishes, cold dishes, dumplings, noodles, seafood, and vegetables, although, his eyesight not being what it once was, he could no longer be expected to carve melon rinds into the shapes of dragons or phoenixes or other mythical creatures. Of course, he had slowed in his old age, needed more time to prepare each dish, and could not always be trusted not to cut himself with the cleaver. Plus, he sometimes forgot the recipes, salting some dishes twice and leaving the centers of others uncooked. And once, he'd actually dropped the ashes of his cigarette into a bowl of curry. But Uncle said he had learned to work around these minor problems.

While we waited for customers, Uncle told us how everything was now in place for success. "Now that you are here," he said to Ma with a smile, "our luck will certainly change for the better."

When Uncle had first purchased the Palace, he'd seen the Native Americans walking on the sidewalks, their dark straight hair, their chiselled faces, and he thought to himself, with all these Chinese here, why didn't they open a restaurant before?

Everything was perfect: no gangs, no competition for forty miles— the next nearest Chinese restaurant being in Sioux City, Iowa, and in the winter, forty miles was too far to drive just for a meal—no unexpected taxes, no bribe to this health inspector or that police officer who just happened to have ties to another restaurant. Everything was just as the Chamber of Commerce brochure had said. Small Town America at its best.

Except that no one had mentioned that in Small Town America people wouldn't like our food.

At eleven-thirty on our first day of work in the Family Business, two men in black suits came in carrying a Bible. They ordered two iced teas and talked to Uncle about Jesus. When they departed at eleven-forty-seven, they left behind a pile of illustrated Bible stories for us on the end of the counter by the door.

At a quarter after twelve, a woman came in with three sweating, red-faced children. She explained the toilet at the laundromat was broken and could they use ours? Uncle said that they could. When they emerged from the restroom, Ma was waiting with menus. She opened one for the woman and placed it in her hands. The woman looked at it as though poisonous snakes might leap from its pages, then set it down carefully on the edge of a table and told Ma she had to "think about it" and they'd come back some other time, but she had to get back to the laundromat before someone stole their clothes from the dryer.

I watched them scurry across the parking lot, like mice fleeing a sleeping cat.

Three people came for a late lunch as all the other restaurants in town were closed between two and five and they were driving through town on their way north to the Black Hills. A couple came in for dinner, the man complaining that he'd lost a bet at work. They both ordered the same thing, fried rice and a Bud.

"It always takes time for a new business," Uncle said, "time for people to get used to something new."

He said the same thing every evening, while we sat around a back table after we'd locked all the doors and turned off the neon "OPEN" sign, and ate leftovers for dinner. In the beginning, Ma had made an effort to agree or at least to nod enthusiastically, but this night, the seventh night of our first week in the Family Business, she continued to chew her rice in silence, as Auntie did, every night, not bothering to lift her eyes from her bowl to watch her husband's sweating face as he quoted from the inspirational books he checked out of the town library, two per week: "Genius is one percent inspiration, ninety-nine percent perspiration," and "With the faith of a mustard seed, man can move mountains," and "There is no hope for the satisfied man."

While Uncle lectured, Auntie chewed her food carefully, spitting gristle and bone delicately into her napkin. When he finished, she rinsed her mouth out with tea, then picked her teeth with a wooden toothpick from the tabletop dispenser, carefully shielding her mouth with one hand.

However, this night, Uncle said something new.

He said that he was going to take another job, working in a Sizzler in Sioux City. "Just until business picks up," he said. "Just for a little extra income."

Auntie looked up at him for the first time in seven days. "And you expect me to run everything by myself while you're gone?"

"Of course not," Uncle said. "Your sister can help you. And all the children." Ma did not look up from her rice bowl. She bent her head towards the table and scraped the last grains of rice from her bowl into her mouth. It was understood that we were here to earn our keep. What was there for Ma to say?

As for Auntie, she folded her arms across her chest and stared off into the distance past Uncle's shoulder, past the empty tables and booths. Perhaps she was looking out the windows into the dark of the empty parking lot, perhaps she wasn't looking with her eyes at all, but was looking into her memories, remembering when she had a house full of servants and a closet full of French silk dresses.

And while she remembered these things, her face began to change. Her scar was still there, dividing her face into its light and dark halves, but I thought I could see something new growing, a hardening around the edges of her mouth where before there had only been slackness, a set to her jaw, a gleam to her eye. And for the first time, I began to worry about what it might be like to work for a woman like Auntie who had been wealthy once, a woman who had grown used to servants, the kind she punished when her own children had done something wrong.

I looked over at my sister Sourdi then, but she was following Ma's example, casting her eyes down at the table.

All at once, Ma stood up abruptly and gathered up the empty rice bowls, the platters of food, the soup tureen. She balanced them against the length of her arm and then carried everything back into the kitchen.

Sourdi rose next and gathered up the chopsticks and spoons, the dirty napkins full of bones and gristle, scraping the dropped and dribbled food from the table top into her cupped hand, and then followed Ma into the kitchen.

Auntie turned to stare at me, her dark eyes glittering above her serpentine scar, and I stared back at her until she grew uncomfortable, or perhaps merely bored, and she turned away again.

I could not sleep that night. The wind blew fiercely, making the cornfields across from the house creak like bamboo. Wispy clouds covered the moon, its blue light only able to seep out in milky strands. It was a night when the dead could roam freely, when the souls of the unburied and the unblessed rode on the wind, whispering in the dark.

The house creaked and groaned, little feet scampered in the attic, the pipes in the walls hissed. When I closed my eyes, I could feel the dark pressing closer, sitting on my chest, icy hands around my throat.

I tried to keep Sourdi awake as long as possible. I begged her to tell me stories, but she was tired. She had helped Ma and the cook all day in the kitchen, preparing the dishes no one would order. She fell asleep almost as soon as her head lay back against her pillow. I tried to burrow closer to her, but the scents of the kitchen still clung to her skin. She no longer smelled like my sister, but burnt chilies and congealed fat, overcooked chicken and too many shrimp.

I lay on my back, listening to the house teeter in the wind.

Finally, when I could stand it no more, I got up and went to look for Ma. The hallway outside our room was dark as a midnight river and drafty from the window opened in the stairwell. The wind swirled around me like a swiftly moving current. The voices of the dead were louder now, impossible to dismiss, hissing directly into my ears. And then I realized, the voices I heard were coming from Auntie and Uncle's bedroom at the end of the hall. Auntie and Uncle were arguing, their voices circling each other like caged tigers, round and round, a snarl here, then a growl. I couldn't make out everything they said, my Khmer was very rusty, but they were clearly arguing about us.

"You should never have invited them . . ."

"What choice?"

"I can't bear to see her face—"

I pressed my ears shut with my fingers and crept down the stairs towards Ma's room, just off the kitchen. But when I got downstairs, I saw light spilling out the kitchen door, and found my mother sitting at the table, drinking a cup of hot water, and smoking.

"You should be in bed," she whispered to me, spotting me peering in the door, but then she smiled and nodded for me to join her at the table. I slid onto one of the wooden chairs besides Ma; it felt cool against my bare legs.

"We should go, Ma," I said. "Let's just pack everything up again and go home."

"This is home," Ma said, blowing a perfect smoke ring towards the ceiling. It rose unsteadily, wobbling like a spinning saucer. "Why do you want to leave so soon? We have such a nice, big house to live in. Our own business."

"It's not ours, it's Auntie's. And Uncle's. And they don't need us here. There's no customers. Even if Uncle's gone to work, Auntie could run everything herself."

"That's why we're lucky," Ma insisted. "They don't need us, but they invited us to come anyway."

In the smokey yellow light of the kitchen, Ma's face almost seemed to glow. The shadows under her eyes were less visible, the lines that pulled at the edges of her mouth were almost gone. She reached across the table and caught hold of my wrist with one hand.

"I'm not afraid of hard work," Ma said, smoke emerging from her mouth in a series of small, blue clouds. "Nor should my children be afraid." Her fingers tightened uncomfortably around my wrist then, but I didn't try to pull my hand free.

"I'm not afraid," I said, and Ma nodded happily.

"That's my good girl." She patted my wrist, her fingers stroking my skin softly, and for that moment her rough fingers felt smooth again, like silk, like smoke.

I let her be happy then. I let her think that I was a good daughter, the kind she wanted, the kind she deserved. But really, I was a terrible daughter, the kind who lied.

CHAPTER 8

Auntie

Auntie, I soon discovered, liked to complain about unusual things.

"The sky is too large. I feel I am being swallowed alive." She waved her hand airily in the direction of the cornfields and the soybean fields and the blue dome of the sky that seemed to stretch all the way to Minnesota.

"And the wind here is too fierce. It is treacherous and uncivilized." Auntie drew her arms across her chest then and shivered.

When Auntie talked like this, Ma laughed. "You haven't changed at all," she said cheerfully as though saying something with enough confidence would make it so.

Auntie turned from the glass of the front door of the Palace where she was surveying the empty parking lot. "Time to practice our English." And she turned on the television set Uncle had set up behind the counter next to the soda machine and the metal cabinets for the plates. "You must all lose your Texas accents or none of the people here will ever understand you, Sister Dear."

Then Auntie sat down on one of the swivel stools to watch her favorite soap opera, which consisted of nothing but people getting married and then divorced then married again, as far as I could tell.

While Auntie watched TV, mouthing the lines along with the actors, Ma cleaned the Palace, scrubbing everything in sight, the tables and the counters, the metal cabinets, the soda pop dispenser, the cigarette machine by the front door. She joked about the customers and the strange ways they seasoned the food, adding soy sauce to their rice, salt to their vegetables, sugar to their tea.

Auntie didn't know how to cook or clean, of course, not when she'd always had servants for such matters, and so Ma didn't expect her to help.

"Nea, take the children outside to play. I can't have them running around when I'm busy," Ma commanded as she mopped the floor. "Sourdi can help me inside."

I was only too happy to obey. It was hot outdoors, but the cold inside the Palace frightened me.

I immediately installed myself in the shade behind one of the large green dumpsters where I could read one of my favorite books, a dog-eared copy of *The Martian Chronicles* that I'd borrowed from the public library in East Dallas before we left. Reading about the adventures of astronauts on Mars appealed to me in a way that watching my younger brother and sisters throw scraps of garbage to the seagulls did not. It's true; by now, even the once miraculous appearance of the gulls no longer thrilled me.

Time passed while I explored an empty Martian town, eerily reminiscent of my hometown on Earth, but empty and ancient.

"Ugh! Filthy birds!" Sourdi said, emerging from the kitchen with a dun-brown Hefty bag. She tossed it into the dumpster where it split, exposing the chicken bones and cabbage hearts and tin cans inside.

She swatted the air as the birds swooped closer for inspection.

Sourdi wiped the sweat beading across her forehead with the back of her hand. Her skin was moist, her pink T-shirt ringed with dark bands beneath her armpits. Her black hair was pulled back into a ponytail off her neck, but her face was red all the same. She looked miserable. Because she was almost sixteen, she couldn't sit in the shade and hide from the adults like me, but had to keep busy all the time.

"Who all wants to help me peel the shrimps?" she asked hopefully.

I ducked my head back into my book. They were not just shrimp, I knew, but in fact the Special of the Day, $8.95, Imperial Prawns. They didn't entail peeling so much as ripping their long, black spinal columns from their fat, spongy bodies.

"Not me!" Sam squeaked up immediately.

"Not me!" the twins repeated.

"Come on, y'all like to eat 'em," Sourdi cajoled us.

"We do not," Maly said, which was true enough. The twins had come to like only the most American of foods, cheese that came wrapped in plastic, soups that came out of cans, meat that sat between buns. They constantly astounded us with their strange eating habits.

"I only like them if they're cooked," Sam said.

Sourdi sighed. More sweat was gathering across her forehead. She blotted her face daintily now with the edge of a tissue pulled from her pocket. She was having trouble with acne and no longer indiscriminately wiped her face on the hem of her T-shirt like the rest of us.

"Don't any of y'all want to help me?"

"I am helping," I insisted, pointing to our siblings. I tucked my book beneath my legs surreptitiously.

"You monkeys," Sourdi said, but then she smiled, unable to hold a grudge. My older sister had been cursed with a sweet disposition. She dabbed the sides of her nose carefully with her tissue one last time then went back inside the steamy kitchen.

We were all relieved that she had not made us go back inside, especially me, although I felt guilty admitting as much. Sourdi reminded us of what was to come when we were adults, or at least old enough to be considered an adult by our mother. I didn't look forward to the prospect.

"We're gonna show you how to pray to the Holy Ghost," Maly announced next as I tried to return to my book. My twin sisters now jumped up and, standing side-by-side, rolled their eyes back into their heads so that only the whites showed. Then holding their arms outstretched, palms upwards, they began to make crazy noises, looping nonsense syllables that rose up and down in pitch. Their eyelids fluttered rapidly over the whites of their eyeballs.

"Cool!" Sam exclaimed.

"Yo, that's whack," I said. "Y'all act like that, the police gonna come lock you up like you on some kinda drugs." I hoped I could shame my sisters back into normalcy. The last time I'd seen anything like this, it was in a movie, and the little girl's head had started to spin around her neck like a top.

"Ubba ubba ubba," my sisters moaned, their voices rising. They flailed their arms in unison.

"You're acting like freaks, don't you get that?" I forced my voice to sound calm, a little bored even. Sam, switching allegiances now, giggled.

My sisters' eyes flapped open. "Y'all don't know nothin'! That's how the Holy Ghost is s'posed to talk!" Maly announced indignantly.

We were all arguing like this about nothing when the boys came. Three of them, on bicycles. They circled at first from afar, in large swooping arcs, then suddenly one of them yelled, "Japs!" and they started throwing rocks.

I bent over the twins, trying to protect them, while I shouted, "Help! Help!" as if someone could hear me. But the cook had the radio on, and there weren't any customers pulling up, so of course no one came to our rescue. I felt a sharp stone strike my head, and for a second, I couldn't see a thing for the pain, as though a knife had been inserted into my temple. I was so surprised, I couldn't remember how to breathe.

And then I was angry.

The boys had stopped circling to watch me as I held my head with my hand. They were standing over their bicycles, doubled over laughing.

"Get behind the dumpster," I hissed to the girls and Sam, and then quickly I gathered up as many of the boys' stones as I could find on the asphalt.

"Hey, *pendejos!*" I shouted. While the boys pointed and laughed at me in an exaggerated fashion that made them seem simple, I grabbed another rock and another. I saw clearly that the boys were at a disadvantage. They couldn't ride their bikes if they had to stop and pick up more ammunition, and they had run out. "Hey, your mother suck the dick!" I shouted in English. This elicited a satisfying gasp. Then I took aim and smashed one of the boys in the face—a scrawny kid with orange hair and skin pale a toadstool. He clutched his nose with both hands, blood gushing through his fingers. Then he jumped back on his bike and rode away.

The remaining two boys called after their friend, but he didn't turn back. The boys hopped off their bikes and set them up like a shield while they scoured the parking lot for ammo. They shouted, "You eat dogs!" and "Go back to Japan!" but their momentum was clearly lost. I lobbed their rocks back at them, and then trash from the dumpster: chicken carcasses, fruit cocktail cans, beer bottles that shattered on the metal spokes of their wheels.

Even Sam and the girls joined in, hurling whatever they could find at the boys.

This time the cook could hear our racket. He came running out the back door with his bloody apron on, and the boys looked shocked, then jumped back on their bikes and took off, pedaling as fast as their legs could manage across the parking lot and down the street.

All in all, I considered the fight a success. I'd been hit a couple times, to be sure, and I could tell that I'd have a shiner for a couple weeks to prove it, but the boys had fled, not us.

Auntie, however, was horrified. She'd watched the whole ugly spectacle unfold from the windows of the dining room: the circling hooligans, my cowering siblings, and me throwing rocks in public, in the parking lot, for everyone in the world to see.

"Just like a street boy!" Auntie said, her voice rising and crashing in indignant waves. "Just like a hooligan! Nea acts like a girl who has had no mother! No mother at all!"

Sourdi was applying ice to my eye in the kitchen, and we both heard Auntie as she lectured Ma in the back of the dining room.

It was then that Auntie launched into a long speech detailing all my shortcomings: I was loud, demanding, bold; I had no grace; I clomped when I walked; I slouched when I stood; I mumbled when I spoke except when I cursed. I even fought with boys in public. I would be the ruin of my family. I was every wrong thing that America could do to a Cambodian girl.

I was hoping that Ma would defend me, that she would point out that I was brave and kind, that I got good grades in school, what a wonderful daughter, but Ma said nothing. Peeking through the kitchen door, I saw that Ma's cheeks were flushed pink, her head bowed in apology. In shame.

I wanted to cry then, I wanted to shout, I wanted to break everything I could get my hands on, but I didn't. Instead I stole one of the little knives from the cutting block in the kitchen and took it with me to the bathroom. I locked myself in the stall then and drew the blade lightly over the skin of my arm, just deep enough to draw a line of blood. Three times. After the wound began to throb, I didn't feel like crying anymore.

That evening, I found myself alone with Ma, just the two of us to close the Palace.

I was setting the chairs atop the tables as Ma mopped the floor. We had the radio on, Tanya Tucker was singing about love gone wrong.

The only stations we could get here played country music. I watched my mother out of the corner of my eye. She was more than twelve years younger than Auntie, but squinting, I could see a resemblance, in the way their nostrils flared, the width of their foreheads, the spacing of their eyes, and I could almost imagine Ma as an old woman, too, with snaky white hair, her body fragile and weak, with a heart that stopped beating in the middle of the day. She'd be sorry that she had been mean to me, when she was old and needed my help. But it would be too late. When I grew up, I was going to go far away, and I'd never come home again.

Ma stopped mopping to smoke. She took her lighter from her apron pocket and flicked it open with one smooth snap of her fingers, the blue flame jumping to life. Then she bent close to the fire, as though she meant to kiss it, her cigarette dangling from her lips. She opened one eye and stared at me.

"What's wrong?"

I shrugged and pretended to go back to work, vigorously wiping the counter with a dishrag.

Ma closed her eye and took another drag off her cigarette. Blue smoke emerged from her nostrils. "What's wrong?" she asked again.

"Auntie hates me."

Ma opened both eyes. "Don't be ridiculous. You're her favorite."

"That's not true!" I cried out. "She absolutely hates me!" I couldn't believe that Ma would lie to me like this, as though I were still a baby who would believe whatever she said like my brother or the twins, as I though I didn't know anything. "I heard her talking to you today," I said. "I know."

Ma shook her head tiredly. She leaned her mop against the table and held her elbow in her right hand, her cigarette in her left. "You don't know anything." Ma brought her cigarette to her lips but then didn't inhale. "It's hard for my sister. She's not like me. She lost everything in the war, her beauty, her children, her mind, everything."

Ma stretched her arm between the chairs and placed her cigarette carefully on the edge of a fire-red ashtray. She picked up her mop. "Auntie likes you very much. That's why she wants to teach you things." Ma's voice was firm, her tone final. It was the voice she used to end an argument. It was the voice that meant there was nothing to discuss.

"You wouldn't let Auntie say those bad things about me if Pa were alive. He wouldn't let her say those things. He loved me. He wasn't like you."

Ma pressed her lips together very tightly. Her eyes narrowed. I thought she might grow angry all at once, grab up her mop and strike something with it. I thought she might knock the chairs to the floor, she might shout or stamp her feet. She might turn her back to me and leave me in the dining room, refusing to say another word. But instead Ma exhaled slowly, blowing her breath through her teeth. "You remind my sister of the daughter she used to have. My sister likes you all right. It's me she doesn't approve of."

Ma walked over to the window, dragging the mop with one hand, leaving a glistening trail behind her on the floor like a snail. She stared into the parking lot as though she could see something in the dark that deserved her full attention.

"You look like him. Your father, I mean," Ma said, without looking at me. "You have his face. The same eyes. The same expressions. Sometimes I can't stand to look at you."

I put my hands to my face.

"I'm not like my sister. I married a poor man for love against my family's wishes," she said. "But my husband was a good man, and I know he'll have a better life next time. I know this. We were never wealthy in our time together, so I don't mind working now. It helps me to bear my memories.

"But for my sister, it's different. She was so beautiful. Her face was like the moon, white and round. Perfect. Her beauty made her ambitious. She married a man above her rank, a man with a government position. She had money and all those servants. Because she was beautiful, she thought she was special. She thought she could have anything she wanted. People always treat a beautiful woman like that when she's young, like the world will stop turning just for her.

"She never learned to bear things."

Ma turned away from the window and looked at me with her dark, sad eyes. "I'm a lucky woman. My sister is the unlucky one. She isn't used to that. When she sees you, you remind her of everything she's lost. And everything I still have."

Ma took one last puff from her cigarette before stubbing it out gently in an ashtray. She then picked up her mop with both hands. "Just try to be good. Just try a little harder. Okay?"

I nodded. She smiled, the edges of her lips pulling up quickly before dropping back down again, and then her face resumed its usual, neutral expression, the one that was neither sad nor happy.

I tried to obey my mother, I really did.

But as our days in the Palace turned into weeks, Auntie's complaints only increased. She said her head hurt, as though the plates of her bones were drifting apart. And her heart beat funny—stopping, she claimed, for minutes at a time. She retreated to her apartment above the Palace, drawing the shades and the curtains, lying on her bed in the gloomy darkness, refusing to come down at all.

On these days, Ma sent me to check on Auntie with a tray of food and a pot of tea. Ma told me to be good and do as Auntie instructed. But sometimes Auntie said nothing at all, only staring at me, her eyes glittering in the dark, and sometimes she complained to me nonstop because nothing I did was ever right.

If I massaged her neck and back and arms, knotty as tree branches, she grimaced and grunted and said I might as well have been born a boy, all the use I was, I only made her bones ache more. When she wanted me to rub her back with spoons to promote healing, she yelped with pain and said I was trying to take the skin off her body. When she handed me her bottle of essential oil, which she wanted me to rub into her joints, I managed to spill the foul-smelling green liquid onto her sheets.

"In Cambodia," she told me, clicking her tongue against the roof of her mouth, "children learned to take care of their parents." She said as a girl, she had bathed her own mother every Buddhist New Year, in water that was filled with herbs and flowers, to ensure her mother's longevity. She had done so willingly, and her mother had lived to be quite an old woman.

I was afraid then that Auntie would want me to bathe her next, so I said quickly, "Ma likes to take showers. She says modern life, that's really living."

Auntie fell silent for a long period, in which she merely glared at me with her dark, unblinking eyes, disappointed by my obtuseness. I pretended not to notice as I went about tidying up her apartment, dusting the television set and the end table, the reading lamp and its plastic-covered shade, and finally the tiny shrine to Buddha she had set up in the far corner, where the light never seemed to reach, not from her dim-bulbed lamp, not from the sunlight seeping beneath the edges of her tightly drawn drapes. Still, the whole time I could feel her snaky eyes staring at my back, as though she were waiting for just the right moment to strike.

CHAPTER 9

Summer Storms

One morning the clouds gathered along the horizon, inky and menacing, unfurling across the sky like smoke at a funeral. By mid-afternoon, it was as dark as dusk. I was standing in the parking lot, showing my little sisters and brother how to hunt for the nails that somebody kept dropping there, bagfuls, when the wind changed tone. For a second, it was completely still, and then the air began to hum, as though a cloud of locusts were about to descend from the sky. I looked up and saw the tip of a tornado, shaped like a baby boy's penis, suddenly poke through the black clouds boiling over the cornfields just west of town. Then just as suddenly it disappeared, sucked back up into the thunderheads. The wind began to howl.

"I'm flying, I'm flying!" my little sisters shrieked with delight, their arms outstretched.

"Fly inside!" I commanded and chased the kids back into the Palace. By this time, hail the size of small fists pounded our backs and heads.

Ma and Sourdi were gathered around the television behind the counter. The Doppler radar showed angry red squares advancing across a map of Nebraska like an enemy army conquering territory.

We could hear the faint wail of the tornado siren going off in town. It was very dark now, like nightfall.

"The weatherman says we should go to the basement," Sourdi said, but of course we didn't have a basement in the Palace.

"I hope he's not out driving in the weather," Ma said, thinking of Uncle. "The hail will ruin the car." She fumbled for her cigarettes.

"Don't smoke, Ma!" I said in a panic. "A tornado's coming!"

Outside the Palace, the rain blew in a horizontal sheet. Lakes formed in the potholes in the parking lot. Hail thundered across the roof. Then suddenly the electricity cut out. As the wind raged outside, shaking the windows, Sourdi and I forced the little kids to crouch under the table in a rear booth away from all the vibrating glass.

Lightning flashed like the glare of a bomb. Then a BOOM, directly overhead. The dishes in the cabinets chattered like teeth.

"You'd better go bring Auntie downstairs," Ma said. "The storm will make her nervous."

At first I didn't understand that Ma was speaking to me. I watched her lips move as though she were a character in a foreign movie, dubbed and slightly out of synch. Then she handed me the umbrella.

I did not want to bring Auntie downstairs. She'd complained of a headache the moment after we all arrived at work in the morning, had gone straight to her apartment above the Palace, and hadn't come down since. If Auntie was nervous upstairs, she could come down herself. I was going to point this out to Ma, but the storm was too loud for my voice to be heard.

Ma gave me a little push. I felt her hand between my shoulder blades, a small hand but a firm shove. She pointed me toward the door.

I tightened my grip on the umbrella. There was no roof over the wooden staircase that snaked up the side of the Palace to the apartment. I walked calmly through the kitchen to the back door, thinking how sorry Ma would be when I was struck by lightning or carried off by the tornado. Sourdi would cry at my funeral, and Ma would feel guilty for the rest of her life. She would realize what a fool she'd been to sacrifice her daughter just because she was worried about her crazy sister. Ma might even shave her head like the women who used to become nuns after some tragedy befell their families. Thinking how sad and small Ma would look with no hair and nothing but a coarse ash-white robe to wear, I took a deep breath and flung the back door open.

I felt as though I had jumped into the ocean. The air had turned to liquid. The wind battered me, I could barely stand upright. The umbrella shriveled up, turned inside out and flew away into the storm like a bat. I hunched my shoulders and ran like a crab to the staircase and pulled myself up the steps.

I moved one foot then the other but I felt more as though I were swimming. Or drowning. Finally, I was at Auntie's door. I burst inside.

Auntie was seated in her chair in the dark facing the window. She looked surprised to see me. "You're wet," she announced.

I struggled to shut the door behind me, but then the wind took hold of it. It slammed like a gunshot.

"You're wet," Auntie repeated.

"COME ON!" I shouted, my ears still filled with the roaring wind. "YOU HAVE TO GO DOWNSTAIRS!"

Auntie winced. She grabbed me by the arm and began to beat me all over with a piece of cloth.

"OW!" I tried to break free. Then I realized Auntie was trying to dry me off. She rubbed me briskly with a towel. I couldn't feel my skin, but I could feel the pressure of her hands on me. I was shivering.

"Crazy girl," Auntie was saying. "What kind of crazy girl goes out in a storm?" She muttered some other things, but I couldn't hear properly. My head shook back and forth as she tried to dry my hair.

"Ow ow ow."

"Take off your clothes," Auntie said, clicking her tongue against the roof of her mouth.

"I can't," I said. My voice almost sounded normal to me, only one ear was still plugged. "Ma says you have to come downstairs. She told me to get you."

"I'm not going out in this weather." Auntie drew her arms across her chest and sniffed. "What an idea!"

"She thought you'd be afraid." Something about Auntie's tone made me want to defend my mother, who after all had sent her daughter out in a terrible storm for her sister's sake. The sacrifice ought to be worth something. Gratitude at least.

But Auntie only laughed. It was not pleasant, Auntie's laugh. It sounded like a person choking.

For the rest of the storm, I stayed with Auntie upstairs in her apartment, while she sat in her chair facing the window without talking. Auntie made me take my clothes off, and I stood naked with her sheet wrapped around me as I watched the storm, too, my face pressed close to the window glass. I was no longer afraid; rather, I felt detached, as though I were watching some kind of disaster movie on late-night TV. Banks of hail formed in the parking lot, which was rapidly turning into a lake. I could see just a corner of the cornfields, which were flattened now, water rushing through the fields into the drainage ditches like a river that had changed its course. Waves like breakers foamed white against the asphalt.

Eventually the wind died down, the howls giving way to moans and then whispers as the rain grew steady and began to fall in a straight line instead of horizontally. The power came back on, and Auntie's TV sputtered to life, the weatherman pointing to his map, where a mass of orange and red squares moved on to Iowa.

I put my clothes back on, although they were still wet, and went downstairs with Auntie. Auntie held a towel over her head, but I got wet all over again.

The sky had lightened to gray, and there was a tiny patch of gold where the sun was trying to burn through, but out of the corner of my eye, I could see lightning forking across the sky, striking the flat fields at the edge of my range of vision.

"Maybe we should wait," I said, but Auntie had already gone on ahead of me, sloshing through the swirling parking lot. I hadn't realized she could move so quickly. I had to run to keep up.

I thought, We're wading through water during a lightning storm. In school in Texas, they'd made us read stories about people who had tried such foolish things, swimming in pools, boating on lakes, wading in rivers, and inevitably they were struck down dead by lightning. There'd never been a story about people wading through parking lots, but I could easily see how Auntie's and my folly would be added to the storm canon. Thunder boomed, and lightning flashed across the entire sky once, twice, then in bolts like pitchforks piercing the fields again and again. I ducked my head and pushed my way through the water, which was rushing around me, as high as my calves. Fortunately, the Palace itself was on a slight incline or it would have flooded.

At last we were at the front door just as another round of thunder fired. But Auntie kept going. She walked past the front door towards the street, then crossed the street. She was headed towards the flattened cornfield. Water was pouring off the field into the ditch that ran alongside the road. "Come back!" I shouted after her. "It's dangerous!" But she didn't seem to hear me.

I ran after her. The ditches were filled with runoff from the fields. They were roaring with foaming water, the waves turgid as a river, loud as the ocean. Auntie stood on the edge of the road and looked into the swirling water. For a moment, I thought she might jump. I grabbed hold of her arm. "Don't!" I shouted, but my voice was lost in the wind.

Auntie, however, did not try to break free of my grip. She stood facing the ruined fields, her chin lifted into the wind. Her white hair whirled about her head and her black eyes shone as she surveyed the banks of hail that had flattened huge swaths of corn, the green stalks bent and broken as far as we could see. Her mouth was opened slightly, and she was panting. "It's beautiful," she seemed to say, over and over.

Then I felt a hand tighten around my arm, and I was jerked back from the edge of the newly created river. I turned and found Ma staring at me. She was squinting into the wind, scowling at me, shouting something that I couldn't hear. Then she grabbed Auntie with her other hand and pulled her back from the water's edge.

Ma gestured with her chin for me to take Auntie's other arm, and the two of us brought her back to the Palace. She didn't really resist, but she didn't seem eager to come in either. She kept turning her head to look over her shoulder at the rushing water, the ruined fields, the distant lightning.

By the time we had managed to drag Auntie inside, I was thoroughly wet again, and chilled to the bone. My teeth chattered inside my head. As we came in the door, Sourdi handed me a bunch of dishrags as well as paper towels from the restroom. I wiped myself repeatedly with them, but I could barely feel my own skin.

Ma swatted Auntie on the shoulder. "What's wrong with you?" she scowled. "Why didn't you come inside?"

"Do you think I'm going to listen to a child?" Auntie said at once. She was standing facing the windows, as Ma rubbed her down with a dishtowel, jerking her limbs this way and that. "I had to see for myself. The sound of the water reminded me of the sea. When I felt the wind against my face, I couldn't help myself. I wanted to lift up my legs and be carried away."

"You're crazy," Ma muttered. She let Sourdi finish drying Auntie off and now bent over at the waist, wringing out her own wet hair. "You could have fallen in the water and drowned. You could have been struck by lightning."

Auntie laughed then, not in her usual way, the sound like something sharp breaking, but a real laugh, a happy sound, as though she were still imagining how the wind had felt against her skin. "Heaven would not be so generous," she said. "I'm not going to die like this." Then she smiled at my mother, not unkindly. "Did you feel the wind, Little Sister? It felt so strong, I felt as though I could fly."

Ma sighed then and shook her head. "I sound like our mother. Afraid of a storm. She would have laughed to hear me." She smiled then, remembering something, but she didn't say anything more.

We went home early, closing the Palace. Ma figured no one would be coming out to eat after such a storm. After we dried off and changed our clothes, Auntie was still in her good mood, and she offered to teach us how to dance.

"My sister is a wonderful dancer," Ma gushed, pressing her hands together before her heart. "She could turn all the men's heads."

Auntie brought out a cassette tape of music that she said she'd been able to purchase in Houston off a couple who'd immigrated years earlier. Sourdi and I pushed the sofa in the front room against the wall, clearing a space while Auntie put her music in our tape player. Suddenly, the room filled with the sound of summer in a hot climate by a fast river, with a track of electric guitar and drums with a go-go beat that must have been added to compete with the Western pop music that had flooded Phnom Penh before the war. Then a woman's voice joined the music, a soft voice, a sad voice, singing about love.

Auntie stood in the middle of the room with her eyes closed and then slowly began to unfold. Her arms rose into the air, her fingers bent gently as though she meant to caress someone's cheek, and all at once she began to step in time with the music. She moved so gracefully, like a statue come to life.

My sisters and I lined up behind her, trying to imitate her motions, our hands sweeping the air, our feet stumbling on the carpet. We giggled as Auntie danced round and round.

Finally, she noticed Sam sitting in the corner. "Here, we'll show you the man's part, too. You'll have to help me, Little Sister."

"I'm not sure I remember." Ma took her place before Auntie.

But then they danced around the room, Ma and Auntie, each moving in time with the other, a step forward, a step back, swaying left then right, Ma giggling into her hand from time to time, Auntie correcting her steps. "Like this, like this," she said, calling over her shoulder to Sam. We followed them around in circles, all of us trying to dance, Sam and the twins, Sourdi and me, dancing until we were dizzy.

We didn't notice that Uncle had come home until the tape stopped. We looked up and Uncle was standing in the hall, grocery bags at his side on the floor, staring. He'd heard about the storm and decided to come back early to check on us. He'd found the note Ma had taped to the door of the Palace and come to the house.

Ma pushed her hair back behind her ears, laughing. "Now you can have a real partner," she said to Auntie. She rushed to turn the tape over.

"We're teaching the children," Auntie said to Uncle. She beckoned to him with her hand.

Uncle nodded, and, without speaking, joined her on the carpet.

The music started up again, and Uncle and Auntie began to dance. They moved together in perfect harmony, Uncle moving side by side with Auntie, their hands in the air, not touching, but stroking the space between them. The sun was setting now, and the living room was wrapped in shadows, but I didn't want to turn the harsh lights on. I sat on the floor, my arms around my knees, watching Auntie and Uncle dance as though they were a much younger couple. They moved in and out of shadow, turning slowly, as a man and a woman on the tape sung a song about the spring. I could almost imagine what they had looked like when they were young and in love, when their family was still whole, and their future seemed to be filled with only bright prospects. And seeing them this way, I finally understood very clearly what they had lost.

Then all at once, Uncle stopped. He turned away from Auntie, from all of us, facing the wall, as he put his hands to his face, his shoulders shaking. He stood hunched over, bent like a comma, while the music played around him.

Ma turned the tape off.

"I don't remember anymore. The children will have to find a better teacher," Auntie said, her voice flat, completely neutral, as though she were discussing the proper way to work a geometric proof or parse a sentence in French. Then she turned on her heel and left us, climbing the stairs slowly to her bedroom.

I never learned any of the old dances.

CHAPTER 10

When I Was a Boy

Late at night we could hear Auntie and Uncle arguing in their room, their voices snaking through the heat vents, entering Sourdi's and my bedroom like poltergeists, rousing us from our sleep.

"You were a fool to take that money!"

"What choice did I have?"

"And when the loan shark comes?"

"He won't come—"

"His thugs then. When they come, you think they're going to take another excuse?"

Sourdi and I plugged our ears with our fingers, we held our pillows over our heads, we kicked at the sheets, we hummed to ourselves and sang the lyrics to TV show tunes and pop songs, and still their voices wormed their way into my skull.

"You shouldn't have—"

"I'll think of something—"

"What will I do? What will we do? And all those children to look after! All our expenses!"

"Stop. They'll hear."

Sobbing.

Even after they stopped arguing and fell asleep, I could hear their anger and fear in my head, vibrating in my bones. Their arguments gave me nightmares.

I dreamed once that I was back in the village, and the soldiers were walking in pairs along the banks of the paddies with their guns drawn, their eyes darting back and forth inside their skulls, never closing, always watching. The soldiers used to say Angka was like the head of a pineapple, covered with eyes. Angka was their name for the new government, which could see everyone everywhere all the time so there was no escape. In my dream, the soldiers' eyes multiplied across their faces, sprouting in the backs of their skulls, peering through their greasy black hair. Eyes fell like seeds from the soldiers and sprouted on the ground, sending up tender green stalks, and at the end of each, a tiny black eye grew.

The Witch took me by the hand and pulled me from the fields where I was watching a tired water buffalo, its ribs pressing at its hide, and dragged me to the river bank. She said it was time for me to go, and she pushed me into the muddy water. I fought her then. "The soldiers will see me! They'll shoot me!" I cried, but her hands were firm and heavy across my shoulders. She pushed me deeper and deeper into the water until I thought I would drown, but suddenly I found myself afloat, caught in the current.

The eyes on the ends of the reeds along the banks all turned towards me now, and the reeds began to sway back and forth, faster and faster, with the sound of an angry wind, and I knew the soldiers would soon come with their guns. My limbs grew heavy and I could barely swim. Water splashed into my ears. Then all at once, the Witch began to sing. Her voice was low and deep, like an animal growling. The sound throbbed across the river, moving among the rustling reeds, until it was the only sound, louder than the splashing river and the treacherous wind. She sang until the eyes growing from the earth began to droop, their tiny lids sliding over the black irises, until the whole world turned dark.

When I woke the next morning, the sky was charcoal, filled with angry looking clouds pushing towards the earth. The rain fell steady as a heartbeat.

Sourdi was already up, her side of the mattress was empty.

Downstairs in the kitchen, I found Uncle and Auntie seated at the table, drinking tea, while Ma prepared noodle soup on the stove. They were laughing together about something as I entered, their voices erupting all at once like a cloudburst. They laughed as though Auntie and Uncle hadn't kept everyone up half the night arguing. I looked at Ma carefully to see if I could read any special clues in her face, a message just for me, such as don't-worry-I'm-laughing-now-because-we're-going-to-pack-up-everything-and-leave-here-forever, or how-lucky-we've-won-the-Iowa-state-lottery-all-our-problems-are-solved, but in fact I could read nothing of the sort in her expression. She looked the same as she always did in the morning before she'd had her breakfast, her eyes a little red still, her skin a little pale.

And hearing Ma's laughter emerging from her tired face, I realized then what good liars adults were.

As the summer wore on, Auntie grew more and more depressed, staying in her apartment above the Palace almost every day, claiming her head hurt worse than ever, her body ached without relief. Once, she announced that her heart had stopped beating for five entire minutes. She knew because she'd counted the seconds, one by one by one. Uncle, too, stayed away from the Palace, working later and later at his job in Sioux City, often returning only as we closed. Even then he never asked how Auntie had been or, for that matter, about the day's receipts. Instead he talked to Ma about unrelated things, details that he recalled suddenly from their life before the war, the color of a favorite pet parakeet, a line from a poem he'd learned in school.

When he talked like this, he leaned back on his heels, his toes tapping on the floor, his head tilted back so that he could look into the sky. He looked like a man without a care in the world.

Sourdi and I liked to make fun of him, his outlandish charm. I think we wanted a more serious uncle, the kind who talked about money and business, the kind who could pay his bills on time and didn't have to worry about loan sharks. But maybe we were jealous, too. To think someone could have such pleasant memories.

We hid in the restroom, pretending to clean the stalls.

"I remember when I was a boy," Sourdi began, making her voice low and gruff like Uncle's, "even our servants had proper manners. Our servants knew they were better than other servants simply because they worked in our house."

"When I was a boy," I began, "I had a dog that could talk. I had a cat that could sing in French. I had a goldfish that could dance on two fins."

"When I was a boy, I set my sister's hair on fire, and she was punished instead of me," Sourdi added.

"When I was a boy, I ate two hundred and forty-three red bean paste buns in a row. I drank cow's milk for breakfast, honey for lunch and ice cream for supper. I weighed three hundred pounds." I thrust my belly out and patted it with both hands.

Then Sourdi and I laughed out loud, hysterically, bumping into each other and the prep table and the metal shelves of pots and pans once we'd returned to the kitchen. We laughed until the cook looked up from his movie-star magazine, until Ma came in from the dining room and told us to hush up, until we had to run outside into the parking lot with our mouths hanging open, to let the brisk wind fill us up inside and quiet our restless voices.

Left on her own to run the Palace, with Auntie in the attic and Uncle away in the city, Ma decided to make some changes, using the Chinese restaurants where she'd worked back in Texas as models. She told the cook to take the heads off the fish and throw them away and never, ever put them in the soup. She added less spice and more sugar to the sauces, as well as pineapple chunks and peanuts. She thought of the one-dollar-one-item lunch buffet and all-you-can-eat Saturdays. She had my sisters and me write a new slogan on the back of the Grand Opening banner—"All New! Special Taste! Low Price!"—and hung it across the facade. She hired a white girl as a waitress and a white boy to do the dishes to give the Palace a more "American" atmosphere. Ma even persuaded Uncle to put a red-and-blue neon Budweiser sign on the wall next to the picture of Angkor Wat. To set the mood, she said.

And Ma was right. People liked the changes. As the summer progressed, customers began to trickle in for the buffet, for the daily specials, for the sweet and sour fried pork balls in the bright pink sauce, the chop suey and the egg foo young, the cocktails with the pretty paper parasols perched on the ice.

But if Auntie or Uncle noticed, they didn't say anything, not that I heard.

Instead, one night when Uncle returned before closing, he surprised us all while we were eating our dinner at a back table, bounding through the glass doors and asking, "Did you see the moon tonight?"

"Moon? Who has time to look at the moon?" Auntie grumbled into her soup.

"Quick, children, come!" He gestured to Sam and the girls to join him by the windows. "You can see the rabbit in the moon very clearly."

They stood in a booth, pressing their faces to the glass.

"Can you see his whiskers? There and there?" Uncle laughed. "A moon like this is a good sign. Our luck is changing. I know it."

"If our luck changes with the moon, it will be very fickle indeed," said Auntie.

But Uncle was unperturbed. He insisted we all come outside with him to the parking lot, even the cook, to stare at the moon, which was in fact very full and bright, hovering in the sky like a giant silver dollar. It had stormed earlier in the day, and the parking lot was still filled with giant ponds from the rain. The sky was reflected in each puddle, so that it seemed the parking lot was littered with moons, like so many mushrooms after a shower.

And then Uncle began to tell us a story he remembered, something his father had told him, about the rabbit that lived in the moon. Once the Lord Buddha in one of his many incarnations had walked the earth as a beggar, he said. He had walked from village to village, begging for food, when he came upon a fox and a monkey and a rabbit in a clearing, huddled around an open fire. The Buddha asked them each for something to eat, and the fox had quickly run into a farmer's henhouse and returned with an egg in his jaws for the old man. And the monkey had scampered into the jungle and returned with a bunch of bananas in his paws. And finally the rabbit began to cry, because he was too small and weak to steal food from anyone or to climb tall trees in the jungle to fetch the fruit that grew there. He himself ran about the earth, looking for roots and vegetables, wary always of the bigger animals that could eat him in one bite. The rabbit cried because he had nothing to offer the beggar, when suddenly he knew what he could do. The rabbit leapt into the flames, immolating himself so that the poor old man would have some meat for his meal. "And that is why the Buddha put the rabbit in the moon," Uncle concluded, his head tilted towards the sky. "So that we will all remember the kind rabbit's sacrifice."

I waited a moment, thinking there might be more to the story. Such as how the rabbit enjoyed living on the moon because he was free from predators and had plenty of food to eat, also supplied by Buddha, and how wonderful it was to gaze at the earth in the sky like a blue-green pearl. Perhaps the Buddha sent more rabbits to the moon, so that he wouldn't feel lonely. But no, Uncle had finished talking. That was it.

Auntie clicked her tongue against the roof of her mouth, annoyed, and announced she would catch a chill if she stayed outdoors this late at night, what an idea, and she turned on her heels, a hand on her hip, and went back inside the Palace. The cook finished his cigarette and tossed it into one of the moon-adorned puddles then headed back to the kitchen. My little brother and sisters began to play tag, chasing each other across the parking lot, while Sourdi ran after them, trying to keep them from splashing through the water and ruining their shoes. Only Ma and Uncle remained in place, side by side, staring at the sky.

In the strong moonlight, their faces glowed perfectly white.

I felt angry at Uncle all at once, for his horrible story, for his impractical ways. I wanted Ma to laugh out loud, to laugh at him, to show that she wasn't going to be fooled, she wasn't going to be talked into admiring a silly rabbit. She was a monkey or a fox. She was not a small, weak creature, but wily and fast. I wished, I wished, I wished.

I didn't understand then how Ma could like this kind of thing, how she might find such talk romantic. I didn't see how it might be refreshing after a day and evening of standing in a hot kitchen, staring into plates of congealing ginger beef and curry prawns, speaking in a foreign tongue that scratched the roof of her mouth. I didn't see how a few honeyed words at the end of the day might make all the difference in her life, might tip the scales between what was bearable and what was not.

Instead I felt only anger, only the heat of my own heart rising to my cheeks, and I turned away from my mother and ran back inside the Palace, where Auntie ignored me as she stood at the window, staring outside not at the burning moon but at Ma and Uncle standing side by side in its light.

CHAPTER 11

The September I Turned Twelve Again

We started school in September only to discover we were late. School began early here, two weeks before the end of August. Here I was no longer a city girl, but a girl who went to school with the sons and daughters of farmers, and their school year still followed an agricultural calendar from back in the days when kids had to work on their parents' farms. Still, despite the mix-up, I discovered there was one advantage to starting at a new school again. I had turned twelve in August, and back in my old school in East Dallas I used to pretend that my birthday was in June so I could have a party. So this year I told my teachers that my birthday was the day after Labor Day, (which I figured would always be a school day).

Just as I thought, this school like my old schools made a big deal out of birthdays, unlike Ma. My first period class—chorus—prepared to have a party, and we were all required to bring in some kind of junk food to celebrate. I suspected that Ma would make me bring in spring rolls along with take-out menus from the Palace, for advertising's sake. She wasn't going to let me waste her money to buy brand name food and hand it out for free. All weekend long, I thought about the goodies I hoped my classmates would bring, forbidden foods like Twinkies and Ding Dongs, Devil Dogs and Cheetos, Doritos and Pringles, Kool-Aid, Coke and Pepsi. But on the morning of the sixth, after the chorus teacher, Mr. Olson, made everyone sing "Happy Birthday" to me in a four-part harmony, I suddenly found that I was not actually hungry. It was first period, after all, which began at 8:38 in the morning now that I was in junior high, and I'd just eaten breakfast. Now with all the bags of technicolored, processed, sugar-laden treats before me, I stood at the desks of food, a paper plate in my hand, and had no desire to eat any of it. I took a couple

Ding Dongs and a Twinkie to be polite, it was my birthday after all, but I stuffed them in my backpack when nobody was looking. I knew Sam and the twins would eat this kind of food whether they were full or not.

Was this what it meant to grow older? I wondered. My hunger for American junk food abating?

Then that afternoon, the taunts began after lunch, during P.E. This was nothing strange, I had expected as much. I'd been at this school for one week, time enough for kids to stare, to decide whether or not they wanted to like me or hate me or ignore me, time enough for those prone to action to act.

We were forced to play horseshoes outdoors under the supervision of the two gym teachers, a game whose point I could not grasp, which was not surprising. I rarely understood the point of the games we played in gym, but at least the iron horseshoes were too heavy to hurl through the air, for example at me, while my back was turned. So I actually enjoyed standing outside in the sunshine, the wide open sky above me like a distant ocean, the wind whipping through my hair, cooling the sweat on my neck. Then the gym teachers blew on their silver whistles, and it was time to run inside and shower.

I never showered. I'd learned it was a bad idea in my last four schools. Usually I waited until all the girls went into the shower room, and I then changed out of my shorts and T-shirt and back into my school clothes—a different set of shorts and a different T-shirt—as quickly as possible, locked my locker, tied my sneakers again and tried to get back out into the open again as soon as possible. But today, my official twelfth birthday, I found my way blocked as I made it past the rows of gray half lockers and worn wooden benches. A group of three girls were waiting just inside the doorway, arms crossed against their chests. I slowed my pace and carefully folded my towel and placed it in the used towel bin as I watched them from the corner of my eye. They were trying to look non-chalant, but I'd seen this pose a thousand times before. The tallest girl was blonde, with a Farrah cut that was several years out of date, even I knew this. The shortest girl had bright blue eyeshadow that made it hard for me to concentrate on her facial features. She had a low center of gravity and enormous breasts. The middle girl looked mousy, pale, freckled. She turned her head to look at the tallest girl, as if waiting for a cue. She was it, the weakest link, so I ran up to her and punched her in the nose as hard as I could. The blood bloomed down her T-shirt, staining her training bra. I could see the contours through the thin cotton.

To my surprise, the other two girls laughed. Apparently, watching me beat up their accomplice was more entertaining than what they'd planned for me.

"What are you, some kind of *gut?*" the short girl asked. She scowled at me, but let me pass now into the gym and then into the hallway. I made it safely through all my afternoon classes. The girls hadn't reported me, claiming instead that their friend had fallen and bumped her nose.

Strange.

That evening as I lay in bed next to Sourdi, telling my sister of the puzzling end to my fistfight, Sourdi raised her head onto her fist.

"What does that mean?" I asked her. "Gut?"

"Don't you know? 'Gut' means Indian."

"Indian?"

"You know, like cowboys and Indians." We'd watched a steady course of John Wayne's cinematic treasures on our scrolling black and white TV in Texas. *Stage Coach, Rio Grande, Rooster Cogburn, True Grit, Red River, Fort Apache* and *The Comancheros.* I must have seen *The Alamo* at least thirty times. In the beginning Sourdi and I had liked how John Wayne talked. Slow enough so that we could understand. By my second month in America, I could imitate him even if I had no idea what he was saying.

"That girl thinks I'm an Indian?"

Sourdi rolled her eyes. "What do you think?"

"Is that good or bad?"

"I don't know." Sourdi sighed and scooted away from me, onto her back. "But there are more Indians than us. So maybe that's why they didn't report you."

I stared at her profile in the dark. Her long eyes stared at the ceiling, ignoring me. "How you'd learn all this stuff?"

"Duke. He knows everything."

The skinny new busboy? Without understanding why, I felt immediately jealous, heat rising to my cheeks. "Chopstick Boy? What does he know? He probably made that all up. He's a *dork,*" I said proudly, using this new word, which I had heard often enough in the halls just before one boy decided to shove another one.

Sourdi sat up and pulled my hair. Hard.

"Ow!"

"Take it back!"

"What? Ow!"

"Say you're sorry!"

"What's wrong with you? Ow! Let go of my hair!"

But Sourdi only twisted harder.

"Okay. I'm sorry. Chopstick Boy's not a dork."

Sourdi let go of my hair.

My scalp stung. I rubbed my head while pretending it didn't hurt so much. There were long black hairs on the pillow, black cracks along the white cotton, all the hairs Sourdi had pulled from my stinging head. I pretended not to care. I made my face blank.

"When did you get so worked up about Chopstick Boy anyway?"

"What do you know? You're only in *junior* high."

I could have said something mean. It was on the tip of my tongue. I just couldn't understand Sourdi's shifting loyalties. We'd both called the busboy "Chopstick Boy" since he'd started working at the Palace. He was tall and long and as skinny as a chopstick after all. He'd even overheard me once, but he'd only smiled. He probably thought it was a compliment. Now he was making me argue with Sourdi, who never argued with anyone, especially not me. I was her favorite.

She was the one who had taught me how to put on makeup when Ma was at work and the little kids were watching TV. She'd bring out her stash of makeup, the pieces she'd bought one by one with our share of the spring roll money, and in the safety of the locked bathroom, she'd outlined my eyes in thick, black swaths, she curled my lashes, she dabbed layer and layer of pale liquid Cover Girl Fair Ivory foundation on my face and showed me how to change my skin from tan to pink. She made me pucker my lips as though I'd eaten something too sour and colored them in red. Then she piled my unruly thick hair on top of my head and, using what seemed like a million metal bobby pins, made it all stay in place, so that I seemed extra tall.

"You see, you're beautiful!" She smiled at me in the mirror then. "Better than Phoebe Cates. Better than Jaclyn Smith." She named our favorite brunettes from TV. (There was also Valerie Bertinelli, but her name had too many syllables for us in those days.)

I looked at myself, this stranger with heavy lidded eyes and too bright lips, and nodded to make Sourdi happy. I knew she'd tried her best. But I also knew that I wasn't beautiful. Sourdi was the beautiful one.

Now in our bed, side by side, we didn't speak. Sourdi was still angry at me, my head still tingled.

Sourdi eventually fell asleep, her breaths deepening, almost turning into sighs, but I tossed and turned. I couldn't get comfortable. My feet were cold and my stomach hurt. Finally, I got up to go to the bathroom down the hall.

There in the yellowish light from the low-wattage bulbs that Uncle and Auntie used to save on money, I lifted my nightgown and discovered that I was bleeding.

My period was like nothing in the films that the school nurse had started showing in fifth grade. My period was nothing like I imagined it would be, a few red drops of blood like discarded flower petals. My blood wasn't even red in my pants. It was dark, almost black. I thought I might faint. I took my underpants off and wadded them up tightly and buried them in the very bottom of the trash can. Then I tried wiping the blood away from my bottom. I used an entire roll of toilet paper, running it first under a stream of cool water from the faucet and dabbing at myself, but the toilet paper kept turning pink then red then darker still.

Finally, I was too panicked to care about angering Sourdi all over again. I ran bare-bottomed back to our bedroom and shook Sourdi awake.

"What? What's wrong with you?" She squinted in the dark.

"Help me," my voice was tiny, not my voice at all, a mouse's voice. "There's something wrong."

"What's wrong?"

"I think, I think..." my mouse voice shrunk even more, until it was an ant whispering in Sourdi's ear. "I think it's my period."

"Your period!"

"Sssh!"

"I didn't get my period until I was fourteen. You're too young."

"No. No, I'm not. Help me."

Sourdi shook her head and rubbed the sleep from her eyes, and then she took me by the hand, leading me back to the bathroom.

There I demonstrated for her how I could not stop the flow of blood from my hidden wound. I held the square of rouge-colored toilet paper up for inspection.

"Oh. You're right," she said. Then her voice grew very gentle, and I was her favorite again. "Sit on the toilet. I'll get you some new underpants. And I'll show you where I store the tampons."

I nodded. My stomach still hurt, but I wrapped my arms around myself and waited calmly. I was no longer scared. Sourdi would know what to do.

The next day, as I waited outside school for the bus to come, standing not so close to the brick wall of the school so that I could be cornered against it, but not so far away that I couldn't flee back inside if I were attacked by a group, I heard a familiar rumble, and saw Chopstick Boy's, I mean, Duke's pickup idling across the street. He waved at me, and then I saw that Sourdi was in the cab as well.

"What are you doing in there?" I growled at Sourdi after I climbed in. "Ma's gonna be mad."

"Ma's not gonna know." And Sourdi looked at me pointedly, her black eyes warning me that she'd pull every hair from my head if she had to.

I shrugged as nonchalantly as possible.

"All righty, Ladies. Next stop, Hawkeye Elementary." And Duke put his pickup into gear.

From that day onward, Duke picked us all up from our respective schools, letting Sam and the twins ride in the back of the truck.

To be truthful, I enjoyed not having to ride the bus where the boys threw spitwads continuously and sometimes drooled long brown streams of chaw-stained saliva onto the floor or else spat it against the windows, no matter how many times the driver yelled at them not to. And I didn't miss the girls who scowled at me and pulled the skin back from their eyes, or put a finger on the tips of their pointy pink noses, flattening the cartilage just for my benefit. But at least they didn't try to punch or poke or scratch me. Word of my fight in the locker room had gotten around.

When the weather was good, not stormy, which turned the country roads to mud, Duke took us for rides before dropping us off half a block from the Palace, where the buses would have dropped us off had we ridden them.

We had time to take this detour so that Ma wouldn't get suspicious. If we arrived at the Palace too soon from school, she might have noticed that we weren't taking the bus anymore. And even though Ma hadn't said anything about taking or not taking the bus, hitching or not hitching a ride with the busboy, none of us chose to mention our new arrangement to her.

Duke liked to play his radio full blast, and when we got to a certain hill a few miles outside of town, he could pick up stations from as far away as Sioux City, Iowa, and once, when the wind was blowing the right way, Omaha. We could hear all the hits, Survivor's "Eye of the Tiger," Hall and Oates singing "I Can't Go for That," Juice Newton's "The Sweetest Thing," and even Paul McCartney and Stevie Wonder crooning "Ebony and Ivory." Sometimes Duke would sing along with Paul and Stevie, and this made Sourdi giggle.

I didn't mind riding in Duke's pick up with the windows rolled down, the wind whipping my hair into a black cyclone, the music thumping in my ears, Sam and Maly and Navy squealing with delight from the bed as the truck hit another bump in the gravel road. But Sourdi's giggling. That bothered me. My oldest sister had always had a full-throated laugh, a deep sound more like a rumble. When she allowed herself to cut loose, she laughed the way that I imagined that earthquakes deep below the sea began: her entire body shook silently, tears gathering on the tips of her thick lashes, and then she would explode with a snort. Sourdi's laugh was the only thing that wasn't graceful about her. I loved to hear her laugh.

But this giggling. I found it strange and unsettling. I had no idea then what trouble it portended.

CHAPTER 12

The Gamblers

A few days after Labor Day, the J.C. Penney's went out of business downtown, and someone shot out the front window of the Palace. We arrived at work Saturday morning to find the glass shattered, shards sprinkled across the sidewalk like an early frost.

The week before, someone had put a dead snake with a drawing of the American flag across the welcome mat. There had been letters to the editor of the local paper about "foreigners taking American jobs," and there'd been some stories on the TV about the threat from Japan's rising economy; "The next Pearl Harbor?" the newscaster asked. Another farm had been marked for foreclosure. Men in town wore black armbands over their shirtsleeves. Perhaps we shouldn't have been so surprised about the window then, but at the time we didn't see how any of these events were connected.

Uncle stood rooted in place a long time, just staring at the hole in the Palace. Ma ran inside and brought out the broom, then Sourdi swept the shards of glass into a pile while Ma knocked the last pieces of glass from the window frame, running the plastic edge of her dustpan over the wood, back and forth, back and forth, the raspy sound like a song played on a broken instrument.

Finally, Uncle said, "It's lucky they didn't steal anything."

"What's there to steal?" Auntie scoffed, pacing on the grass.

"Everything!" Suddenly Uncle grew angry, his face reddening, the veins on his forehead throbbing. He waved his hands helplessly, at the Palace, its tables and booths exposed to the air, as though he wanted to scoop them up into his arms. "Our future!" he shouted. "The children's future!"

"Junk," Auntie spat. "Worthless. I told you we should never have invited them to come. Now it's too late. Now everything is ruined."

Uncle rushed towards Auntie then, his right arm raised, and Auntie shouted, "Go ahead, hit me! Hit me!"

Then when he didn't, she bent over the pile of glass, picked up a large jagged shard and waved it at Uncle's face. He took a step backward, and she took a step forward, swinging the glass before her like a scythe.

My brother and little sisters stood motionless on the sidewalk, shocked, their mouths hanging open, their eyes widened into circles, watching Auntie and Uncle fight. They looked terrified.

Uncle put his hands before him, palms upwards, and took a step towards Auntie. She struck at him with the glass, and he stepped back again.

Ma stepped forwards now, a look of concentration in her dark eyes. I tried to grab her arm, but she brushed me aside. She had her loving face on, which was not to say a tender face, or a gentle face, but rather the fierce expression that meant she was ready to walk through fire.

It was time to leave, I thought. Time for us to jump back in our car and drive away, as fast as we could. Forget about packing. We could start over wherever we ended up. We wouldn't have to stop in Dallas, we could keep going this time, all the way to the sea. I wanted to grab hold of Ma and shout this in her ear until she heard me, until she listened, but when I opened my mouth, no words came out.

All at once Ma spoke up.

"It's just some boys playing a joke," she said, her voice loud and firm. She took the broom from Sourdi, holding it before her like a sword. She slipped between Uncle and Auntie, taking little steps until she was close enough to grab hold of Auntie's wrist. Still, Auntie did not put down her wedge of glass. "They don't know any better, farm boys," Ma said, shaking her head. Her voice sounded as though it wanted to laugh, although her face remained tense, alert, full of her love for Uncle. "They don't have anything to do in this kind of little town. They go drink too much, and then this happens. They think this kind of thing is funny." Slowly Auntie put her arm down, and the glass dropped onto the sidewalk, shattering around her feet.

"Yes," said Uncle. "It's just a joke."

"Just a silly joke," Ma said. She was, in fact, laughing now. "Just some boys' joke." Ma laughed without covering her mouth. She laughed until tears ran down her cheeks.

Auntie pushed Ma aside, walking right through the pile of glass, scattering it in her wake, as she marched inside the Palace. She let the door slam shut behind her.

Uncle looked at Ma briefly, his expression stricken, his old man's face melting around the edges, like a candle left in the sun. Ma, for her part, looked away. She lowered her arm, the one holding the broom, and began to sweep up the glass. Her shoulders shook with her sobbing laughs. The broom scraped the sidewalk with a sound like sandpaper moving over bone, scruhscruhscruh.

Long after Uncle left to call the police, long after the glass had been swept away, Ma continued to sweep the sidewalk.

With the insurance money, Uncle managed to have the window replaced and even bought a couple of outdoor lights for security, one to shine on the Palace and one to shine on the American flag that Ma put up by the front door. The police promised to investigate the crime and even though they never charged anyone, the fact they went around asking questions made people nervous and for a while no one dared to bother the Palace, no more dead animals were deposited at our door, no more cryptic messages were left for us to decipher, no one shot out the new window.

But Auntie and Uncle continued to argue. They fought as though their lives depended on it.

Once Ma and I walked in on them while they were arguing in the kitchen. We were coming home from the Palace, it was late, and we were both tired, but when we stepped into the house, we could hear Auntie and Uncle's voices moving in a slow, circling dance, accusation and counter-accusation. They were arguing about the loan shark, and the money Uncle had borrowed, and what would happen if he couldn't pay the interest, especially what would happen to his legs, his knees, his tender and fragile joints. Apparently the loan shark had called Uncle this day and said he would be coming soon.

However, when Ma and I entered the kitchen, Auntie and Uncle stopped arguing abruptly. They were both seated at the table, facing each other but not looking at each other. Auntie announced with a sigh that she'd like some tea. Immediately Ma went to make it for her although it had been Ma who had stood on her feet all day, all night, working. Then Auntie turned to Uncle and began to complain again, about the changes in the Palace, the ones Ma had made, the bland way the food tasted, the strange food coloring in the sauces, the all-you-can-eat lunch buffet. "These farmers eat, eat, eat. They will eat until we are bankrupt," she said. "Who runs a business like this?"

Uncle sat very still, silent now, while Auntie talked on and on, her complaints circling around him in the air like the cactus fences that farmers back in Cambodia used to grow around their houses. I looked at Uncle very carefully to see if I could read his face, but he looked neither angry nor sad, only tired.

Ma brought the teapot over and poured both Auntie and Uncle a cup. She acted as though she did not hear Auntie's voice at all. Her face was as blank as Uncle's and when she bowed her head to refill Auntie's cup, she might as well have been one of Auntie's servants, a woman of little means and fewer options, a woman struck deaf and dumb by her circumstances.

I wished then that the loan shark would come immediately and eat us all.

One Friday in mid-September Uncle announced that he had some good news. In fact, he declared, he very well may have found a solution for all our problems. He said this at dinner, as we sat around a table in the back of the Palace, and immediately both Ma and Auntie stopped eating, mid-bite, and turned to stare at him. Neither looked hopeful, only curious.

Then he explained that he'd been invited to play cards in Omaha this weekend with some important businessmen. He'd heard about the game through some Chinese men he'd met in Sioux City. A cook and a busboy. They weren't Cambodian, but Uncle could speak their southern dialect. Anyway, the gambling was good in Omaha, they said, and they'd invited Uncle to join them. Everyone knew all really important business deals were made while playing cards, Uncle said. He was lucky to have been invited.

Auntie waited a minute after he finished speaking to see if he was truly done or if he had left some important detail out, such as how exactly this was going to solve all our problems. When she was certain he'd said everything, she dropped her soup spoon onto the table with a clang. "Have you lost your mind? Gambling with a cook and a busboy? If they know such important businessmen, why are they working in the Sizzler?"

Before Uncle could answer, Ma spoke up. "You don't have to gamble," she said. "We can sell the Palace. We can use the money to pay your debts. We can move away. We can find a new place to work."

All at once Uncle began to laugh. "That's just what I was thinking! We two think alike."

Auntie rolled her eyes at this, and even Ma seemed unsure. "I'm not going to gamble!" Uncle smiled patiently, as though everything were clear. "I mean, I will play a few hands, but just to be friendly. No, don't you see the opportunity? I can meet contacts. *Les vrais hommes d'affaires.* That's what we're missing here."

"You'll gamble the Palace away," Auntie announced, pointing her chin at Uncle. "I can't say I care. Good riddance. We can let the loan shark come then. When we'll have absolutely nothing. Let him take one of the children, why don't you? My sister's got too many to keep track of anyway." Then Auntie laughed at her own joke.

"You'll see," Uncle announced, tilting back on his heels, looking off into the distance above our heads, as though he could see a bag of money there, a guardian angel with a winning hand. He smiled confidently. "I know what I'm doing."

Ma didn't say anything more, but she stopped eating, even though she'd barely touched her bowl of rice, and went back into the kitchen immediately to finish washing up.

That night, Uncle and Auntie did not argue in their room. Unaccustomed to their silence, Sourdi and I tossed in our bed, this way and that, kicking each other in the shins, knocking our sheets to the floor.

"We should run away," I whispered. "Before he comes back. Before he's lost everything."

"Uncle won't lose. Rich men know how to gamble," my sister said, squinting into the dark.

"That's not true," I said. "Rich men don't care if they win or lose because it doesn't matter, they already have all the money they need. And besides, Uncle isn't rich anymore."

But in the end, Sourdi was right.

When Uncle returned from Omaha after dawn on Monday morning, he was bearing flowers. I recognized this from all those afternoons of "Days of Our Lives" as a good sign.

In fact, Uncle had neither won nor lost. Instead he had met a friend named Chhay, a dear old friend of his he'd known since before the war. What a surprise to see him again after all these years! They'd been classmates in lycée, and now the man lived just one state away in Des Moines, Iowa. He'd been a rascal in school, never very serious about his studies, although he'd written several very good poems, and one had been published in France. His father had even threatened to disown him, his only son, because he'd refused to become a lawyer. What use was a poet? the old man had asked. At home, the friend had lived in near poverty, barely able to make a living, selling his poems as best he could. The last time Uncle had seen him, before the war, he was living in a tiny apartment, wearing ratty clothes, spending all his money on feed for the twenty singing canaries he kept in bamboo cages that hung from the ceiling. And yet now, here in America, he was a successful businessman, prosperous, the owner of many properties. Uncle smiled proudly, remembering the rascal his friend had once been, as though the bohemian youth and the successful present were Uncle's own memories, his own achievements.

(*When I was a boy*, I thought, hearing Uncle speak in my head, *I had a friend who could walk on water, who could raise the dead with his own two hands, who could buy Palaces like knickknacks, like flowers to press in a book of memories.*)

After they'd both had too much to drink, Uncle had explained to his friend about our financial problems, and the man had said he might be able to help. He had some business contacts, men who might be interested in purchasing a restaurant.

Auntie clicked her tongue against her teeth then and sighed. "You shouldn't have told him everything! What kind of men would buy a restaurant that's failing?"

Uncle smiled then, and nodded, rubbing his hands together, as though he'd been waiting for just this question. "Men who are looking for a tax write-off!" he proclaimed. And then he explained how in America there were some men so wealthy, they needed to own a business that lost money.

"They must be criminals." Auntie nodded. "No one honest could have that much money."

But Uncle only shrugged. He said his friend would be bringing the men in a week's time, Auntie could judge for herself then exactly what kind of men they were.

The day Mr. Chhay would arrive with his business contacts, Ma was still working frantically to get the Palace in order. She'd tried to make the Palace look as run-down as possible when we thought the loan shark was coming to collect his money, but now she wanted to spruce things up.

"Maybe we shouldn't make it look too good," I warned her. "Don't these guys want to buy a losing business?"

Ma glared at me then, her eyes narrowing. "A friend is coming! Uncle's dearest, oldest friend. What kind of face will he have if we look bad?"

Ma was embarrassed because Uncle's friend had known Uncle and Auntie when they were wealthy. She didn't want him to see how far the family had fallen.

By evening, Ma went into overdrive, ordering us about. "Go find the red paper tablecloths! Go!" she commanded. She had Sam wash all the windows, inside and out. She set Sourdi and me to sweeping and mopping and scrubbing and shining. Ma, and even Auntie, scurried about the kitchen helping the cook to prepare the banquet food: spring rolls and curry prawns, bean noodle soup, ginger-sauce fish, sticky rice, and the lobster we'd ordered special and kept in a tank in the back in case any customers happened to feel like eating something expensive.

By the time Mr. Chhay was about to arrive, the Palace was ablaze in good-luck red. Red tablecloths, red napkins, little votive candles in the red ashtrays. Ma had insisted that Sourdi and I go home and change into our best dresses. When we returned, we found that Ma and Auntie had transformed themselves as well. Ma looked good, less tired, and healthy with pink cheeks and red lips, but Auntie had become another woman entirely. The two halves of her face were gone, hidden by the magic of Mary Kay. Her hair was combed neatly, pulled back from her forehead. She smelled of flowers. If not for her raised scar, she would have looked beautiful.

When Uncle and the men pulled up to the Palace, Ma made us get away from the windows. She banished Sam and the twins upstairs to

Auntie's apartment but allowed Sourdi and me to stay in the kitchen, in case she needed our help.

Then the men were coming in the doors, we could hear their voices booming off the walls. Uncle was talking too loudly, nervously. Another man told a joke, and Uncle laughed loudest of all. Ma was flying about the kitchen, rearranging the platter of prawns, restacking the spring rolls, ladling broth into a bowl then testing the noodles for elasticity. "Oranges, where are the oranges?" she asked no one in particular. "We should have bought pears!"

Sourdi found Ma's Virginia Slims and handed them to her. Ma nearly dropped the pack as she tried to shake one out. I flicked her lighter open for her, held the flame up between us. Ma nodded at me but didn't speak as she leaned towards the fire, her cigarette dangling from between her lips.

She inhaled the smoke in gulps, and then set the cigarette carefully on a saucer. She smoothed her hair down one last time, picked up a tray of spring rolls, and rushed out into the dining room.

From inside the kitchen, Sourdi and I watched the adults through a crack in the door.

None of Mr. Chhay's friends had normal names, it seemed, but called themselves by sobriquets: Uncle Chapeau, Third Younger Brother, Big Nose. The final man had no name at all, not that anyone called him at least, but sat quietly while the others spoke, his eyes darting greedily over everything, the tables and the candles, the glowing Budweiser sign and the print of Angkor Wat. The way he sat on the edge of his chair like a cat ready to spring, his tongue licking his lips, I could tell he liked the Palace all right.

Uncle Chapeau was an ancient wrinkled man with white hair and a long, thin face who rarely spoke but drank quite a bit. Third Younger Brother and Big Nose were younger, perhaps in their thirties, although Big Nose had acne that ran across his cheeks in an angry red swath. They sat on either side of Uncle Chapeau like bodyguards, pouring him tea and scowling. The remaining man was Mr. Chhay, but because he sat with his back to the kitchen, I could not see him very well. I was disappointed because I had wanted to see what a first-born son who had defied his father to write poetry and keep canaries looked like. Wild, I had imagined. With long poetic black hair and a wandering eye, the kind that could make a person look crazy or else very wise. However, from behind, Mr. Chhay looked quite ordinary, merely middle-aged and a little slumped in the shoulders. He asked Uncle many questions and wrote the answers down in a tiny notebook that fit into the pocket of his suit jacket.

After the fourth course, Mr. Chhay stopped asking Uncle questions, and the old man began toasting everyone, holding his tiny wine glass up with both hands and bowing slightly at the end of each toast.

It felt odd watching my family entertain guests. I couldn't make out what they were saying, they spoke so quickly and my Khmer had grown so slow and awkward, but I could tell when they were talking about business, the serious way Uncle nodded and gestured with his hands, and I could tell when they were being charming, the way Auntie tilted her head as she spoke, waving her hands daintily about. She seemed almost flirtatious, smiling as though she were a young girl again. And I could tell she was witty, too, when everyone laughed at her jokes.

Even Ma seemed like a different person. She looked young, younger than I had imagined possible. Maybe it was the makeup, maybe it was the wine, but her face had softened, so that she smiled easily, so that the worried lines that had chiseled into her forehead were nearly gone, and once she actually laughed so loudly, tossing back her head, that she forgot to cover her mouth with her hand.

That night I saw my family as they might have once been, holding dinner parties, chatting about politics, joking about the state of the world, sophisticated, prosperous, healthy. I could almost believe that this scene would continue even after the night had ended. I could almost believe this pageant was real, and the rest of our life a dream, except that Uncle's teeth were still missing, and Auntie's face was still ruined, and the men were not really friends but strangers, possibly criminals, and Ma was not really happy and gay but desperate that this scheme work.

Finally, after many hours, after the men had eaten all that we had prepared, and drunk a lot, five bottles total of three different kinds of wine and the Chinese clear rice liquor that Uncle had brought all the way from Houston, which smelled like lighter fluid when I had put a glass to my nose, they left. Uncle escorted the men out the door, pressing his palms together before his face, bowing his head as they staggered to their cars. I could see him bowing through the windows.

We all stayed up very late that night, washing the dishes and woks and pans together in the kitchen. But even after we had finished cleaning up, the adults seemed reluctant to leave the Palace, even Auntie. Perhaps because it seemed as though we might be able to really sell our restaurant and leave this town, the Palace suddenly seemed very precious to them. All at once, they started talking again, pulling down some chairs from a back table and sitting as though it were noon and not two in the morning.

We'd turned off all the lights except for the red candles on either side of the Buddha shrine and the red-and-blue neon Budweiser sign. Still, I could see that their faces were flushed from the wine.

Uncle said something funny and both Auntie and Ma laughed, covering their mouths in the same way, tilting their heads together, Ma's arm lacing through Auntie's as though they were young girls again.

My head felt very heavy. I curled up in a booth, resting my chin on my arm atop the table, wishing I were in my bed.

The adults laughed and laughed.

Then Auntie began to talk about a woman who had been sent to her work camp during the war, and her face began to change before my eyes. The corners of her lips pulled downward, her skin sagged, her eyes narrowed, her skin creased into wrinkles as she grew old again.

Auntie said, "Of course, I recognized her immediately. Madame Yu. Their restaurant had been so famous. I remember our father invited three of his classmates to one dinner, and it cost him five hundred dollars. Afterwards he said he could die a happy man because he had tasted the Yu clan's shark fin soup. Even the French waited in line for a table. After the CIA arrived, the Americans."

Ma whispered something into Auntie's ear that I couldn't hear.

"No. Why would she know me? The Yu family was very secretive. They wouldn't hire anyone but their own relatives from the countryside to work in their restaurant. They were afraid someone would steal their recipes. They used to place big men, angry-looking men at the kitchen doors, armed with clubs, in case anyone should try to sneak inside while they were cooking. I thought it was excessive. But it's true, the thieves were clever in those days."

Auntie rubbed her face with one hand tiredly, inadvertently removing much of her makeup. When she stopped, her purple scar throbbed, dividing her face in two again.

"I saw how she died, Madame Yu. She wasn't used to working, planting the rice. She was very weak and sick. Everyone was weak and sick. I don't know what she did wrong, but the guards decided to make an example of her. They beat her to death with shovels in front of everyone. They said she was an enemy of the people. They made us watch. I had to stare at the ground beside her body, I couldn't look at her. I didn't do a thing. I didn't say a word. I just sat there while they beat her to death."

There was a long pause. In the red light, the adults seemed frozen, like puppets in a play, at rest between acts. I wanted to stuff Auntie's words back inside her mouth. I wanted to sew her lips shut so that she could never use her poison talk again. From now on, I would only allow Ma and Auntie and Uncle to speak about happy things, the stories that had made them laugh. But it was too late. Auntie had ruined everything. It was as though a clock had struck twelve in a fairy tale. Ma and Uncle were changing back to their old selves. Growing older. More tired. Resigned. Until they looked the way they did every day.

Ma pulled out her cigarettes from the pocket of her apron. She lit one quickly, the orange flame of her lighter hissing as it touched the end of her cigarette. She closed the lighter with a flick of her wrist as she exhaled a cloud of blue smoke.

"I had to pretend to be so stupid," Ma said. "Every day. I had to pretend I could remember nothing. I spoke in simple sentences. No French. No Chinese. The guards, they would test us. They would shout out a word, a phrase to each other, to see if we would react. To see who understood. I had to pretend all the time. I told them my husband was a taxi driver. I told them I had sold fruit in a stand in the city. They believed me.

"It used to be so hard to deceive everyone. To remember to act so mute. But now I've become stupid. In America, people they hear me speak, they hear my accent, they can't understand. I don't have to pretend anymore. I have become dumb."

"No, not you," Uncle said. "Not you."

"When I was a little girl, my classmates used to tease me. 'You're so ugly! So dark!' I remember what they all said," Ma whispered. "Mother used to complain, 'How did you get to be so black? Not from my side of the family!' But because of my skin, the soldiers believed me when I told them I was originally from the countryside, that I had only moved to the city during the civil war, after the Americans started bombing the farms. I used to hate my skin, but it saved my life."

"Your skin," Auntie said. She stroked the scar that ran across her cheek, her eyes glittering. "Your skin is perfect."

I couldn't hear Ma's reply. I could only see the smoke that emerged from her mouth as she leaned against her older sister, their heads touching, their arms entwined.

"I should have died," Auntie said. "I should have died in that minefield, the same as my sons."

"Don't," Uncle said loudly. His voice was too loud, awkward from all the wine he'd had to drink. "Don't talk that way," he said, his syllables were stretched too thin.

"Don't you wish I was dead? Don't you wish I had been the one to die and our children—"

Uncle stood up abruptly. His chair scraped against the floor then fell over with a bang. He rushed out of the dining room and into the kitchen, the door swinging open and spilling golden light everywhere, messy as water from a broken pipe. Ma and Auntie did not move from the table. They did not stir or lift their heads even when we heard the back door open and slam shut, loud as a gunshot in the hush of the Palace, as Uncle ran outside into the black night. Ma and Auntie sat like statues, frozen in their embrace, their heads pressed together, the smoke from Ma's cigarette rising above them like a shroud.

That night, although it was very late, although I was exhausted, my limbs heavy, I could not sleep.

The moon was shining through the bedroom window, directly into my eyes. I tossed and turned, tried burying my head beneath my pillow, pulling the sheets up to my nose, but I could still feel the moon on my back, its cold light penetrating to my bones. Finally, I rose and headed to the kitchen, thinking a glass of hot water might soothe my nerves, a bowl of leftover noodles might calm the knot in my stomach.

Uncle was speaking so softly, I did not hear him until I was at the kitchen door. I was surprised because the light was off, and I had not realized he and Auntie were still awake nor that they were in the kitchen. The door was opened just wide enough for me to see Uncle's back as he sat at the kitchen table, a teacup before him. Moonlight poured through the kitchen window, like the blade of a sharp knife slicing through the darkness. I couldn't see Auntie completely either, just her arm. It lay exposed and glowing on the kitchen table at the end of the shaft of cold light.

I smelled the smoke before I saw it, twisting through the air, like milk through tea. And I realized that Uncle was speaking not to Auntie but to Ma.

His voice was soft in my ears. He wasn't whispering, but I had to slow my breathing to hear him correctly. His voice was that soft, like water seeping through a crack in a wall.

"The moon always reminds me," he said.

"My wife was pregnant again. She had given birth to our first two sons a few years earlier, but then she lost the next baby, a girl. Afterwards, she had grown quite depressed and withdrawn. I hadn't known what to do. She would cry for days on end, lock herself in her room, refuse to come out, to eat, to do anything. She wanted nothing to do with me. She couldn't even take care of our sons. I had to hire a woman to look after them. It was as though I'd lost not only the baby but my wife as well. This depression lasted more than a year. But then little by little, she regained her strength, and we were able to conceive another child.

"When she found out she was pregnant again, she was naturally very nervous. She went to see an old fortuneteller who told her the baby was not safe until the fifth month; before that anything could happen. The woman told her that she should hide from the world, not let anyone know she was with child. But if she made it to the fifth month, the baby would be fine. My wife could be very superstitious sometimes.

"To celebrate when the fifth month finally arrived, we went to see the ocean. We bought ices to eat as we walked along the sand. Ices and fresh lychees. She had been feeling very sick to her stomach the first four months but now she ate so many lychees, handful after handful. I began to laugh. I teased her, Are you sure there's not a little monkey inside you, the way you eat? 'How dare you call our child a monkey!' she said, but she laughed too. When she laughed, her eyes became perfect crescents, like the quarter moon.

"There were many people at the beach, all kinds of people in those days, French, Chinese, Vietnamese, Cambodian, everyone together.

"My wife insisted upon paying money to release some caged birds. Young boys used to line the boardwalk, with their wooden cages of songbirds. You paid them some coins, and they would say, 'Bless you,' as though they were monks, and release a bird from its cage. I told my wife it was foolish, because these boys were not as innocent as they looked. They trained the birds to come back every evening. They would wait for them with all the cage doors open, and the birds would fly right back inside because then the boys would give them food. They were trained birds who no longer knew how to survive in the world. What kind of merit could you have for releasing them?

"But my wife insisted. 'Maybe they like to fly in the air for a day. Even if they return at night, how do you know they don't enjoy their freedom during the day?' So I gave her the money and she paid to have five birds released. We watched them swoop through the sky in arcs as though they were writing poems in the air. They even began to sing. And I saw that my wife was right. The birds obviously enjoyed their freedom, even if it lasted only a few hours.

"That evening we watched the moon rise over the sea. The ocean was dark and calm and the sky clear all the way to the edge of the world. The moon shone onto the water so brightly, we could see fish leap up from the waves, snapping at air. I put my hand on my wife's belly then. I told her I could feel the baby leaning against my palm. 'You are going to have a little girl who will look just like you,' I said. 'She will have your beautiful, round moon face.' My wife laughed at me and said now I was the one who said foolish things, but I was right. When our baby was born, she was a girl and she looked just like her mother. So we decided to call her 'Channary.' Moon-faced girl. My wife always said we were blessed because she had freed those birds that day.

"Maybe it's true. When I think how blessed we were . . ."

Uncle stopped speaking abruptly. I waited for Ma to say something. I was sitting in the hallway outside the kitchen, in the shadows, my back against the wall, my arms wrapped around my legs. I hadn't realized that I was spying, that I was eavesdropping, that I might be doing something very bad until the silence that followed Uncle's speech. And even then I couldn't stop myself, I couldn't make myself move, I couldn't force my legs to stand up and walk away. The strange silence seemed to grow and spread, pushing out of the kitchen into the hallway, stronger than the smell of Ma's smoke, softer than Uncle's voice, but all-pervasive and in-escapable. It found me in the shadows and wrapped me up with Ma and Uncle, binding us together, flies in a spider's invisible web.

Instead of fleeing back to my room, I crept towards the kitchen door, drawn by the silence, and I peeked through the narrow opening. At first I could not make out what I was seeing, and then it was clear to me, my mother was standing next to my uncle. He was still seated at the table. She was bending over him, her two arms cradling his head, as he leaned against her body, his face in her ribs. They held completely still, as though they were not alive but frozen, a black and white photograph captured in the odd, colorless light of the waning moon. Then Uncle gasped, and I realized he was crying.

"I'll always be grateful to you. Even then, before the war, you took care of our daughter when my wife . . . when she was not . . . when she wasn't herself."

"Sssh," Ma said, her voice soft as smoke. "Sssh."

And then I saw her kiss him. First on the cheek, then on the forehead, and then on his mouth.

I turned then, ashamed, the full sense of my crime hitting me at last. I slunk away, on tiptoe, like a thief, like a murderer, like a soldier in the night, and hurried back to my bed.

In the eight big Hells and the one hundred and eight little Hells that governed the souls of Cambodians who had sinned too greatly to be born again, I was certain there were places reserved just for people like me, for disloyal daughters, for girls who should have plucked their eyes from their own heads, who should have turned into a pillar of salt, but instead had stayed alive, had continued to live knowing that they had seen too much.

As I crept into our room, I saw that Sourdi was still asleep, her breathing even and deep and peaceful. I climbed into bed beside my sister, pulling the sheets up to my chin, as I shivered, so cold, as though I had swallowed all that moonlight and it had turned my blood to ice.

I slept too late the next morning, waking only after the sun was streaming into our room. Sourdi had already risen, and I could hear the sounds of my family in the house, the little kids running in the hallway, a toilet flushing, the television in the living room blaring the theme from *Tom and Jerry*. When I thought about what I had seen, it seemed as though I must have been lost in a dream, the kind that seemed completely real and normal until something odd happened. I had lain in bed the whole night, I had not risen and walked to the kitchen, my dream had only seemed real, but in the light of day, in the sun's warm rays, I knew it was impossible, what I had thought I'd seen.

I got up then and hurried downstairs. I didn't bother with going to the bathroom or putting on my clothes or combing my hair. I rushed straight to the kitchen to remind myself what was real and what was not, to shake this strange image that had lodged itself in my memories, sticky as a spider's silk. But then I found Uncle's teacup on the kitchen table, the tea leaves sodden at the very bottom, a fortune I didn't try to read, and Ma's cigarette on the saucer before it, her lips traced in red around the end, and I could feel once more her smoky voice in my ears, and I knew that it hadn't been a dream.

CHAPTER 13

Frying Shrimp

I did not know then how to feel happy for my mother. I did not know what a precious thing it was to be able to fall in love, for the heart to heal enough to beat passionately for another person after it had been broken, again and again.

I did not see my mother as a woman with a phoenix heart. I only knew how to think as a child, a spoiled girl who wanted her mother's love all to herself. I didn't understand anything about love in those days, only jealousy, my constant companion.

During the day, I began to talk back to Ma. When she asked me to do something, like de-vein the shrimp, or wash the counter, or walk through the dining room with a pitcher of iced tea and see if any customers wanted refills, I would sigh and roll my eyes first, as though whatever she asked me were a great burden, too much for me to bear.

She looked at me crossly and told me to hurry, and I only sighed some more.

"What's gotten into you?" she asked me once. "What's wrong with you?"

And I said, pointedly, "What's wrong with you?"

Ma shook her head then and threw her dishtowel over her shoulder. She rolled up her sleeves and began to chop a mound of chives with a cleaver. She worked very fast, reducing the long green stalks into a mound of tiny shards like identical beads in a matter of seconds. The prep table shook from the force of her cleaver. After she finished cutting the chives, she rubbed her eyes on the back of her hand to wipe away the tears that were welling up in her burning eyes.

I wanted to apologize to my mother then for my rude behavior. I wanted to put my arms around her waist as I had as a small child and bury my face in her back. I wanted her to put her knife down and put her arms around me, too, and tell me as she had when I was very young that she loved me and that I needn't be afraid because everything was going to be all right. She'd never had to ask me what I was afraid of when I was little, and I'd never had to tell her either. She understood me without my having to say a word. And in those days, it was enough that my mother reassured me to make me believe that whatever she said was true.

But now that I had turned twelve, I felt I was too old for such things.

Instead I rolled my eyes once more and said, "You don't cut those right. If you cut them under water, you wouldn't have to cry." And then I shook my head, sadly, as though Ma were impossibly incompetent, a complete embarrassment, and being her daughter were a trial indeed.

I don't know if Uncle and Ma's love ever went beyond the kiss I had witnessed in the kitchen. Physically, I mean. I never witnessed them so much as touch again.

And yet all the same, it was plain, their love for each other. The way they glanced at each other when they thought no one else would see, the way they seemed more alert in each other's presence, the way the hairs stood up on Ma's arms when Uncle brushed past, the way Uncle smiled easily in her presence, the way the air in any room they entered at the same time took on a different quality, as though lightning were about to strike.

I took to talking back to both of them, my jealous heart pounding in my chest. I complained about my chores at home and in the Palace. I sighed and shuffled, I yawned and shook my head. I provoked Ma until she slapped me once in front of customers, and even then, unabashed, I looked her in the eyes and clicked my tongue against the roof of my mouth as though to say, we both knew who really was at fault.

Then I discovered that I was not the only one who had noticed.

One night when Uncle and Auntie were arguing in their bedroom, I heard Auntie's voice cry out, sharp as broken glass, "I see how you smile! I see how you look!"

Uncle's voice, low and tired, like an animal caged too long, growled, "What should I do? Treat her like a servant?"

Auntie cried out again, "You treat me like a wife who's been abandoned. You treat me like a wife who's already dead. Hasn't that woman taken enough from me already? Now you take all that I have left. I have no face, I have no dignity."

Sourdi buried her head under her pillow, she put her fingers in her ears, just as I had always done in the past, but this night, I lay flat on my back, my eyes wide open, because I knew then that Auntie had decided to fight for her husband. Even if she didn't love him anymore, he was still hers to have.

The next day Auntie began to treat Ma differently as well. Instead of retreating to her apartment upstairs, she now stayed in the kitchen of the Palace, the dining room, the parking lot, wherever Ma happened to be. She insisted upon helping with the prep work, although this usually entailed her sitting on a stool watching Ma work while she gave directions. She called Ma "dearest little sister" and "sweetness" and "kindness," every sugary thing she could think of. But when she used these words, they seemed to lose their sweetness on her tongue. Instead her lips puckered slightly, curling away from her teeth, as she spat them from her mouth, like the sour pits of rotting fruit.

As we prepared shrimp in the kitchen, a pile of limp bodies between Ma and Sourdi and me on the metal table, Auntie put her hand to her eyes and sighed. She sighed several times, loudly, until she felt she had our attention, then she cried out that she was certain Uncle was cheating on her.

"It's some young refugee girl, I bet," Auntie said. "That's why he stays in the city so late. These girls today, they have no shame."

"Uncle wouldn't do such a thing," Sourdi said, shocked. "He loves you."

Auntie picked up a shrimp between two fingers and pinched the feelers off. She waved them in the air for emphasis. "It's true, he'd never leave me. He might have his fun with one of these cheap, low-class girls, but I'm his wife. I'm the true mother of his children. He can't forget that. Not after what I've been through."

"Of course not," said Ma. Without looking up, she ripped the feelers, eyes and spinal column from shrimp after shrimp, her fingers moving faster than my eyes could follow. Soon there was a mound of gray bodies before her on the table. "He's an honorable man."

I looked at Ma then, out of the corner of my eye, but her face remained completely still, her eyes fixed on the dead, gray prawns breaking beneath her fingers.

At the end of the month, Uncle's friend, the erstwhile poet, the best last hope, the successful American entrepreneur Mr. Chhay, called to say his business associates had decided not to buy the Palace. They'd found a better losing proposition somewhere else.

I don't know how things would have turned out, what the loan shark would have done to Uncle, what would have become of us all then, if Ma hadn't found out about Sourdi and the busboy.

CHAPTER 14

Dragon Chica

Once when Sourdi and I were working alone in the Palace that fall, just the two of us and the elderly cook, some men got drunk, and I stabbed one of them.

I don't remember where Ma had gone that night. But I remember we were tired and it was late. The Palace was one of the only restaurants that stayed open past nine. The men had been growing louder, until they were our only customers, and, finally, one of them staggered up and put his arm across Sourdi's shoulders. He called her his "China doll," and his friends hooted at this.

Sourdi looked distressed and tried to remove his arm, but he held her tighter. She said, "Please," in her incense-sweet voice, and he smiled and said, "Say it again nice and I might just have to give you a kiss."

Now I was panicked. I wanted Ma to be there. Ma would know what to do. She always did. I stood there, chewing my nails, wishing I could make them go away. The men's voices were so loud in my ears, I was drowning in the sound.

I ran into the kitchen. I had this idea to get the cook and the cleaver, but the first thing that caught my eye was this little paring knife on the counter next to a bowl of oranges. I grabbed the knife and ran back out to Sourdi.

"Get away from my sister!" I shouted, waving the paring knife.

The men were silent for about three seconds, then they burst into laughter. "Ooooh, lookee here. We got a little dragon lady on our hands now!"

"That's dragon chica to you, old man!" I thought and charged, stabbing the man in the sleeve.

In a movie or a television show this kind of scene always unfolds in slow-motion, but everything happened fast-fast-fast. I stabbed the man, Sourdi jumped free, Ma came rushing in the front door waving her arms. "Omigod! What happen?"

"Jesus Christ!" The man shook his arm as though it were on fire, but the paring knife was stuck in the fabric of his jeans jacket.

I thought Ma would take care of everything now. And I was right, she did, but not the way I had imagined. She started apologizing to the man, and she helped him take off his jacket. She made Sourdi get the first-aid kit from the bathroom, "Quick! Quick!" Ma even tried to put some ointment on his cut, but he just shrugged her off.

I couldn't believe it. I wanted to take the knife back and stab myself. That's how I felt when I heard her say, "No charge, on the house," for their dinner, despite the $50-worth of pitchers they'd had.

Ma grabbed me by the shoulders. "Say you sorry. Say it." I pressed my lips firmly together and hung my head. Then she slapped me.

I didn't start crying until after the men had left. "But, Ma," I said, "he was hurting Sourdi!"

"Then why didn't Sourdi do something?" Ma twisted my ear. "You don't think. That's your problem. You always don't think!"

After the men left, Sourdi said I was lucky. The knife had only grazed the man's skin. They could have sued us. They could have pressed charges.

"I don't care!" I hissed then. "I shoulda killed him! I shoulda killed that sucker!"

Sourdi's face changed. I'd never seen my sister look like that. Not ever. Especially not at me. I was her favorite. But she looked then the way I felt inside. Like a big bomb was ticking behind her eyes.

Sourdi frowned at me grimly. "Oh, no, Nea. Don't ever say that. Don't ever talk like that."

I was going to smile and shrug and say something like, I was just kidding, but something inside me couldn't lie this night. I crossed my arms over my chest, and I stuck out my lower lip, like I'd seen the tough girls at school do. "Anyone mess like that with me, I'm gonna kill him!"

Sourdi took me by the shoulders then and shook me so hard I thought she was going to shake my head right off my body. She wouldn't stop even after I started to cry.

"Stop, stop!" I begged. "I'll be good! I promise, I'll be good!"

Finally she pushed me away from her and sat down heavily in a booth, with her head in her hands. Although she'd been the one hurting me, she looked as though she'd been beaten up, the way she sat like that, her shoulders hunched over her lap, as though she were trying to make herself disappear.

"I was trying to protect you," I said through my tears. "I was trying to save you. You're so stupid! I should just let that man diss you!"

Sourdi's head shot up, and I could see that she had no patience left. Her eyes were red and her nostrils flared. She stood up, and I took a step back quickly. I thought she was going to grab me and shake me again, but this time she just put her hand on my arm. "They could take you away. The police, they could put you in a foster home. All of us."

A sharp pain coursed through my whole body, as though Sourdi had handed me the hot end of a live wire. We all knew about foster homes. In Texas, Rudy Gutierrez in fourth grade was taken away from his parents after the teacher noticed some bruises on his back. He'd tried to shop-lift some PayDays from the 7-Eleven and got caught. When his dad got home that weekend, he let him have it. But after the school nurse took a look at him, Rudy was sent to live in a foster home. The Gutierrezes couldn't speak English so good and didn't know what was happening until too late. Anyway, what kind of lawyer could they afford? We heard later from his cousin in Mrs. Chang's homeroom that Rudy's foster-dad had molested him. The cousin said Rudy ran away from that home, but he got caught. At any rate, none of us ever saw him again.

"You want to go to a foster home?" Sourdi asked me.

"No," I whispered.

"Then don't be so stupid!"

I started crying again, because I realized Sourdi was right. She kissed me on the top of my head and hugged me to her. I leaned my head against her soft breasts that had only recently emerged from her chest and pre-tended that I was a good girl and that I would always obey her. What I didn't tell Sourdi was that I was still a wicked girl. I was glad I'd stabbed that man. I was crying only because life was so unfair.

When we were little kids in Texas, we used to say that we'd run away, Sourdi and me. When we were older. After she graduated. She'd be my legal guardian. We'd go to California to see the stars. Paris. London. Cambodia even, to light incense for the bones of our father. We'd earn money working in Chinese restaurants in every country we visited. We had enough experience; it had to be worth something.

We'd lie awake all night whispering back and forth. I'd curl into a ball beside my older sister, the smell of Sourdi like salt and garlic and a sweet scent that emanated directly from her skin. Sometimes I'd stroke Sourdi's slick hair, which she plaited into a thick wet braid so that it would be wavy in the morning. I would stay awake all night, pinching the inside of Sourdi's arm, the soft flesh of her thigh, to keep my sister from falling asleep and leaving me alone.

So when she first started seeing Duke, I used to think of him as something like a bookmark, just holding a certain space in her life until it was time for her to move on. I never thought of him as a fork in the road, dividing my life with Sourdi from Sourdi's life with men.

I didn't understand anything.

I'd underestimated Chopstick Boy. At first, Sourdi and I had paid him no mind. He was just this funny-looking kid, hair that stuck up straight from his head when he wasn't wearing his silly baseball cap backwards, skinny as a stalk of bamboo, long legs and long arms that seemed to move in opposition to each other. Later he'd seemed cheerful enough, though he wasn't much of a talker. I hadn't seen any danger in accepting his rides to the Palace after school. I hadn't understood at all.

Now I could see why he fell in love with Sourdi. My sister was beautiful. Really beautiful, not like the girls in magazines with their pale pinched faces, pink and powdery, brittle girls. Sourdi looked like a statue that had been rescued from the sea. She was smooth where I had angles, and soft where I was bone. Sourdi's face was round, her nose low and wide, her eyes crescent-shaped like the quarter moon, her hair sleek as seaweed. Her skin was a burnished cinnamon color. Looking at Sourdi, I could pretend I was beautiful, too. She had so much to spare.

At first, Duke and Sourdi only talked behind the Palace, pretending to take a break from the heat of the kitchen. I caught them looking at the stars together.

The first time they kissed, I was there, too. Duke was giving us a ride after school in his pickup. He had the music on loud and the windows were open. It was a hot day for October, and the wind felt like a warm ocean that we could swim in forever. He dropped Sam and twins off at the Palace, but then Duke said he had something to show Sourdi and me, and we circled around the outskirts of town, taking the gravel road that led to the open fields, beyond the highway where the cattle ranches lay. Finally, he pulled off the gravel road and parked.

"You want us to look at cows?" I asked impatiently, crossing my arms.

He laughed at me then and took Sourdi by the hand. We hiked through a ditch to the edge of an empty cornfield long since harvested, the stubble of cornstalks poking up from the black soil, pale and bone-like. The field was laced with a barbed-wire fence to keep the cattle in, though I couldn't see any cows at all. The whole place gave me the creeps.

Duke held the strands of barbed wire apart for Sourdi and me and told us to crawl under the fence.

"Just trust me," he said.

We followed him to a spot in the middle of the field. "It's the center of the world," Duke said. "Look." And he pointed back to where we'd come from, and suddenly I realized the rest of the world had disappeared. The ground had appeared level, but we must have walked into a tiny hollow in the plains, because from where we stood there was only sky and field for as far as our eyes could see. We could no longer see the road or Duke's pickup, our town, or even the green smudge of cottonwoods that grew along the Missouri River. There was nothing overhead, either; the sky was unbroken by clouds, smooth as an empty ricebowl. "It's just us here," Duke said. "We're alone in the whole universe."

All at once, Sourdi began to breathe funny. Her face grew pinched, and she wiped at her eyes with the back of her hand.

"What's wrong?" Duke asked stupidly.

Then Sourdi was running wildly. She took off like an animal startled by a gunshot. She was trying to head back to the road, but she tripped over the cornstalks and fell onto her knees. She started crying for real then.

I caught up to her first—I've always been a fast runner. As Duke approached, I put my arms around Sourdi.

"I thought you'd like it," Duke said.

"We're city girls," I said, glaring at him. "Why would we like this hick stuff?"

"I'm sorry," Sourdi whispered. "I'm so sorry."

"What are you sorry for? It's his fault!" I pointed out.

Now Duke was kneeling next to Sourdi. He tried to put his arm over her shoulder, too. I was going to push him away, when Sourdi did something very surprising. She put both her arms around his neck and leaned against him, while Duke said soft, dumb-sounding things that I couldn't quite hear. Then they were kissing.

I was so surprised, I stared at them before I forced myself to look away. Then I was the one who felt like running screaming for the road.

On the way back to the Palace, Duke and Sourdi didn't talk, but they held hands. The worst part was I was sitting between them.

Ma didn't seem to notice anything for a while, but then with Ma it was always hard to know what she was thinking, what she knew and what she didn't. Sometimes she seemed to go through her days like she was made of stone. Sometimes she erupted like a volcano.

Uncle fired Duke a few weeks later. He said it was because Duke had dropped a tray of dishes. It was during a slow Saturday afternoon when Sourdi and I weren't working and couldn't witness what had happened.

"He's a clumsy boy," Ma agreed after work that night, when we all sat around in the back booths and ate our dinner.

Sourdi didn't say anything. She knew Ma knew.

She kept seeing Duke, of course. There was only one high school in town. Now when I leaned close against Sourdi in bed at night to stay warm, when she talked about running away, she meant Duke and her. I was the one who had to pipe up that I was coming with them, too. What we didn't know was that Ma was making plans as well.

In November, Uncle invited his friend, Mr. Chhay, back to the Palace. Even though Mr. Chhay's friends hadn't wanted to buy our restaurant, Uncle said he wanted to show there were no hard feelings.

I had a strange dream the night before he came. I hadn't remembered it at all until Mr. Chhay walked inside the Palace, with his hangdog face and his suit like a salesman's. He sat in a corner booth with Uncle and, while they talked, he shredded a napkin, then took the scraps of paper and rolled them between his thumb and index finger into a hundred tiny red balls. He left them in the ashtray, like a mountain of fish eggs. Seeing them, I remembered my dream.

I was swimming in the ocean. I was just a small child, but I wasn't afraid at all. The sea was liquid turquoise, the sunlight yellow as gold against my skin. Fish were swimming alongside me. I could see through the clear water to the bottom of the sea. The fish were schooling around me and below me, and they brushed against my feet when I kicked the water. Their scales felt like bones scraping my toes. I tried to push them away, but the schools grew more dense, until I was swimming amongst them under the waves.

The fish began to spawn around me and soon the water was cloudy with eggs. I tried to break through the film, but the eggs clung to my skin. The water darkened as we entered a sea of kelp. I pushed against the dark slippery strands like Sourdi's hair. I realized I was pushing against my sister, wrapped in the kelp, suspended just below the surface of the water. Then I woke up.

Seeing that old guy with Uncle, I thought about that dream, and I knew immediately they were up to no good. I wanted to warn Sourdi, but she seemed to understand without my having to tell her anything.

Uncle called over to her and introduced her to his friend. But Sourdi wouldn't even look at Mr. Chhay. She kept her eyes lowered though he tried to smile and talk to her. She whispered so low in reply that no one could understand a word she said. I could tell the man was disappointed when he left. His shoulders seemed barely able to support the weight of his jacket.

Mr. Chhay wrote letters to Uncle, to Ma. He thanked them for their hospitality and enclosed pictures of his business and his house, plus a formal portrait of himself looking ridiculous in another suit, standing in front of some potted plants, his hair combed over the bald spot in the middle of his head. He sent a poem, too, in French, which none of us could read.

The next time he came to visit the Palace, he brought gifts. A giant Chinese vase for Ma, Barbie dolls for my younger sisters, an action figure for Sam, a Christian music cassette tape for me, and a bright red leather purse for Sourdi.

Ma made Sourdi tell him thank you.

And that was all she said to him.

But this old guy was persistent. He took us all out to eat at a steak-house once. He said he wanted to pay back Uncle for some good deed he'd done a long time ago when they both were students and Mr. Chhay's father first threatened to disown him. I could have told him, Sourdi hated this kind of food. She preferred Mexican, tacos, not this Midwest cowboy stuff. But Ma made us all thank him.

"Thank you, Mr. Chhay," we said dutifully. He'd smiled so all his yellow teeth showed at once. "Oh, please, call me 'Older Brother,'" he said.

It was the beginning of the end. I should have fought harder then. I should have stabbed this man, too.

Just as winter was settling over the state, dark clouds racing across the sky like endless layers of smoke, dropping snow like ash, burying the world in white, Mr. Chhay decided to pay off the loan shark for Uncle himself. He said he'd always wanted to own a restaurant, it'd been a dream of his ever since he'd come to America more than thirteen years ago. He'd only gone into nail shops because of economics, the law of supply and demand in Des Moines, where he'd settled. But really, he told Ma, the romance of the restaurant business was what called to his heart.

Called to his heart. That's the way he actually talked. But we all knew what his heart really wanted, and it wasn't the Palace.

Sourdi and I began to argue, more and more frequently. She no longer wanted me to sleep beside her. She said I kicked. And snored. Uncle bought a second mattress just for me, so that I'd have my own bed, he said, but I knew what was going on. We were to sleep apart so that my sister could grow into a woman without me to hold her back.

In December, the wind howled outside the window in our room like a woman in mourning, an angry sound. My mattress lay beneath the window so I couldn't ignore the sound, nor the chill that slipped through the glass and into my bed, unwelcome and sharp as needles on the sheets.

One night when the moon was too bright and the wind too loud, I crept from my bed across the inky carpet and climbed in beside Sourdi. Her bed was warm; my sister always had the cat-like ability to throw off heat. The sheets and comforter smelled like my sister too, a summery scent, good enough to eat. I burrowed down into the smell, rubbing the edge of the blanket against my nose, as though I could inhale my sister's fragrance into my body and keep it there, like the embers of a fire I might need to rebuild someday.

"We can still run away," I offered now. "We can go in the spring. We can go to California and see the ocean."

"Mmm-hmm." My sister's voice grew drowsy, faint. I could feel her slipping away from me. Desperately, I huddled closer to my sister, grasping her arm in my hands. She pushed me away irritably.

"You're too old to sleep with me, Nea," Sourdi said. "You should go to your own bed." Then she kicked me sharply with her pointy big toe.

I had no choice but to return to my exile across the room.

That night, my sister tossed and turned in the dark, sighing now and then, but refusing to answer when I whispered from my bed, "What's wrong?" Even after she fell asleep, Sourdi seemed to be having angry dreams. She kicked at her sheets and made a sound deep in the back of her throat like a growl.

I knew because I lay awake, in my cold distant bed, watching her, all night long.

CHAPTER 15

Silent People

After Mr. Chhay paid off the loan shark, Uncle didn't have to worry about the lack of profits and the growing interest on his debt, the threat of men coming to break his legs, or worse. He no longer had to work his second job at the Sizzler. He could stay in our town and work in the Palace, full-time.

Ma took to whistling in the kitchen and singing in the shower. She clipped pictures out of bridal magazines to show to Sourdi and tacked them up on the refrigerator at home with magnets. She smiled all day because the Palace was ours for real, and Sourdi was marrying a wealthy businessman, and Uncle worked beside Ma in the kitchen day and night.

However, Auntie's headaches suddenly grew more severe, her dizziness more pronounced, the pains in her heart more frequent, just when it seemed she and Uncle had nothing to argue about at night, no accumulating debts, no unpaid bills. But their arguments had never really been about money. They had argued about trivial things to keep from thinking about their real losses, all that they no longer had, their children, their family, their sense that their future lay bright and bountiful before them, stretching infinitely forward through the generations, children, grandchildren, and beyond. Now the future was a stone wall and their past lay before their eyes, every day, mocking them, their memories a catalog of loss.

Now the silence between Uncle and Auntie grew day by day, until it was a presence that couldn't be ignored, its chill went to our very bones. And what was worse, Auntie no longer retreated to her apartment during the day but insisted upon staying in the Palace, sitting stubbornly by the cash register (although she refused to speak English to the customers) or scowling like a bad-luck idol from a back booth, watching, waiting, radiating unhappiness.

At first Ma had seemed too preoccupied to notice.

And then Auntie's unhappiness became impossible to ignore.

One evening, she grew ill, her heart beating so rapidly she had to press on it with both hands through her ribs. She insisted then that we take her back to the house even though it was a busy night, every table and every booth filled, and a family waiting by the door. We were all working together, the little kids upstairs doing their homework and watching TV in Auntie's apartment since she no longer used it, the rest of us working in the kitchen and the dining room. But Auntie said, she had to go home immediately. She couldn't wait. She'd forgotten her medicine. There was no telling what would happen if she delayed.

So Ma gave Sourdi the keys and had her drive Auntie back to the house while Ma and I waited on tables and Uncle and the cook manned the woks. Sourdi returned twenty minutes later, saying Auntie had found her pills and was lying on the sofa before the TV. She'd sent Sourdi back to work, saying she didn't need anyone hovering over her, it made her feel like a monkey in a cage, like an animal in a zoo, not even a human. She'd complained like that continuously, so Sourdi had come right back.

My sister looked weary, a little more worn around the edges, and I could hear Auntie's voice in my own ears. I'd heard that tone enough times, when she spoke as though she wished we were all dead.

It was after nine when Uncle went back to the house. He said he forgot something, but later I thought he must have known, he must have had a premonition. Once, many years ago, after Auntie had just arrived in America, she had tried to commit suicide. I'd overheard Uncle telling Ma how he'd found Auntie in the bathroom of their apartment in Houston when he came back early from a night shift. He'd realized he'd forgotten his wallet and he'd owed another waiter some money, so he came back during his break and he found her coiled upon the bathroom floor, choking on her own vomit. He'd called for an ambulance, and they pumped her stomach. After that, the doctors changed Auntie's medication. They said she was depressed. They gave her pills to help her with that, in addition to the pills for her headaches and for the pain she felt because of her scars, and the pills that helped her to sleep and the ones that helped her to wake in the morning.

Tonight he found Auntie in the garage, smelling like gasoline. Uncle's first thought was that she was trying to kill herself again. Trying to asphyxiate herself somehow, although she pretended that she'd merely been looking for something and knocked the spare gas can over accidentally.

He urged her to come back inside the house and fixed her some jasmine tea and a bowl of rice congee, and he'd waited with her until it was time for her to take her sleeping pills. And only after he'd seen her fall asleep, her breathing rhythmic and deep, did he dare return to the Palace.

The fire changed everything.

Two weeks before Christmas, someone set fire to the Palace after we'd locked up for the evening and gone home. I remember almost everything about that night.

My insomnia had grown worse since Auntie and Uncle no longer argued endlessly when I tried to sleep. Now I had no excuse, as I lay on my own mattress, apart from Sourdi, tossing this way and that, listening to the sighing wind and imagining it was Auntie's voice I heard hissing through the cracks where the window did not fit perfectly into its pane.

My ears hurt from listening to the silence. I heard Sourdi's soft breath across the room from me, as she sighed in her sleep, lost in dreams that did not include me. The water running through the pipes in the walls caused the radiators to ping and gurgle. Small paws scampered across the ceiling, most likely a mouse in the crawlspace beneath the roof. We'd put out traps but only managed to catch a rat's tail and a gray left hind leg on separate occasions. Both times, our bait had been eaten.

The rodents were so brazen, we'd even heard them running through the walls while we sat in the living room watching TV. I told Sam and the twins that very evening that they must be ghost mice that we were hearing, more powerful than ordinary mice, and that's why they had no fear and could not be killed. Sam hadn't turned from "World Wide Wrestling," live from Sioux City, Iowa, and the twins had only stared at me in their wide-eyed owlish ways, inscrutable. Then they whispered to each other, giggling. It was too late to scare my younger siblings with ghost stories. They were too American now. So I gave up.

But now I'd scared myself. Why couldn't mice become ghosts, too, like people whose souls hadn't found peace and been reborn? If people could be reborn as mice to pay for their bad actions in a past life, then why couldn't mice souls be left as ghosts to haunt our house?

This is the kind of question I would have liked to have asked Sourdi, but now she was a grown woman, engaged to be married, and I was an annoying kid.

More footsteps converged upstairs, and I thought they must be rats, not mice. They sounded so heavy. I sat up in my bed, pulling my blankets around me to protect myself from the draft, and cocked my ear toward the ceiling, the better to hear. All our bait had done nothing but make them gain weight. Perhaps they considered us friendly, feeding them as we did with leftovers from the Palace. Had they become rat pets, spying on us from the corners of the floorboards, from cracks in the ceilings? Listening to us through the walls just as I listened to them now?

I'd read a book once about a world of rats that lived just as we humans did. They even had royalty. A king rat and queen rat. They wore crowns and red robes with ermine trim. I read this book in Texas; it was a children's book but I'd had to look up the word "ermine" in the school librarian's dictionary. I thought it strange that rats would wear the fur of other animals, and in my book report to my teacher I said the book made the rats seem *barbaric*, a word I'd heard and liked very much. "It's like if we Americans wore the skins of people from other countries, like Canadian-trimmed robes," I wrote. My teacher didn't like that and sent me to the school nurse, saying I needed to see a psychiatrist. But our school didn't have its very own psychiatrist, so the nurse, who was annoyed and busy dealing with actual emergencies like kids with nosebleeds or the girl who threw up in music class, let me sit and doodle in my notebook for twenty minutes then sent me back to class.

But now the drawings of those rats were like memories. I could literally see them holding court in our dusty attic. There were rats from all over town convening, as though for a grand ball. They marched in rows before the king and queen, bowing deeply, before scampering off to dance. The sound of hundreds of little paws moving in unison sounded very loud indeed. Thump, thump, thump!

The wind through my window no longer sounded like Auntie complaining, but had become a kind of music from a breathy flute, rising and falling, rising and falling, eventually drowning out even the dancing rats.

Suddenly, a bomb siren wailed. Ringing louder and louder. And the rats threw off their pretend-human clothes and ran fast away on all fours before the bombs could fall.

Then I woke up. The phone was ringing.

Our room was completely dark.

The ringing stopped, and I could hear Uncle's voice shouting into the receiver.

"What? What?"

I jumped out of bed to see what was happening.

But he was already hanging up by the time I got downstairs.

He looked startled to see me on the stairs as he stood in the kitchen door, his hand still on the phone on the wall.

"There's a fire," he said. "At the Palace."

"A fire!"

"I have to go see." Uncle seemed dazed, uncertain. Old. I didn't want to see him like this. I'd rather hear him arguing furiously with Auntie or waxing poetic about his wonderful youth than see him looking almost frail.

"I'll go with you," I said, and I raced to the door to put on my shoes. I threw my coat on over my pajamas.

Ma was padding down the hall now in her slippers. "What happened? Where is she? Is she all right?"

"It was the fire department," Uncle said, and they exchanged glances that I couldn't understand. "There's a fire at the Palace."

Ma put a hand to her mouth.

"Don't worry," Uncle said. "I'm sure she's not there."

"The Palace is on fire?" I shouted. "Who's not there? What's happening?"

"Sssh. Don't wake everyone with your loud voice." Ma shook her head at me. "You go with Uncle. You talk to the firemen if he needs you to."

Ma nodded at Uncle. "I'll wait here. She'll come back. If we go together, it will only make her angrier."

"Who? Auntie? Did Auntie run away?"

"What did I tell you? Sssh." Ma frowned at me. Then she touched Uncle's elbow just briefly, a reassuring kind of touch, as she went into the kitchen. She turned on the light and began filling a kettle with water for tea.

Uncle was grabbing a coat from the closet. "I should put on pants," he said, as though he just realized he was wearing pajamas still. Then he hurried back to his bedroom.

Uncle drove us to the Palace in Ma's car. His car was missing. I assumed Auntie took it, which is why he and Ma were wondering where she was, but I didn't say anything. Uncle didn't speak at all, so I tried to be polite and not ask questions. There was still a lot of snow left from the last storm, banks and banks where the plows had created miniature mountains to clear the roads. Everything glowed blue in the dark night. It was clear out, and I tried to see the moon, but there were too many trees in town. Their leafless branches looked like crooked fingers reaching for the sky.

I could smell the smoke before we got to the Palace.

"Oh, no!" Uncle exclaimed as we turned the corner round Tom & Bud's and the Palace came into view.

The town's two firetrucks were in the parking lot. Black smoke still hung in the air, fluttering in the wind like giant flags at the funeral of somebody important.

At least there were no flames—that I could see—and the Palace was still standing.

Uncle pulled up front, and we both got out of the car. The night air slapped me in the face, hard. I was definitely awake, although I wished I were still dreaming.

The fire chief walked over to us. "Looks like somebody tried to burn you down," he said to Uncle. "Good thing Shirley over there in the Super 8 smelled the smoke and called us in time."

"Thank you," said Uncle. "Thank you for saving our business."

The fire chief nodded. He pulled a glove off and put a hand on Uncle's shoulder. "Let me show you the damage. Looks like it started in the kitchen."

"We turned off all the stoves!" I cried out. "We always do and we always check. Every night."

Ma was meticulous about this. Even the cook. Even Sam and Maly and Navy knew how to check the burners. We knew enough about restaurants. We weren't stupid after all.

"Oh, it wasn't from the stove, little lady," the fire chief said. "Let me show you the damage." We followed him around to the back. His boots crunched through the snow and slush. There was water running through the parking lot from where they'd had to hose the Palace down, I imagined, and it was fast freezing into ice. I was wearing my sneakers. I stepped into a puddle and now my feet were wet. My toes were cold.

The rest of the firemen were folding up the giant hoses, which glowed white and snakelike from the lights in the parking lot.

Smoke billowed from the back door. "Is there still a fire?" I blurted out.

"Naw, it's okay now. And with this wind, the smoke'll disperse soon enough. But you're sure lucky we caught it in time. With a wind like this, coulda spread to the roof. Coulda burned your whole restaurant down."

"We are very grateful to you," Uncle said. "When we re-open, free food to the fire department. On us. Just come in anytime."

"Just doin' our job," but I could tell the fire chief was pleased by the idea.

"No, no. I insist. You save everything."

Then the fire chief took out this monster flashlight and showed us in the back door. The smell of smoke was so thick, I immediately started coughing. I pulled my scarf up over my nose.

"Here. And over there. See that? That's where somebody poured the gasoline. Fire like this isn't natural. It's been set."

I translated for Uncle and he nodded.

"How'd they break in? They do this to the door?" I asked. The back door was completely smashed to the ground.

"Uh, no. That was us trying to get to the fire. We had to ax the door down. Sorry bout that."

"No problem, no problem," Uncle said. "We are very grateful to you."

"Here's the thing. The door was good and locked. You think any of your employees would do this? Anyone else but you got the keys?"

I translated again as best I could. The fire chief had a funny accent as though he were chewing an apple while he spoke that made it difficult for Uncle to understand him.

"No, no one," Uncle said.

"Mighta broken in the window, I suppose. But the heat busted the glass, so we can't tell anymore. Damn shame. I'm sorry for your loss."

"No one is hurt. This is the most important thing," Uncle said.

They both nodded.

We stepped back out into the parking lot. I slid a bit on the ice, but I didn't mind the cold anymore or the wind. Anything was better than breathing that terrible smoke smell. It reminded me of something. Something from the war, I figured, because I couldn't remember what exactly, and I didn't want to try harder to think what it might be.

The fire chief told Uncle they'd investigate more in the morning so he'd appreciate if Uncle held off on the cleaning up until he and his men had finished. Uncle said that was fine, just fine. I got the chief's personal phone number. Then the police came over, too. The cops had been waiting in the Super 8, drinking free coffee, waiting for the fire to be put out. The policeman said they'd investigate in the morning as well, since the "situation was under control now" and it was "butt cold" out. I got this man's name and phone number, too. Just in case. Then a couple cops strung up some yellow tape across the back door. It made me sadder than I would have imagined, seeing the Palace turned into a crime scene.

Uncle thanked everyone again.

The cops drove off and the fire men too, one of them letting off a WHOOP of the siren to signal…that everything was okay? That they were headed home? That someone liked to run that siren?

"No use standing here in the dark. Let's go home." Uncle seemed strangely serene.

"Does this mean Mr. Chhay will want his money back?" I asked hopefully once we were buckled in the car. "Maybe he won't marry Sourdi now."

"I have insurance. It's okay," Uncle said. "At least they didn't find any bodies there."

I thought, *Would've served the arsonists right!* but I didn't say it. I was going to be good tonight. Ma would want that, considering the disaster and all.

As we pulled into the garage, I noticed Uncle's car was back in place. He didn't say anthing so I didn't either.

Inside the house, the light was on in the kitchen. I shook the snow and slush off my sneakers and left them by the door. I took off my socks, too, since they were wet. Nobody came rushing to greet us, or to ask if the Palace was still there, or to find out if anybody had died. Again, the silence of adults perplexed me. The things they chose to talk or yell about versus the things I'd expect they'd want to know, I just couldn't figure it out. I wondered if every family was like this.

Uncle went straight to the kitchen, and I followed him. Ma and Auntie, fully dressed, were sitting at the table, drinking tea. They looked up at us expectantly as we came in.

"The fire? It's all over?" Ma asked. Her brows furrowed.

Uncle nodded. "The fire was already out, thank Heaven, when we arrived. No one was hurt."

Ma sighed, relieved.

Auntie stared into her teacup.

"You two put your clothes in the plastic bag." Ma got up and rummaged under the sink where she kept the Hefty bags. "I'll wash everything in the morning. You smell like smoke!"

I nodded, but we weren't the only ones who smelled. Auntie, I noticed, smelled like gasoline.

Naturally the adults forced me to go to bed then. They said I needed my rest after such excitement.

"What if the fire department calls again? What if they need me to translate?"

Ma gave me a stern look. "Then we'll wake you up again. Go upstairs."

There was no arguing with that tone, so I obeyed, slowly, dragging my feet as though they were made of lead, as I tried to eavesdrop. I could hear Auntie's voice, small and anguished, speaking slowly, then Uncle replying rapidly, anxiously in Khmer. They were talking about the fire. That's all I could make out before Ma shut the kitchen door tight.

I couldn't sleep the rest of the night. I wanted to wake Sourdi and tell her about the strange goings on, about the whispers and the secrets and Auntie's gasoline-scented clothing. But my sister lay on her mattress like a princess in a fairy tale, looking so peaceful and remote, I let her sleep. There would be time enough for discussing our disasters the next morning. And the morning after that, and the next day, and the next.

As I lay under my blankets, listening to the wind hiss, I kept wondering, *Why would Auntie do such a thing? Why would she set fire to our own restaurant?*

The next morning, none of the adults wanted to talk much about the fire at all. They simply told Sourdi and Sam and the twins the news, and Uncle said everything would be all right.

Later I told Sourdi what had really happened, of course, that Auntie had set the fire, but my sister refused to speculate with me about her reasons. She merely frowned and shook her head. "Poor Auntie," she said.

"Poor Auntie!" I exclaimed. "She's nuts!"

Then Sourdi looked at me sadly, pursing her lips. Then she looked off to the side, her long dark eyes staring away from me, as though she could see something in the corner of our room that was invisible to me.

Funny thing is, a couple weeks later, the police chief found two young men who confessed to the crime. They admitted they'd been drinking when they got this idea, something they'd seen in a movie. They put rags in their beer bottles, after filling them with gasoline, and set the ends on fire. Then they'd tossed them into our dumpster.

The flames must have jumped out and spread to the rest of the building, they claimed. They said they'd never intended to burn the whole place down.

The police chief said he'd suspected this pair from the get-go. They were up to no good. Local boys who'd gone bad. If they weren't trying to shoplift at the Tom & Bud's, they were starting fights in the bars. He'd known them since they were in grade school, and they'd been trouble even then.

The only odd thing, he noted, was that the fire chief had said with some certainty that the fire had originated in the kitchen.

"Maybe they threw some of them Molotov cocktails high," the police chief speculated over the phone as I listened in. "Broke a window and tossed a couple in. You never know. Memory's a funny thing and they were good and drunk."

Uncle assented politely.

But after he'd hung up, Uncle kept shaking his head. "Why? Why would they do that?" he asked over and over.

And none of us had any answers, because we didn't know why these boys would confess to a crime they hadn't committed. Because by this time we all knew who had started the fire, even the little kids.

Auntie had finally admitted everything just a couple days before the police chief called. That she had planned it, too, for weeks, just how she'd do it. How she'd make it look like an accident. Something catching fire in the kitchen and then burning and spreading. She said she and Uncle could take the insurance money that way, and they could leave, move far away, start over. Let Ma run the Palace if she wanted to, but they could go.

She'd waited till everyone else was asleep, and she'd gotten up and gone to the Palace by herself and then set the kitchen ablaze.

"She's like the first Mrs. Rochester," I whispered to Sourdi in our bedroom that evening. "She'll stop at nothing."

"What on earth are you talking about?" My sister frowned. "Who's Mrs. Rochester?"

"Auntie."

"Don't you start talking crazy now, too, Nea. I'm trying to sleep." And Sourdi turned her back to me, pulling her pillow round her head like armor.

After the fire, Ma and Uncle no longer worked together in the Palace. While Uncle took stock of the damage to the kitchen, while he filled out the forms for the insurance company, Ma stayed at home, cleaning the house, cooking supper, helping Auntie. Only when Uncle returned home did she go to the Palace with Sourdi and me to help with the clean up and repair work. Luckily the damage wasn't too bad, Ma said, as Sourdi and I pulled broken tiles from the walls. "We'll be able to open for business again, no time flat."

I said, "What if Auntie was right this time? Maybe we could just take the insurance money, all of us, and leave. Now Sourdi doesn't have to get married, right?"

Ma glared at me, tossing down her cleaning rag. I thought she was going to strike me, but it was Sourdi who piped up first, "Don't be stupid, Nea. And don't ruin my wedding. I never thought you of all people would be so jealous of me."

I was so shocked, I couldn't reply. I wished Ma had hit me instead then. I wished she'd hit with something harder than the palm of her hand, something made of metal, something sharp that would draw blood. Because even that would have hurt less than Sourdi's words.

The week after the two boys were arrested for setting the fire, their mother came to the Palace to talk to Uncle. She even ordered a plate of the Daily Special, although she didn't actually eat any of it, just pushed the eggroll from one side of the plate to the other with her fork. She was the kind of thick-necked, ruddy-cheeked woman who was common here. Her hair was mostly gray, her skin was lined and rough, her voice was flat. She could have been forty or fifty. It was hard to say.

"They're good boys," she told Uncle over and over. "Good boys."

She explained that they'd had a bit of family trouble in the past few years. They'd had to sell their dairy farm although they kept a three-hundred-acre back lot that her husband still farmed. But there was nothing left for the boys.

"They didn't think we'd ever have to sell. It's been in the family five generations," she said, her blue eyes dry, her tone calm. "You must understand that. What it's like to lose your home."

Uncle told her that he understood all right.

When Uncle told the police chief he wasn't going to press charges, the police chief said he was crazy. He told Uncle to think it over some more. But Uncle said he'd made up his mind. The boys were young, he said. Still teenagers. They hadn't understood what they were doing.

The police made some kind of plea agreement with the boys and they ended up serving time for some other crime, shoplifting, bad checks, something like that. We read about it in the paper.

"A miracle," Ma told Auntie while Uncle was at the Palace, supervising the carpenters fixing up the kitchen since the insurance money had come through. The rest of us were at home, supposedly doing our homework. We could all hear Ma talking to Auntie in the kitchen. When she was upset, Ma's voice could be quite loud.

"If not for those boys, just think!" Ma said. "What if they found out who really did it? Then what do you think will happen to all of us? What?"

I didn't hear Auntie's answer.

CHAPTER 16

Red Lobster

For Sourdi's engagement party to Mr. Chhay, Mr. Chhay insisted on treating us all at the Red Lobster in Sioux City, Iowa. He rented the entire restaurant just for the occasion.

There wasn't an official announcement in the town paper with a photograph of them smiling, Sourdi leaning on his shoulder like all the other brides-to-be, on account of Sourdi being underage. But Ma said it was official all the same; her word made it so. And this party did, too, apparently, even though it was conveniently located in another state. At any rate, Ma said everything would be fine by the time they were to be married in the summer after Sourdi's sixteenth birthday. The wedding was legal then. Ma said she'd asked around.

There were lots of strange people at the party. They were strangers to us, but they also were strange. In addition to some of the Gangsters from Omaha—I recognized Uncle Chapeau and Big Nose—there were a lot of girls with super long nails painted with elaborate designs: the American flag, stripes, flowers, spiders, and even letters that spelled out S-U-P-E-R-S-E-X-X-Y when one of them held all her fingers out. Apparently these were employees at Mr. Chhay's series of nail salons. They brought their boyfriends along too, thick-necked Asian guys with too much gel in their hair and lots of tattoos. (One poor soul had the word "Star Boy" emblazoned on his bicep.) They reminded me of the gangbangers we used to see in East Dallas.

Mr. Chhay gave a long speech into a microphone set up at the front of the restaurant about how everyone here was like family to him. And that's why he wanted to introduce us, his new family, and share his joy. Then he pointed to all of us and called out our names, and Ma made us stand up one by one as Mr. Chhay's bored looking family-like employees clapped very carefully so as not to spoil their nails.

Then it was buffet time. I could tell Ma was casing the competition, trying a little of everything to figure out the recipes so she could introduce them on the Palace's menu. Later I saw her talking to one of the waiters, a white girl with a long brown ponytail. Ma was pointing at various items on her plate, and the girl nodded or shook her head accordingly as Ma tried to figure out which items were most popular with the regular customers.

Mr. Chhay had gone all out for this party. Not only had he invited every single person he knew in America, it seemed, but he'd also rented a karaoke machine and deejay, who told jokes between the songs. All the strangers had a turn, singing mostly country western tunes but some in Khmer, too, while blurry images of Angkor Wat and jungles showed behind them on the portable screen. Even Sam asked to take a turn, choosing to belt out "Fight for your right to paaarty!" while dancing around the floor like George Michael in Wham! I was surprised that the deejay stocked country music, old Khmer songs and the Beastie Boys, but I guess that's how he made his business a success; he came prepared, all right. Then Maly and Navy stood up, giggling, as Ma prodded them, "Go on! Go on! Sing a song for your sister!" They whispered something to the deejay, who was a Chinese guy in his forties, dressed in jeans and a Hall & Oates T-shirt with a suit jacket thrown over it. He looked perpetually bored, and I imagined that Hell itself had to have a deejay, forced to play karaoke hits for eternity.

Then the twins burst out into "Like a Virgin." At first Ma couldn't understand the lyrics and clapped along to the beat. But when Maly began to writhe along the floor as Navy sang on and on, gyrating her hips, Ma stood up and made them stop.

I clapped loudest of all. Thanks to them, I knew I wouldn't have to sing tonight. Ma wasn't going to risk it.

"But Mommy! That's how it's supposed to be sung!" Navy whined as Ma dragged her and Maly by the wrists over to my table.

"You look after them! Be useful," Ma commanded me. Then she plastered a big, fake, aren't-kids-cute smile on her face and rejoined Mr. Chhay and Sourdi at the head table.

"Good jobs!" I gave the twins a thumb's up, but they continued to sulk until I ordered them a couple of virgin strawberry daiquiris in honor of their singing debut.

Still, the horrors of the evening were far from over.

Mr. Chhay stood up, patted his comb-over to make sure it was still in place and then took the microphone. I thought he was going to launch into another speech about family, but no such luck. Instead he sang a long and embarrassing love ballad in Chinese. I don't know where the heck the deejay got the karaoke video that went along with this opus. Must have imported it from the West Coast or Texas maybe. Some of the Red Lobster employees came out just to stare at Mr. Chhay while he sang, really loudly so that the reverb made the water glasses on our tables shake. Or maybe they were watching the endless scenes of pandas frolicking in bamboo glens, the cascading waterfalls, misty mountain peaks, the mandarin ducks circling on a lotus pond, and every other cliché image of China now projected onto the screen behind him. It was all I could do to turn my laughter into a hacking cough before Ma got angry. I looked over at Sourdi, expecting her to be giggling at this display as well, but instead she was carefully patting at her tears with a folded Kleenex.

"Stay here. I'm going to the bathroom," I told the twins. They nodded, sucking away at their straws. Then I scooted over to Sourdi's table, kneeling down just out of Ma's line of sight.

"You don't have to marry him," I whispered into Sourdi's ear. "We could run away tonight. We can go to the bathroom and climb out the window. It's not a long drop. I already checked it out."

But she pulled away from me, and before I knew it, she walked over to Mr. Chhay and took his hand.

Everyone burst into applause. I don't know if it was because they were genuinely moved or because Sourdi's actions finally got Mr. Chhay to stop singing, but everyone clapped and clapped. Even Auntie.

Uncle and Auntie moved away shortly after the engagement party.

They didn't give an official reason for leaving. They didn't say, of course, it was because Uncle had fallen in love with Ma and Auntie couldn't bear the two of them being together, even if she no longer loved Uncle, and so Uncle had decided to move away from temptation before Auntie killed herself or anyone else from despair or rage or a combination of the two. They merely left, and quickly, packing up their things and driving away one day.

Ma, for her part, used to say they moved because of her dream. It was shortly after the fire that Ma announced she'd had a strange dream. In it, Auntie and Uncle's oldest son—the one who'd been sent away to a distant work camp during the war and whom they'd never heard from again—was alive and well and living in California. He was married and had two children already, a third on the way.

Ma told Auntie all about her dream one morning while she was staying in the house and Uncle was gone, still busy cleaning up the damage from the fire. I was home that day from school with a fever. The three of us sat in the kitchen, Ma peeling potatoes and smoking, Auntie sipping tea, me wrapped in a blanket, my throat swollen and throbbing, as I sucked on cough drops.

It hadn't seemed like a nightmare, Ma recounted, peeling the skin from a potato in one long curling spiral. It had seemed familiar, like a memory, like something that had already occurred.

"Where exactly?" Auntie demanded then. "It's a big state."

"I'm not sure," Ma said. "There was a lot of sunlight. It was warm. Like summer."

"By the ocean?"

"I didn't see water. Just palm trees," Ma said.

I thought that Auntie would grow angry then, she would scowl at Ma, she would see right through her, but instead Auntie grew very quiet and very still and stared into her teacup for a long time without asking any more questions.

(I once asked Ma if she had made up this dream, when I was older and feeling intellectual, and she had replied haughtily that a dream was too important to make up.)

If anyone had asked him, Uncle might have said they moved because of the business opportunity he'd discovered. Now that Mr. Chhay owned the Palace, Uncle needed something of his own to manage. He couldn't just work in another man's business his whole life.

Uncle received a letter from a friend who had a cousin who operated a donut franchise in San Bernardino, and the friend said he'd get Uncle set up, too. He wouldn't need to put up a lot of money to begin. He needn't worry about involving another loan shark.

Donuts were really something in California, the friend wrote. Donuts were dollars in the bank.

Uncle nodded, thinking it over. To be a *pâtissier*, he said, was an honorable profession, celebrated for centuries in France. A noble tradition. A dying art. When he was a boy, in fact, he had loved the *pâtisserie* around the corner from his uncle's bookstore, and he had often stolen money from his mother's petty cash drawer just to buy himself a buttery *pain au chocolat*, a glazed *religieuse*, an *éclair* so rich that the cream and chocolate melted into a brown stream in the hot sun even before he could greedily stuff the pastry from his sticky fingers into his gaping red mouth. Yes, when he was a boy, he had learned the taste of love from eating French pastry.

After Uncle and Auntie decided to move to California, we packed up all our things as well. We would no longer be living in the big house Uncle had rented but would move to a smaller rental in town, something more modest, more practical.

During this period, there were some days when Auntie felt well enough to help pack, and some days when she lay upstairs in her bedroom, resting.

Once while everyone was busy packing up the kitchen and the living room, Ma sent me upstairs with a lunch tray, and I was surprised to find that Auntie wasn't lying in her bed as I'd expected but was instead sitting upright by the door, waiting for me.

Auntie gestured to me with a finger across her lips. "I want to show you something," she said. "Open the curtains for me. We need some light."

With the curtains drawn, it seemed as though all the air had been sucked out and replaced by inky water. The room was sparsely furnished—there was only a bed against the wall, a nightstand with Auntie's pill bottles on top, Auntie's chair, and a short dresser with a tiny shrine on top—just a framed picture of the Buddha clipped from a National Geographic and a saucer of oranges. There wasn't even a mirror. Now I pulled the red cotton draperies apart and raised the shades so that the harsh sunlight cascaded inside. Auntie blinked rapidly and held a hand over her eyes.

"You want me to shut them again?"

"No."

Auntie shuffled across the floor and opened the closet door. "There," she said, pointing inside to the top shelf. "I need you to get my box down." She folded her arms across her chest and waited.

I peered inside. Besides clothes, there were a couple shelves stacked with spare lightbulb boxes, sixty watt, seventy-five, one-fifty, fluorescent, Christmas lights, refrigerator bulbs, and indoor/outdoor fog lights. There were enough spare bulbs there to keep every light in the house and the Palace burning for years. At the very top of all the light bulb boxes, I spotted a shoe box, near the ceiling. "That box?" I asked.

Auntie nodded.

I dragged Auntie's chair over to the closet and, standing on tiptoe, I was able to grab the shoe box. I wondered how Auntie had managed to put it up so high.

"Here it is," I said and Auntie reached for it greedily with both hands. She took it over to her bed, where she sat down, holding the box on her lap without opening it. Instead she poured herself a cup of tea then shook out a couple teeth-white pills from one of the bottles on her nightstand. She swished some tea around in her mouth then swallowed her medicine. Exhaling slowly, like a balloon losing its air, Auntie eased herself back against her pillows.

"I used to have it on the shrine, so that I could see it every day, but your uncle took it down. He couldn't bear it anymore." From inside the box Auntie pulled out a glamorous-looking photograph in a cheap frame. It was a black and white picture of a family, taken long ago in some forgotten studio in Phnom Penh. The name of the studio was embossed in the corner. A father and mother and four children, dressed elegantly in Western-style clothes before a backdrop of a park in Europe, complete with a kiosk and swans and willow trees.

The father stood in a suit and tie, his chin high, his two sons at his sides. The eldest, a teenager, stared straight into the lens proudly, but the little boy of about seven was a blur. He must have moved his head at the last minute. There was a baby boy propped up in a bassinet next to a little girl, who was maybe all of three, in a stiff, starched dress, with a bow in her dark wavy hair. She looked spoiled, and I guessed it was she who used to pull Sourdi's hair and caused so much trouble. But it was the mother who really captured my attention. She did not sit so much as recline atop a cushioned divan, dressed in what could only be silk, the creamy folds falling suggestively over her body, her hair framing her face in soft waves. She was beautiful, in a standoffish, movie star kind of way. She looked like a woman who was used to being looked at. I held the picture closer to the lamp on the end table.

Auntie smiled slightly at me. "You don't recognize me? It's all right. Of course you don't." She took the picture frame out of my hands and held it, lovingly, on her lap. She traced the outline of the faces with her index finger, one by one.

"You were so beautiful," I said, not thinking how terrible that might sound now. But Auntie wasn't upset. In fact she seemed so pleased, she almost laughed.

"Yes, wasn't I? It's not immodest to say so now. That beauty is gone. Completely gone."

I didn't know what else to say about that so I changed the subject awkwardly. "These are my cousins?"

"Do you remember their faces?" She leaned towards me eagerly. "Look closely." She handed the picture back to me.

"Maybe a little," I said slowly. "The girl, I think I remember. We used to play together."

"You all played together." Auntie's voice grew fainter, more breathless as she settled back into her pillows again. Her eyelids fluttered. Her medicine would make her fall asleep soon. "Do you remember anything, Nea?"

"Yes," I lied. "She pulled my hair once. I pinched her back."

"My daughter was very bold for a girl. So naughty. I spoiled her." Auntie's eyes closed.

I tried to remember what Ma had told me about our cousins, something that would make Auntie feel better, but I couldn't think of anything specific. "They all look so perfect," I said.

"I would have done anything for them." Then Auntie told me a story from the war, something that had happened after she'd been evacuated from the city to a village far from Phnom Penh. There had been a blind widow and her mentally retarded son, and Auntie and her children had been assigned to live with them. At first Auntie had felt sorry for the woman and had genuinely tried to be kind to her. When the cooking was done in one main kitchen, and everyone was sent there to get their food, Auntie had volunteered to help the blind woman by bringing back food for her and her son. However, there wasn't enough food, and everyone grew so hungry, and Auntie's children began to get sick. That's when Auntie began to lie and steal. Before she gave the blind woman and her son their bowls, she divided most of the rice up for her own children. The retarded boy grew so hungry, he tried to steal someone else's rice bowl and was punished by the soldiers. He was sent away to another camp. Or so they said. Maybe the soldiers really killed him. At any rate, they had taken him away from his mother, and the blind woman had cried and cried, while Auntie had held her head on her lap, as though she were a kind person and not a thief.

"I wanted to help my children," Auntie said. "I did anything I thought would help. Anything. Can you forgive me?"

"Don't think about it," I said. "It's not your fault. It's the soldiers' fault."

"I used to think the most important thing on earth was to survive," Auntie said.

I sat next to Auntie on her bed and tried to take her hand in mine, but she pulled it away and put her hands over her eyes. She turned her head back and forth on her pillows, squinting, her face twisted into a grimace as though the light still pained her, as though it could penetrate through her hands and her bones and her eyelids. I got up then and shut the drapes once more. After a while, Auntie stopped tossing about.

I waited for her to say something more, but she didn't stir. I placed the picture back in the shoe box and set the box next to her on the bed. I poured her a fresh cup of tea and placed it on the nightstand where she could reach it easily when she woke up. Then I tiptoed to the door. I hesitated before I left, turning back to look at her, and the unpleasant thought came to me that this was what Auntie would look like when she finally died, stretched out on a bed with the photograph of her dead children at her side.

Then Auntie stirred. "Nea?"

"Yes?"

"When I look at you, I see my little girl. As though nothing has changed. You know why?"

"Why?" I asked.

But Auntie had drifted off back to sleep, and I never learned what she had intended to say.

After Uncle and Auntie moved away, not even waiting for spring, Uncle didn't write any letters, not to any of us kids, and not to Ma, as far as I know. Auntie wrote from time to time. Progress reports on the search for their eldest son. They put up flyers in the local Cambodian-run groceries, she said, in restaurants, in curio shops, in the small stores that immigrants were managing to put together all over Southern California in the eighties. In every letter, Auntie was certain she would find him soon.

CHAPTER 17

St. Agnes

I almost didn't go to Sourdi's wedding. The night before, she and Ma had stayed up extra late, giggling together in the kitchen after everyone else had gone to bed. As usual my insomnia kept me up, but Sam and the twins were tired out from the rehearsal at the Catholic church. Mr. Chhay's family had converted to Catholicism back when the French had ruled Cambodia, and so he'd wanted a wedding mass to honor his deceased parents' religion. At least I didn't have to see him at the rehearsal. Sourdi didn't want him to see her wedding dress so he agreed to stay in his motel room.

I don't think most people wear their fancy clothes for the rehearsal, but Sourdi wanted to practice so that everything would be perfect. The twins needed to navigate the slipperly waxed wooden floors in the fancy patent leather shoes she'd ordered for them from the Sears catalog along with the matching puffed-sleeved dresses. They loved their new shoes so much, instead of pretending to spread flower petals on the ground, they tap-danced their way to the altar. Ma chastised them, but I could tell there was going to be trouble during the actual wedding. Not that I cared.

Sam was the ring bearer, and he walked stiffly in the tux Mr. Chhay had rented for him from Des Moines. He hadn't quite got Sam's size right, so the poor kid had to walk in stiff, robot-like steps so his too-big shoes didn't fall off and his too-tight pants rip, but he seemed proud to be wearing such grown-up clothes, and he carried the red silk pillow between his hands as carefully as if the diamond wedding ring were actually tied to it.

Since I was Sourdi's maid of honor, it was my turn next to walk up the aisle. Ma had done my hair up so that it hurt and some of Mr. Chhay's nail girls, invited for the ceremony, had done all our nails. My two-inch long plastic talons clicked against each other as I tried to mime carrying a bouquet. I started laughing, then I couldn't stop.

Ma marched right up to me, and I know she would have slapped me good if not for the fact that the priest had stopped by to open the church for us and was waiting for us to finish so he could lock it up again. So instead, Ma took me by the shoulders, planted me beside the altar, and glared at me so fiercely, I swear I could see the flames of Hell burning in her dark irises, showing me my fate if I messed up again on Sourdi's actual wedding day.

Then it was Sourdi's time to walk down the aisle. She was wearing her prom dress, the one that had been her favorite out of the vast selection of all the shops in all the malls in Sioux City, Iowa. She hadn't worn it to prom, since she'd gotten engaged and she couldn't exactly go with Duke as originally planned, and it wouldn't have looked right to go with her really old fiancé. So she was wearing it now, even though it was pink.

The nail girls had done her makeup, a trial run before the Big Day, and though they'd tried to make her look older, plucking her eyebrows into arches as slender as bows, powdering her face until she was as white as a sheet of blank paper, gluing thick false eyelashes like tarantulas above her long dark eyes, the overall effect only made her look younger, like a child playing dress-up in a pink lace party dress.

After I saw Sourdi walk up the aisle, careful careful in her new high heels, I didn't feel like laughing anymore.

That night, as Ma and Sourdi whispered and giggled in the kitchen, upstairs in our bedroom I emptied my backpack of all my school supplies and began stuffing it with socks and underpants, T-shirts and jeans. The things I thought I'd need on the road. I was going to run away. For real this time. For good. I could walk to the exit off the interstate and hitch a ride south to I-80. From there I'd head west. Maybe I'd be able to reach a city with a Greyhound bus depot. Mr. Chhay had given us kids red envelopes at dinner after the rehearsal, after Sourdi had changed out of her dress. There was more than a hundred fifty dollars in my envelope, crisp bills, fresh from some bank. Maybe that was enough to get me to California. I could go look up Uncle and Auntie. Or maybe I'd just pretend I was homeless and register at some school. Lie and say that my mother would come later because she was looking for a job right now. If the school started to hassle me, I'd move to a different school. There were homeless kids like that in my old school in East Dallas. They probably were really homeless, and their mothers probably were really looking for a job or working someplace that didn't pay enough or maybe the mothers were drunk or doing drugs or something that kept them from enrolling their kids themselves or showing up for parent-teacher conferences. It didn't seem like the school paid that much attention.

I'd have to go to a city school. One with lots of kids where the principal and secretaries and teachers were too busy to worry about one more new homeless kid.

I was packing everything furiously, finally deciding to bring my dog-eared copy of *The Martian Chronicles* and leave my other novels behind because they'd take up too much space, when Sourdi came into our bedroom without my hearing her first.

"What are you doing, Nea?"

She looked at my notebooks scattered about the floor.

"I…" Biting my lips, I examined the mess. "I'm looking for my math folders."

"School doesn't start for two weeks."

"I've forgotten everything about geometry. I wanted to get a head start. I can't sleep anyway so I wanted to read something boring."

Sourdi sat down on the worn carpet next to me. She picked up one of my discarded paperbacks. "*Do Androids Dream of Electric Sheep?*" she read. "That's a strange title. Maybe if you count electric sheep, you can dream of androids." She smiled.

"It's not really about that. It's about this guy who kills these fake people, they look just like everybody else, but they're not what they seem. They're androids hiding among the real people. And then the killer guy starts wondering if he's an android, too."

Sourdi put her hand to my face, pushing my hair out of my eyes. "You're going to read in the dark?"

Then all at once, without even realizing it was going to happen, I burst into tears. Horrible, wet, snot-running-down-my-chin, nasty tears. The kind of crying jag where my mouth falls open and I can't shut it and I'm making weird gasping noises and still I cry and cry.

Sourdi put her arms around me. I tried to turn my horrible, wet, snot-covered face away, but she pulled me to her, and I was crying onto her shoulder, getting her arm all wet and gross.

"Sourdi, don't get married. Please don't get married. You can still say no."

"Sssh, sssh," she murmured. "You can come visit me anytime you want, Nea. I'm only moving to Iowa. You'll always be my favorite girl in the world, Nea. My special Nea. Don't worry, don't worry."

I cried harder. Gasping for breath now, I couldn't speak anymore but I couldn't stop crying, no matter how much I wanted to. I put my arms around Sourdi and held her tight, as though I could hold her in place, keep her locked in our room, forever.

"Sssh, sssh," she whispered. And then she slipped into a lullaby, a song from long ago, another lifetime ago, her voice soft as the wind in the reeds along side a gentle stream.

Like that, Sourdi rocked me to sleep for the last time.

The morning of Sourdi's wedding day came. My eyes were swollen but it didn't matter. Ma was crying now, too, but out of happiness. Sam and the twins fought out of excitement, pinching each other, pulling each other's hair. Maly even bit Navy. Only Sourdi managed to keep her composure.

I made it through the wedding ceremony, the interminable mass with the priest's voice droning on and on, the terrible organ music, like something that should be played only at the funerals of convicted criminals. I don't remember walking down the aisle. I don't remember Sourdi following me. Just the guests—Ma invited customers from the Palace so the church would be full—everyone standing as the organ music crescendoed, and the world went blurry. I thought I would faint, but I didn't.

Then it was over, and it was too late.

The guests were clapping, the organist pumped and pumped like Satan's personal accompanist, and then Ma was calling to me, her mouth opening and shutting, as she waved for me to follow her next door for the reception.

I was standing inside the bingo hall, before the row of squat windows, my back turned to the festivities, the exploding flash capturing the tipsy toasts, the guests singing off-key to the rented karaoke machine.

Then it really became too much to bear, and I had to escape the

terrible heat, the flickering fluorescent lights. I slipped from the church
into the ferocious August wind and gave it my best shot, running across
the hard lawn, but the too-tight heels pinched my toes and the stiff taf-
feta bodice of the cotton-candy-pink bridesmaid's dress might as well
have been a vise around my ribcage. I had intended to make it off church
property, run to the empty field that stretched low and dark all the way
to the horizon, but I only made it to the end of the walk near the rectory
before vomiting into Sister Kevin's over-tended tulip patch.

That's when I saw him. Duke.

Sourdi had invited him for the ceremony proper, the reception, too,
but instead he was slouching through the parking lot of St. Agnes, wearing his best hightops and the navy blue suit that his mother had insisted
upon buying for graduation. I wasn't used to him looking like a teenage
undertaker, but I recognized his loping gait immediately. He was holding
a brown bag awkwardly behind his back, as if trying to conceal the fact
that he was drinking as conspicuously as possible.

Duke came over and sat on his haunches beside me while I puked.
I let him hold back my hair while the wedding cake and wine cooler that
I'd tried poured from my mouth.

Finally, I spat a few times to clear my mouth, then sat back on my
rear end.

After a few minutes, I could take a sip from Duke's beer.

We didn't talk.

I took out the pack of cigarettes I'd stolen from Ma's purse and lit
one. It took five puffs before I could mask the taste of bile and sugar.

The wind was blowing fiercely from the northwest, whipping my
hair about my face like a widow's veil, throwing dust from the parking
lot around us like wedding rice.

After a long while, Duke stood up and walked back down the sidewalk lined with yellow daffodils. He walked bow-legged, like all the boys
in our town, farmers' sons, no matter how cool Duke tried to be. I buried
my head in my arms and watched him from under one polyester-covered
armpit as he climbed back into his pickup and pulled away with a screech.
As he left the parking lot, he tossed the brown bag with the empty bottle
of Bud out the window. It fell into the street, where it rolled and rolled
until it disappeared into a ditch.

CHAPTER 18

The First Day

The first day of eighth grade, I waited for the bus on the corner as though expecting the ferryman who would take me across the River Styx. As Ma was dropping Sam and the twins off at the elementary school en route to the Palace, I was completely alone. Waiting there was like becoming a refugee all over again. I had that same queasy stomach feeling of not knowing what was next. Not knowing what to expect. Feeling all wrong, inside and out.

I'd never been this kind of alone before. I'd always had Sourdi.

When we first arrived in Texas, we used to have to ride a bus to a bigger town where there was an ESL teacher for "special needs students" like us, as we were called. The teacher didn't speak Khmer, and most of the other kids in the class spoke Spanish, but at least she smiled at us when she spoke slowly, repeating words in English that we couldn't understand, and showing us flashcards with pictures of animals or food on them and letters of the alphabet.

"Buh, buh, bee!" she said, holding up a card with a smiling insect flying over an English letter.

"Buh, buh, bee," we repeated after her dutifully.

I think it was a year and a half later before I realized that she had been sounding out the letter "B" and not trying to teach Sourdi and me to permanently mispronounce the word "bumblebee."

At least she was pleasant enough, and Sourdi and I could sit together. Even though I'd been placed in third grade and Sourdi in sixth, we could be together for ESL.

On the school bus in Texas, we all knew our place. The students who had physical handicaps sat in the very front so the driver could strap their wheelchairs into the special grooves on the floor or just "keep an eye on them," although I don't know how he was supposed to do that and keep an eye on the road at the same time. I don't know what people expected them to do or need that required special attention from our driver. Mostly the kids sat clumped together, trying to make themselves invisible. I could understand that.

The Mexicans sat in the back, even the family of kids who couldn't speak Spanish but another language that the teachers hadn't been able to identify yet. They were from some Indian tribe that no one had heard of. They had round, brown faces and wide-set eyes, and they looked as though they wore masks over their real faces, masks that had been carved from stone. The two girls wore long braids and the same matching T-shirts for the Longhorns. Their brother was bigger, almost too big to be in elementary school, with a faint line of dark hairs sprouting above his lip, but there he was with us, all the same. He had the same round, flat face as his sisters, but narrower eyes, which made him look thoughtful, and his short black hair stuck straight up from his head like a paintbrush. I had a crush on this boy. My first. But not at first.

The Indians wore the same clothes to school, every day. We used to do that, too, until the Church Ladies told us not to. They said Americans expected us to change our clothes, something different every day. We didn't have that many clothes, just what our sponsors had donated to us, so sometimes we just switched among ourselves; Sourdi and I would switch T-shirts, and Ma would make my younger sisters and brother exchange shorts. We didn't want the Americans to think we didn't know how to dress.

But nobody must have told the Indians. Or maybe they just didn't care. The boy wore a brown corduroy jacket over his shirt, even when it was too hot to wear a jacket. It was a nice jacket, new-looking, not second-hand and wornout like our clothes. The jacket had wide lapels, four or five pockets, yellow top-stitching, and large, leather-covered buttons on the sleeves, on the front, on the flaps of the pockets. It wasn't really a jacket for an elementary school student, but the boy wore it all the same.

Some of the other boys had tried to make fun of him, on account of the jacket. They'd crowded round, in the seats surrounding him and his sisters, and began to tease him in a sing-song made-up language that we all recognized as inherently sinister. Some of the boys even reached out and grabbed at his jacket, pulling at its wide lapels, flicking his shoulders with their fingers, index bent behind thumb. One boy pulled off a button, from the sleeve. Then they all laughed. Or started to.

The Indian boy's arm shot out, and he grabbed the button-thief by the neck. His hand tightened around the boy's throat, and the button-thief began to gasp and choke. His friends tried to pry the Indian boy's hand off, but they were just little kids, they couldn't make him stop. It was as though his arm were made of stone and he'd turned into a statue, a statue of an Indian choking somebody to death. He stood and pushed the button-thief to the floor of the bus, and finally the little kid pulled the button from his pocket and gave it back. Then the Indian boy let the button-thief go.

Watching him in action, I fell in love with him, our school bus Bruce Lee.

Sourdi and I sat in the very middle of the bus, in the same seat.

The bigger town was about thirty miles away but we rode for a good hour and a half every morning because it took so long to pick everyone up, the handicapped kids first, then Sourdi and me from the trailer park, and finally the Mexican kids from the houses and apartments scattered where the town ended and the farms and ranches began. Then we headed onto the interstate, past the cattle ranches and the strip malls, the truck stops with the giant signs shaped like coffeepots and cowboy hats, and the dirt roads where we could watch pickup trucks approaching from miles away, trailing clouds of dust the way jets would sometimes arc through the sky trailing vapor.

At the new school, everyone seemed to have a group but us. The Mexicans congregated by the swings. The handicapped students had teachers' aides awaiting their arrival. Even the Indians found some Indian-looking kids they could hang with by the mural of world peace painted on the side of the lunchroom. The white kids were the most numerous so they could control the kickball field, the hopscotch asphalt, the jungle gym, and the school steps. (In those days, we didn't call them the "white" kids, of course; we called them "the Americans.")

Unfortunately, for Sourdi and me, we had no group. We got beat up.

The girls were the worst. The boys only called us names, but the girls hit. They pulled our hair, they pinched our arms with their long nails, they kicked.

We tried to stay on the bus as long as possible and then made a mad run for the school doors, hoping we could make it past the girls who waited on the steps. Sometimes one of the teacher's aides waited in the doorway, arms folded across her chest, blocking our path. The worst of them was a large, angry woman who had a black mole in the middle of her forehead and wore such thick false eyelashes that it seemed tarantulas had taken nest over her eyes. She wore her hair teased into a metallic-looking blonde ball on top of her head, with a silver whistle on a leather cord around her neck. The whistle bounced atop her enormous boobs, menacingly, as she paced in the hallway just inside the doors, looking this way and that, to make sure no errant child ran inside. When she was very angry, she'd blow on her whistle until her face turned a deep red. We know she did this because when Sourdi and I tried to make it past her once, she grabbed us both by an arm and, holding her whistle between her teeth, blew it like a siren until her entire face, neck and cleavage had turned an inhuman scarlet as she dragged us back out the door and onto the playground, right smack into the middle of the group of girls we'd been trying to escape.

We called her The Tarantula.

On days when The Tarantula was guarding the door, we knew there was no hope of making it inside. We'd have to fend for ourselves on the schoolyard.

Sourdi and I would try to keep moving. It was harder to hit a moving target after all. We'd walk behind other groups of girls, the kinds who had lots to talk about and didn't want to beat up on other kids. But sometimes they'd stop and turn, then seeing us, tell us to go away. We'd pace along the outskirts of the ball games the boys played, as though we were watching, like the friends that stood and cheered them on. But once we walked the wrong way, and a group of boys chasing a ball plowed into us, knocking us and themselves to the ground. They got angry then, we'd spoiled their game, and they shouted something, and we tried to smile, as Ma had taught us to do when someone is angry, to show that we meant no harm, but that only seemed to make them angrier.

Then one day, maybe six months into the school year, when we'd started to get sloppy and less vigilant, we didn't watch where we were going. We were following a group of girls as usual when they turned a corner sharply and we found ourselves surrounded.

"Why are you always following us, huh?" one of the girls wanted to know, a girl with pretty curly brown hair that she wore in two pigtails on either side of her head.

"Yeah, what's wrong with you? Find your own friends!" another girl shouted. This one had yellow hair that shone white in the sunlight.

"Can't you talk? What's wrong with you?"

They circled closer. I held Sourdi's hand and she squeezed mine. She smiled as Ma taught us, and so I smiled, too.

"We like to be friends," Sourdi said.

"What? What are you trying to say?"

"What language are you speaking?"

"I speak English," Sourdi replied.

The girls began to laugh. They turned their voices inside-out, making strange high-pitched noises, which was supposed to be Sourdi's voice. "I speakee Chinese," one girl sang. "I speakee Japanese." They pulled their faces down with their hands until their eyes were mis-shapened, drooping, their eyelids stretched taut.

"We go," Sourdi said. "We go now. Good-bye." She squeezed my hand super-tight then let go, and I knew this was my cue to run.

We took off, Sourdi in one direction, me in the other, to maximize our chances of getting away.

But I was grabbed by two girls, much bigger than me, and the rest of the pack went after Sourdi.

This fight drew a crowd. The boys stopped playing ball, the handful of girls jumping rope ran over, there were shouts in Spanish and English. Eventually three teachers moseyed on up, including The Tarantula, blowing her silver whistle, but no one could hear it above the shouting. I was curled up on the asphalt like an armadillo, trying to keep the girls from punching my face or stomach. The Tarantula tried to unroll me herself, and I kicked her in the ankle, not realizing it was her. She hauled me up then, her hands under my arms, her long press-on nails digging into my armpits.

Sourdi was standing in front of me. She had a nose bleed. The blood had splashed across the T-shirt she was wearing, which was really mine. A pink shirt with a picture of Donny Osmond on it, now with a series of red splotches across his big white teeth.

"Who started this? Will one of y'all tell me just which one of you saw what happened?" a teacher was shouting.

Nobody said anything.

Then I saw one of the girls smirk. The one with the curly pigtails.

I didn't care if she was really the one who'd made Sourdi's nose bleed; I decided she was the one who was going to pay.

The Tarantula let go of me to blow on her whistle. Three sharp blows as if she didn't already have everyone's attention.

The moment I was released from her grip, I took off. I jumped right up to that girl with the curly hair and punched her in the stomach.

She bent over then, crying, and the other girls started to shout, and Sourdi tried to explain, but her soft voice was lost in the shouting. I pointed my finger at the groaning pony-tailed girl. "Hey, pendejo! I'm gonna kick your cajones! Tu madre es puta!" I shouted all the things I'd heard the tough girls on the bus say.

After that, The Tarantula hauled Sourdi and me to the principal's office. She said we were going to have to call Ma to make her pick us up from school. But of course we knew Ma wasn't home, and Sourdi said she couldn't remember where Ma worked.

"Well, we'll just see about that," The Tarantula said, as though that made any sense at all.

The principal's office smelled like disinfectant, like the kind of cleaners Ma used in her maid's job at the Motel 6. His office was just a tiny room with a big desk and a lot of books in a case on the wall. Sitting between that tall bookshelf and his big desk, the principal appeared very small. He was a tired-looking man in a wrinkled suit, with no hair on top of his sunburnt head and a thin, graying mustache under his nose. He looked apprehensive when we came in the door, and I thought I could hear him sigh.

The Tarantula told him that we were troublemakers. That we'd started a big fight on the schoolyard. "On school property!" she said for emphasis as though he didn't know where the schoolyard was. She told him what I'd said, and for the first time since we'd come in the door, he looked alert. In fact, he almost smiled, the edges of his lips twitching slightly. After The Tarantula finished laying out our sins, the principal thanked her for bringing this "al-ter-ca-shun" to his attention. She stood there with her chest pushed out, her whistle shining brightly on her boobs, as though she expected him to give her a medal but after a moment when the principal said nothing more, The Tarantula nodded her head.

"You're welcome," she said. Then giving us one last dirty look, she turned on her heels and left.

The principal seemed relieved that she was gone. He gestured for Sourdi and me to sit down on the two chairs in front of his desk; they were cushioned and covered with a slick vinyl. I had to brace my feet against the floor to keep from sliding off. The principal gazed at us tiredly, his heavy eyelids fluttering over his eyes. Then he did sigh. He said some things about getting along, and making new friends, and "a difficult tran-ziss-shun." Finally, he even tried to smile, his lips twitching back from his gray teeth briefly before falling back into a straight line. He talked to someone on his intercom. Then the school nurse came in and gave Sourdi an ice pack for her nose.

I couldn't understand most of what the principal had said, but I realized now that he wasn't going to make us call Ma, and I felt better. The principal wasn't going to do anything about the girls who tried to beat us up either, but at least Ma wasn't going to get angry at us.

I looked at Sourdi then for the first time since we'd been brought into his office, and she smiled back at me, faintly, as best she could with her nose beginning to swell up.

"You look ridiculous," I whispered to her then in Khmer.

"You should see yourself," she shot back.

I touched my face then and everything hurt anew.

"You've got a black eye," Sourdi whispered. "A big one. What will Ma say?" I gasped, but then Sourdi pinched me on the arm to let me know that she was only teasing.

Ma wouldn't have understood about the fights. Ma was pleased that we were going to school in America. She told us she expected us to do well, to make her proud. She told us we should obey our teachers, we should do as we were told, we should smile and be pleasant and helpful and make friends with everyone.

Ma herself was trying her best to follow her own advice, which meant smiling at work at the other maids even when as a result she was always the one who ended up cleaning the toilet bowls. And she smiled at the Church Ladies when they came to visit us in the trailer, with their gifts of old clothes and canned creamed corn, American cheese, Kix, Wonder Bread, generic peanut butter and bunch after bunch of browning bananas. She smiled when they frowned at the kitchen table sticky from

breakfast and the piles of laundry on the floor of the living room and the
way we ran the TV and the radio at the same time, loud, so that we could
hear even as we sat on the front lawn where it was cooler, while the little
kids ran in and out the screen door in their underwear. Ma didn't like to
keep them dressed in their school clothes as they'd only get them dirty.

Ma smiled when the Church Ladies came to pick us up on Sundays,
though as of late Ma had told us kids to go on along without her. She
had a headache, her feet hurt, she suffered dizzy spells, we explained to
the Church Ladies. She had a catalog of ills that might be catching, you
never knew what people like us might be carrying inside.

In truth, Ma didn't like to walk into the small church filled with
people who stared and whispered, who had given us everything we owned
including the clothes on our backs, who might recognize this blouse and
that skirt. She knew full well that not everyone in the church had wanted
to sponsor a refugee family. Not everyone thought America needed any
more foreigners. Especially the kind that didn't speak English and needed
welfare and food stamps and were rumored to eat cats and dogs.

We didn't talk much in those days, any of us, including me. English
was still a ball of steel wool on my tongue. The words scratched and
scraped against the roof of my mouth, the back of my throat. But we
understood what the Church Ladies were saying all right. We understood a squinted face, a sidelong glance, a raised eyebrow. We understood
perfectly.

Sometimes Ma's shoulders felt too heavy for her spine. Just standing
up straight could wear her out. But if anyone would have asked how she
felt, she would have only smiled in reply.

We knew Ma couldn't teach us how to survive the schoolyard. It was
the Indian boy who did that.

That afternoon on the bus ride home, the Indian boy surprised us.
Instead of ignoring us as usual, he and his sisters didn't head to the very
back of the bus but instead sat in the seats directly around us. At first I
was afraid that they were going to try to beat us up, too, now that those
girls had shown everyone how easy it was.

The boy was sitting in front us, one sister to the side, the other behind. This is it, I thought. But then the boy turned around and leaned
over the seat. He pulled something out of the pocket of his leisure-suit

jacket. It looked like a woman's nylon stocking that had been filled with rocks. Then I realized that's exactly what it was. While the sisters kept watch, making sure no one else was looking our way, the boy showed us how he could snap the nylon into the air then pull it back quickly, like a boomerang on a rubber band. He'd used only the foot part of the nylon to hold the rocks, the other end he kept knotted in his fist. And if a teacher should come by, the rocks could be emptied quickly onto the pavement, erasing evidence of the weapon. He demonstrated, letting the rocks fall onto the seat beside him while he stared into the middle ground, maintaining a blank expression of, if not innocence, at the very least indifference.

We made ourselves a pair that evening, while Ma was at work. We found Ma's nylons hanging on the shower head to dry, and cut them up, one foot for each of us. It was too bad, destroying Ma's clothes like that of course, but survival was survival.

Thus, filled with a new sense of hope and possibility, I thought about the Indian boy. That night as I lay beside my older sister, I couldn't sleep, my heart beating too fast in my chest. Not because I was anxious or afraid or hungry or hadn't understood and thus hadn't done my homework, all the usual reasons why I couldn't sleep. No, this night, I lay awake trying to think of words and gestures that I might use to convey my gratitude and hopefulness—as well as the giggly feeling in the very pit of my stomach— to the Indian boy, who was now our savior, better than the Church Ladies' Jesus in my eyes, and better looking, too. Not all pale and stringy and nailed to anything, but live and whole and a pleasing shade of brown. I whispered pleasant sounds that I had heard. "Luf-lee." "San kyoo." "Wun-duh-ful-luh." I watched my hands in the moonlight as I practiced placing them over my heart in a sign of sincerity. I pressed my palms together before my face in a *sompeah* and watched as the shadows of my fingers arced against my bedsheets. I imagined that the boy and his sisters would become friends with Sourdi and me. We would form our very own group. We would devise our very own language, one only we could understand, the better to pass secrets. Finally, after thinking along this line for a very long time, I fell into a deep and peaceful sleep, unimpeded by the night-mares that usually haunted me.

But I never saw the Indian boy again. Perhaps the boy and his sisters had moved away with their family. At any rate, they never rode on our bus again, so I could never thank him. Thus, I learned to recognize the bitter-iron taste of unrequited love.

At any rate, he had been correct.

Once we started fighting back, the girls didn't pick on us so much. They began to squabble amongst themselves, Americans versus Mexicans, blonds versus brunettes, or everybody against the one redhead, calling her names like "carrot-top" and "leprechaun" until she cried. That was the way it was on the schoolyard. It wouldn't have mattered if everybody was the same race, the same color. The kids who wanted to fight would have found somebody to make different.

Now I was going to school alone. Once again, I had no group. Worse, no Sourdi. And now that I was older, 13, a bona fide teenager, I knew a nylon filled with rocks wasn't going to help me anymore.

When the bus came, I climbed aboard quickly with my head down, and took a seat right behind the driver, and stared out the dusty window, ignoring the noise around me.

I would make myself invisible, I decided. I would become a ghost.

When the bus pulled up to the junior high, I made sure I wasn't first off or last, just one body in the stream of kids heading toward the open doors. Some of the male teachers were posted outside the door, and they called out at certain points, "Spit that out!" or "Hand that over, right now!" until wads of chaw were deposited into the grass, packs of cigarettes grudgingly surrendered.

In the hall, all my classmates seemed taller and older and prettier than me. I tried not to meet their gaze. Some of the boys hooted and snickered, but I told myself they were doing that to haze the seventh graders, not me. I was dressed like everyone else. Mostly. I could speak English. I fit in. I belonged here. This was my town, I told myself, over and over.

When the first bell rang, I examined my schedule and wandered the long hallway, trying to find my first period class, room 107, so I wouldn't be late. A boy with acne pushed me so that I fell against a locker and dropped my binder. Then he grabbed another kid, a boy, and actually tossed him against a wall.

"What are you looking at?" he sneered at me.

A group of girls standing nearby, as though they had nothing better to do but stand in a clutch and show off their summer tans, stopped gossiping for a second to watch us.

The boy straightened up. He was going to do something to impress them, I could tell, and I was going to have to hit him hard, and would probably get detention my first day of school, which would be just great. The cherry on this dung sundae. I braced myself, sizing the boy up, figuring out his center of gravity. All I needed was the element of surprise, and I was faster than I looked.

But then one of the girls stepped forward. She was tall and shapely and wore green eyeshadow that matched her eyes. "Don't pick on girls, Bryan," she said. "What's gotten into you? Besides, don't you know? That's that refugee girl. She's a boat person. You should be nice."

Chastised, the boy shrugged in an exaggerated fashion and headed off down the hall.

Then the girl turned to me and smiled tightly, triumphantly, her coven of friends cackling behind her. She tossed her long, permed hair over her shoulder.

I sighed. The whole hierarchy of my school years swirled before me like a mandala of Buddhist Hell. I could see my life here stretching ahead of me like an endless tunnel. The girls would be worse than the boys. And I could say something nasty now, and fight every day from this moment on, or I could turn myself into a ghost and disappear.

A heaviness settled into my bones. There was no point in fighting. I only had to bear things. Like Ma always said. Five years. And then I'd be gone, too. I'd graduate and leave this town forever.

So I said nothing, picked up my binder, and headed to homeroom.

Frankly, I would rather have punched that boy hard, broken his nuts and his nose, and shown them all. But I was alone now. And besides, if I got in trouble and made Ma angry, maybe she wouldn't let me call Sourdi on weekends, the way she'd promised.

And so I vowed that for once, I would be good, the daughter Ma had always wanted me to be.

PART II

CHAPTER 19

The Churning of the Sea

In my first full year without Sourdi, when I was a freshman in high school, it was like the earth itself was mourning with me. It started snowing in October and didn't stop until the next spring. I remember January as a particularly depressing month, when winter seemed to have settled in for good, and the drifts stood three feet high on either side of the streets. All the Christmas decorations that the Chamber of Commerce paid for had to be taken down, but our town only had one firetruck with a crane high enough to do the job, so it took a while. By the end of the month, half the streets still had their giant plastic candy canes and Santa Claus banners dangling from lightposts. The effect was that our town looked like a worn-out Christmas tree, abandoned on the side of the state highway.

By mid-January, the snow plow didn't even bother trying to clear the entire parking lot around the Palace anymore and merely pushed the new snow against the giant mountains of old snow that hadn't melted since the last blizzard, and wouldn't for a while, not till March. As a result, large swaths of the parking lot were unusable, with the snow piles towering more than eight feet high along the edges of the lot.

Once Ma looked out into the parking lot and remarked that the whole sad scene made her think of the story about the churning of the sea of milk. It was a Hindu story originally, but something Ma had learned, too, growing up in Phnom Penh before the war. The way the story goes, in the beginning of time, the universe was made up of a vast, primordial ocean of milk. And because of a minor transgression, the Lord of All Creation had taken away the secret of longevity from the lesser gods and tossed it into the sea. Not knowing what else to do, the gods decided to dredge the waters and see if they could bring the elixir of immortality back up and save their lives. Unfortunately, they weren't strong enough for the job and had to enlist the help of demons.

Holding each end of a giant snake wrapped around a mountain, the gods and demons pulled the mountain back and forth across the universe, churning up the milk in towering waves. Working together in this way for a thousand years, they managed to dredge up thirteen Heavenly wonders, including diamonds and gems, a wish-granting cow, dancing girls, and at long last the magic potion that would grant them all eternal youth. Here's where the truce broke off, and the gods and demons began to fight, each group wanting to keep the potion for themselves. Ultimately, the gods won, but not before one demon managed to swallow a mouthful, ensuring the existence of evil for eternity.

"It just goes to show why we humans don't have a chance," Ma said almost facetiously, shaking her head. "Even gods will ally themselves with demons when they need them."

The snow banks around our restaurant did, in fact, look like giant waves of milk, frozen in place. Sometimes Ma surprised me like this, when she could stare out the window at the endless white fields, and say something profound. However, there were more times when Ma refused to say anything as she stared into the parking lot at the seemingly endless cliffs of snow and instead smoked one cigarette after another, blowing smoke from her nostrils.

I had a dream once that Ma and I were sitting together in the Palace, sipping hot jasmine tea, the light reflecting off the snow through the windows as though through a prism, sending shards of colored gems to dance around us on the walls, on the floor, in the air. We reached our hands into the beams of light and laughed to see spots of red and green and blue alight upon our fingers like rubies and emeralds and sapphire rings.

I felt completely at ease with my mother, because I knew when I opened my mouth and spoke, all my words would be like these colored rainbow lights, they would delight my mother, they would put her heart at ease. And when I asked her a question, she would answer it easily, with a laugh, the way a mother on a television show might, reminiscing about the past, about the first time she fell in love, about the giddy feelings she had as a young girl, a girl my age perhaps. She could remember and smile at the same time, and she could talk to me at length, the warmth of her words, like the warmth of the tea, moving down my throat, my chest and settling into my belly.

When I awoke, the sun was shining through a space in my bedroom curtains, hot white sunshine, surprising for a winter day, and caught momentarily between the warmth of my dream and the brightness of the sunshine, I dipped my hand into the light, as though it were something that could be scooped up in a palm and brought to my mouth to drink.

And then I woke up for real, and it was still winter, and I was still me, and I still did not possess the right words, the ones I needed, to talk to my mother and put her heart at ease.

It was a couple weeks after Christmas when the phone rang early in the morning. I thought it might be Sourdi, so I leapt out of bed and ran to hall to answer it, my toes curling up from the cold floor. But it was a man's voice at the other end, sobbing. "Nea," he cried. "Nea." Over and over like that, and I realized it was Uncle.

My first thought was they'd discovered their oldest son was dead. Something terrible like that. Something that would break Auntie's wounded heart forever.

That's how dumb I was. That's how a real tragedy comes up and gobsmacks you in the face. Just when you think you've figured it out, you realize you didn't even know what was coming.

Ma came into the hallway now; she was already up and in the kitchen, fixing her morning tea. She held an unlit cigarette in her hand.

She looked at me quizzically.

I held the phone out to her. "It's Uncle," I whispered. I wanted to warn her, prepare her, say something, a code word. At least tell her that he was crying. But my voice froze in my throat, and I handed the phone then turned away and leaned my head against my arm on the wall.

"Is it you?" Ma asked in Khmer. And then she fell silent. Her hand with the cigarette dropped to her side. "Mmm hmm. Mmm hmm," she murmured, as though soothing a young child. I was surprised how calm she remained while I found myself shaking, cold sweat running down my sides.

She spoke to him in that soft, calm voice for quite some time. I couldn't make out all the words. But I could tell Ma was saying something about Auntie, telling Uncle he was a good husband, a good father, a good person.

Then at last she hung up.

"What is it? What happened? Did they find their oldest son?" I turned to Ma, expecting to find her standing there as calm as her voice, lighting her cigarette perhaps.

Instead I discovered she was crying. Her hands covered her face, but the tears streaked down her cheeks, her chin, her throat.

I put my arms around her. I was taller than Ma by now, but I'd never thought of her as a small person or a fragile one. But now in my arms, as she shook and sobbed, my mother felt as delicate as an antique doll.

"My only sister is dead! She's dead! My only sister! My dearest sister! Dead!" Ma wailed, and then she clung to me, sobbing into my pajama top, as I patted her back, stroked her graying hair, and cried, too, unable to think of one consoling word to say.

Auntie had died the previous evening. She'd taken an overdose, accidental or on purpose Uncle didn't know, but when he came home from work and found her stretched on her bed, the picture of their family from before the war at her side, she was already cold. He'd called 911 and ridden in the ambulance with her to the hospital, holding her hand in his the entire way, even as the EMT crew wheeled her on the stretcher into the ER. The doctors there had pronounced her dead.

Ma had me call Sourdi and tell her the bad news. My sister remained remarkably calm.

"There's a Buddhist temple, a Cambodian one, here in Des Moines," she said. "I'll send my husband to make an offering for Auntie. The monks can pray for her soul."

"I thought *he* was Catholic," I said. Even now I couldn't forgive Mr. Chhay for stealing away my sister.

"He is. But Auntie was Buddhist. He understands."

Sourdi sighed. "Auntie deserves a better life next time. A kinder life. The Buddha will forgive her. I know her soul will find peace in her next life."

Then my sister told me a story about Auntie, and Ma, too, from before the war.

My mother was a young girl, sixteen, when she met my father and fell in love with him, marrying him against her parents' wishes. She was a headstrong girl, and she was very much in love. She was already working by then, an office lady, a young assistant secretary. She'd lied about her age and gotten the job because she was smart and quick and capable, and she'd wanted to earn her own money. She had a plan. She was going to go on to college, like her older brothers before her, although the family finances were not what they'd once been. It had been expensive to send two boys to school, and she'd finished junior high, already a lot of education for a girl.

But my mother had a plan. She was going to surprise her family. She was going to study on her own, at night, she bought the books herself with the money she earned, and one of her brothers was helpful, letting her borrow his old school books, his old notebooks of composition and mathematics and history. And when the time came in a year, she would sit for the college entrance examinations, just as though she'd been a lycée student. She wasn't yet sure of how she would get herself admitted to the examination hall, perhaps with a forged letter stating she'd been studying abroad?, something exotic and irrefutable like that. At sixteen, she had confidence in her ability to find a way around these kinds of problems, the kind that would stop a less capable and less determined girl.

So during the day she worked in the offices of Biswas, Monthawat, and Chhang, General Contractors, typing and filing and taking dictation, occasionally brewing and serving tea to visitors, carrying the dainty Chinese teapot and tiny porcelain cups on a lacquer tray, and at night she studied geometry and trigonometry and the conjugation of French verbs and the story of the Ramayana as well as the history of the French Republic, both of which seemed equally fantastic and unreal. And her plans were set, her mind made up, determined, until the day that she met my father.

At first she paid him little mind. He was not handsome like the Bollywood movie stars whose faces adorned the posters before the Royal Cinema that she passed by every day on the bus on the way to work. He was neither tall nor muscular, nor was he particularly charming. He was slight and myopic, his glasses forever sliding down his flat nose. But he had an amazing shock of thick black bangs that bounced above his forehead and a smile that blossomed from cheek to cheek. And he smiled a lot at Ma. First, shyly, then more boldly, when he noticed her staring. She'd quickly go back to work, scrutinizing a letter she was typing, holding it close to her eyes as though it were the most important document she had ever seen, and the grain of the paper was something she needed to examine at length. And then when she dared to glance up again, when she was sure it was safe and he had gone back to his duties, she would look up again to watch him.

He had a soft, gentle voice. He had eyes that smiled whenever he looked at Ma. He was smart and hard-working. He was himself a university student, but because his family did not have money, he'd stopped his studies temporarily to take this job, as an assistant to one of the contractors, to earn money for his family. There had been an illness, a debt, a tragic circumstance, but you'd never guess from looking at my father. He carried himself with a cheerful buoyancy, his easy smile belying whatever family tragedy had derailed his studies.

After he noticed my mother noticing him, he began to whistle at work, he smiled all the time, he began to move with quick steps about the office as though he might be dancing to music no one else was yet aware of.

"He's a male secretary!" My mother's mother had exclaimed when Ma had come to her, to tell her the secret longings that had filled her heart. "He's one generation off the farm! He's one generation away from being a peasant himself!"

Ma had tried to explain about his prospects. He was a smart boy, the smartest she'd ever met. He could talk about any subject you could think of. He could quote poetry. When he sang, imitating the famous crooners on the radio, his voice rang out sweeter than theirs. He was kind.

My mother's father tried to dissuade his daughter. He said he regretted now that he had protected her from the harshness of life, that he had not prepared her for The Reality of Life and Living.

My mother looked at her shoes, she examined the coating of fine yellow dust that had settled on the toes of her good leather pumps on the way home from the office, while her father talked on and on about Practicalities.

Love was one thing, but one could not live on love alone. Money, too, was important. And family. And prospects. And all these things were linked. He said he understood, he'd been sixteen once himself, but he absolutely forbade my mother to marry this boy from a poor family, who had had to leave his studies (a bad sign), this boy who they were certain could never amount to much.

My mother married my father anyway. There was no wedding tent, no Chinese banquet in the best restaurant in Phnom Penh as there had been for her oldest sister. There was no announcement in the newspapers. There was no telling of the neighbors or of the cousins or even of her eldest brother who was currently out of the country, on holiday in Thailand.

After the first baby, Sourdi, was born, my mother's mother softened, her heart melting at the sight of such a lovely granddaughter. But after the next baby, a miscarriage, a boy who died before he could be born, my mother's mother whispered that maybe it was for the best. They barely had enough money to feed the three of them, how would have managed with four? And then another baby, and another pregnancy, and my father could not think of going back to school, he needed to work to support his family, he needed to think of his responsibilities. And Ma returned to work again as well. She'd quit her office lady job after the marriage, and now with so many children, it would have been unseemly for her to try to go back, so she opened a small business, close to their apartment, selling cloth and sundries and imported tins of food.

Yet my parents were happy, my father still whistled at work and at home, he sang lullabies to the babies, and Ma smiled too much for a woman in her position. It was generally agreed that she should have been more humble rather than flaunt her happiness when the circumstances of her life were, in fact, nothing to brag about. Other women began to gossip about her, about her happiness. It made them jealous.

And it was at this point that my mother's mother began to say that she had only one daughter.

And then when the babies had fallen ill, and Ma was pregnant yet again (with twins, no less!) and my father had come down with a chest cold and couldn't find work for a while—for his office job had disappeared too, as the civil war raged on and on, foreign companies began to move out of the capital, and there was less need of General Contractors, there was less need of secretaries, male or otherwise—finally my parents began to argue, the nervous kind of arguments that solved nothing but dispelled fear with hot air and bold accusations. Around this time my father found a job as a delivery man, a truck driver. It didn't pay well, this job, plus it was dangerous because the highways had been overrun by soldiers and bandits, and they could stop a truck and take the driver's wares and kill him, or hurt him, or he could accidentally take a wrong turn and trip a mine, the kind that soldiers on all sides were now planting in the countryside, or he could be struck by a stray bomb, either from the Royal Khmer Air Force or the Americans or the mercenary soldiers with weapons that nobody knew how they had managed to obtain. And because of their increasing fear, my parents began to argue even more.

It was during one of the times my father was out of the capital, driving his truck on the perilous highways, that one or all of us children became ill and my mother needed money for the doctor and for the expensive medicine that he prescribed. She had gone to her older sister to ask for money.

This was not the first time that my mother had done so, "borrowing" money, although they both knew the money would never be returned.

My mother left us in a neighbor's care and rode in a pedicab to her sister's grand house. She'd put on her best silk dress, which was only a little frayed at the hem, and only had one missing button. She didn't want to seem like a pauper, come begging, she wanted to seem like a sister who could rightfully expect to "borrow" a little change, a little petty cash, just until her husband returned, just until the war was over and the economy improved, and her husband could find a better position, one more suitable to his talents.

Auntie let my mother into her house, and she listened to the story of the sick children, and the doctor's bill, and the expensive medicine. She cooled herself with a Chinese silk fan, the oblong kind painted with bright peonies, back and forth, back and forth, the breeze lifting Auntie's hair, drying the sweat collecting on her forehead.

And then Auntie had sighed. A long, terrible, drawn-out sigh. The kind the lesser actresses made in the more melodramatic films, just as they were about to be sold into slavery to pirates or tied to railroad tracks to be run over by trains. Then Auntie rolled her eyes. Terribly. As though she were being asked to sacrifice her first-born son to a heathen god.

Ma thought to herself that her sister had missed her calling. She should have entered the Royal Academy for the Dramatic Arts. She should have auditioned for the pictures. But my mother held her tongue, because she knew that she was not really coming as a sister to "borrow" pocket change, she was coming as a desperate woman to beg.

And finally Auntie had risen from her cushioned chair, the one that had been made by a local carpenter in the exact imitation of a picture Auntie had seen of a chair in a foreign magazine, complete with unnecessary stuffing on the arms and rather gaudy brass brads along the edges of the flowered upholstery, and Auntie had walked slowly across her bedroom, to the jewelry box with the hidden compartment where she'd hid her extra money, and she'd turned her back to Ma, and hunched over the box as though she were afraid Ma would see exactly how she coaxed the hidden drawer open, as though Ma were a stranger who could not be trusted, a thief.

And then she had taken the wad of money in her hand and she had languorously made her way across the tiled floors, her slippers flap-flap-flapping the length of the room, and Auntie had stood before Ma seated on the edge of her chair and she held the money before Ma's face.

"I always knew you shouldn't have married that pauper's son. And now look at you. If you had any sense, you'd leave him. Leave him before he comes back in his ridiculous truck. You can stay here if you want. But, mark my words, if you stay with that . . . that . . . beggar of a man, you'll watch your children starve before your very eyes."

And then Ma in a fury rose slowly from her chair and snatched the money in her fist, and then she'd tossed the bills to the floor, so that they fell about the room like so many dried, dead leaves. Ma turned on her heels then and ran from her sister's house, and she vowed she would never speak to her sister again.

That night, she sat at the kitchen table in her tiny apartment, and she cried into her fists because she did not know how she would pay the doctor, and she cried because she had been too proud and should have taken the money. And then her fury returned, and she began to pray. She prayed that her sister would be cursed, that her womb would become barren and her body wracked with ills, boils and tumors, worms and parasites. She prayed that her sister would watch her own children fall ill before her eyes and she would have to beg strangers for money, for food, for shelter. She cursed her sister with every affliction she could imagine, and only then, could Ma stop crying, and wipe her eyes, and go to bed.

Later, Uncle found out about the feud, perhaps Auntie had complained to him, perhaps an eavesdropping maid had reported the fight. At any rate, he paid the doctor's bills himself. And he told the doctor, in the future, should there be any more expenses, the bills should be sent directly to his office.

After Sourdi finished telling me this story, I understood why Ma had put up with her sister's cruelties in the Palace, why Ma had felt guilty every time she looked at her sister, why she was willing to sacrifice her love for Uncle rather than fight for him even though Auntie couldn't love him anymore.

I also understood why she hadn't wanted Sourdi to marry Duke. A poor boy with kind eyes and an easy smile. In Ma's experience, the world eats these kinds of boys up and spits their bones out whole.

CHAPTER 20

Saving Sourdi

I might never have seen Duke again if it were not for Sourdi's strange phone call late one Saturday evening, two and a half years after her wedding. I was fifteen.

At first, I hadn't recognized my older sister's voice.

"Who is this?" I demanded, thinking: heavy breathing, prank caller.

"Who d'you think?" Sourdi was crying, a tiny crimped sound that barely crept out of the receiver. Then her voice steadied with anger and grew familiar. "Is Ma there?"

"What's the matter? What happened?"

"Just let me speak to Ma, O.K.?" There was a pause, as Sourdi blew her nose. "Tell her it's important."

I lured Ma from the TV room without alerting my younger sisters or Sam. Ma paced back and forth in the kitchen between the refrigerator and the stove, nodding and muttering, "Mmm, mmm, uh-hmm." I could just hear the tinny squeak of Sourdi's panicked voice.

I sat on the floor, hugging my knees, in the doorway to the hall, just out of Ma's line of sight.

Finally, Ma said, in the tone normally reserved for refusing service to the unruly or arguing with a customer who had a complaint, "It's always like this. Every marriage is hard. Sometimes there is nothing you can do—"

Then Ma stopped pacing. "Just minute," she said and she took the phone with her into the bathroom, shutting the door firmly behind her.

When she came out again, twenty-two minutes later, she ignored me completely. She set the phone back on the counter without saying a word.

"So?" I prompted.

"I'm tired." Ma rubbed her neck with one hand. "Just let me rest. You girls, it's always something. Don't let your old mother rest."

She yawned extravagantly. She claimed she was too tired to watch any more TV. She had to go to bed, her eyes just wouldn't stay open.

I tried calling Sourdi, but the phone only rang and rang.

The next morning, Sunday, I called first thing, but then Mr. Chhay picked up.

"Oh, is this Nea?" he said, so cheerfully it was obvious he was hiding something.

"Yes, I'd like to speak to my sister."

"I'm sorry, Little Sister." I just hated when he called me that. "Sourdi is out right now. But I'll tell her you called. She'll be sorry she missed you."

It was eight o'clock in the morning, for Chrissake.

"Oh, thank you," I said, sweet as pie. "How's the baby?"

"So well!" Then he launched into a long explanation about his daughter's eating habits, her rather average attempts to crawl, the simple words she was trying to say. For all I knew, Sourdi could have been right there, fixing his breakfast, washing his clothes, cleaning up his messes. I thought of my sister's voice in my ear, the tiny sound like something breaking.

It was all I could do to disguise the disdain in my voice. "Be sure to tell Sourdi to call back. Ma found that recipe she wanted. That special delicious recipe she was looking for. I can't tell you what it is, Ma's secret recipe, but you'll really be surprised."

"Oh, boy," the jerk said. "I didn't know about any secret recipe."

"That's why it's a secret." I hung up. I couldn't breathe. My chest hurt. I could feel my swollen heart pressing against my ribs.

The next afternoon, I tried calling back three more times, but no one answered.

At work that evening, Ma was irritable. She wouldn't look me in the eyes when I tried to get her attention. Some little kid spilled his Coke into a perfectly good plate of House Special Prawns and his parents insisted they be given a new order—and a new Coke—on the house. There was a minor grease fire around quarter to nine; the smoke alarms all went off at the same time, and then the customers started complaining about the cold, too, once we had opened all the doors and windows to clear the air. Fairly average as far as disasters went, but they put Ma in a sour mood.

Ma was taking a cigarette break out back by the dumpsters, smoke curling from her nostrils, before I could corner her. She wasn't in the mood to talk, but after the nicotine fix took hold, she didn't tell me to get back to work, either.

I asked Ma if I could have a smoke. She didn't get angry. She smiled in her tired way, the edges of her mouth twitching upwards just a little, and said, "Smoking will kill you." Then she handed me her pack.

"Maybe Sourdi should come back home for a while," I suggested.

"She's a married woman. She has her own family now."

"She's still part of our family."

Ma didn't say anything, just tilted her head back and blew smoke at the stars, so I continued, "Well, don't you think she might be in trouble? She was crying, you know. It's not like Sourdi." My voice must have slipped a tad, just enough to sound disrespectful, because Ma jerked upright, took the cigarette out of her mouth and glared at me.

"What you think? You so smart? You gonna tell me what's what?" Ma threw her cigarette onto the asphalt. "You're not like your sister. Your sister knows how to bear things!"

She stormed back into the kitchen and ignored me for the rest of the evening.

Ma liked Sourdi's husband. Mr. Chhay had a steady job, a house. Ma didn't mind he was so old and Sourdi just sixteen when they married. In her eyes, sixteen was a good age to start a family. "I was about Sourdi's age when I got married," Ma liked to say.

When Sourdi sent pictures home for the holidays, Ma ooohed and aaahed as though they were winning lottery tickets. Sourdi and her old-man husband in front of a listing Christmas tree, a pile of presents at their feet. Then their red-faced baby sprawled on a pink blanket on the living room carpet, drooling in its shiny high chair, slumped in its Snuggly like a rock around Sourdi's neck.

"Look. Sony," Ma pointed at the big-screen television in the background of the New Year's pictures. "Sourdi says they got an all new washer/dryer, too. Maytag."

When I looked at my sister's pictures, I could see that she looked tired.

I called Sourdi one more time, after Ma and my sisters and brother had gone to bed and I finally had the kitchen to myself, the moon spilling from the window onto the floor in a big, blue puddle. I didn't dare turn on the lights.

This time, my sister answered. "Mmm . . . Hello?"

"Sourdi?"

"What time is it?"

"Sssh." My heart beat so loudly, I couldn't hear my own voice. "How are you doing?"

"Oh, we're fine. The baby, she's doing real good. She's starting to talk—"

"No, no, no. I mean, what happened the other night?"

"What?"

Another voice now, low, a man's voice, just beneath the snow on the line. Then suddenly a shriek.

"Uh-oh. I just woke her up." Sourdi's voice grew fainter as she spoke to *him*: "Honey, can you check the baby's diaper?" Then she said to me, "I have to go. The baby, she's hungry, you know."

"Let him handle it. I have to talk to you a minute, O.K.? Just don't go, Sourdi. What's going on? What did you say to Ma?"

Sourdi sighed, like a balloon losing its air. "Oh . . . nothing. Look, I—I really have to go. Talk to you later, Nea." She hung up.

I called back in twenty minutes, surely long enough to change a diaper, but the phone only rang forlornly, ignored.

I considered taking Ma's car, but then Ma wouldn't be able to get to work, and I wasn't sure how long I needed to be gone. Then I thought of Duke. The last time I'd seen him was at Sourdi's wedding.

Even though it was far too late in the night, I called Duke. He was still in town, two years after graduation. I'd heard he was working as a mechanic at the Standard station. I found his number in the phone book.

"It's Nea. Pick up your phone, Duke," I hissed into his machine. "It's an emergency!"

"Nea?!" He was yawning. "My god. What . . . what time is it?"

"Duke! It's important! It's Sourdi, she's in trouble."

There was a pause while I let him absorb all this.

"You have to drive me to Des Moines. We have to get her."

"What happened?"

"Look, I don't have time to explain. We have to go tonight. It's an emergency. A matter of life and death.'"

"Did you call the police?"

"Don't be stupid. Sourdi would never call the cops. She loves that jerk."

"What?" Duke whispered now, "Her husband, he beat her up?"

"Duke, I told you, I can't say anything right now. But you have to help me."

He agreed to meet me at the corner, where there'd be no chance Ma could hear his truck. I'd be waiting.

It was a freezing night for April. The wind stung my cheeks, which wasn't a good sign. Could be rain coming, or worse, snow. Even when the roads were clear, it was a good six-hour drive. I didn't want to think how long it would take if we ran into a late-season blizzard.

There was the roar of a souped-up engine and then a spray of gravel. Run-DMC rapped over the wind.

"Duke! What took you?"

He put his hand over the door, barring me from climbing up. "You want me to help or not?"

"Don't joke."

I pulled myself inside and then made Duke back up rather than run in front of the house. Just in case Ma woke up.

"How come your Ma didn't want to come?"

"She doesn't know."

"Sourdi didn't want to worry her?"

"Mmm." There was no point trying to shout above "Walk This Way."

He was obviously tired. When Duke was tired, he turned his music up even louder than normal. I'd forgotten that. Now the bass underneath the rap was vibrating in my bones. But at least he did as I asked and took off toward the highway.

Soon the squat buildings of town, the used car lots on the road in from the highway with their flapping colored flags and the metal storage units of the Sav-U-Lot passed from view, and there was nothing before us but the black sky and the slick asphalt and the patches of snow on the shoulders glowing briefly in the wake of the headlights.

I must have fallen asleep, though I don't remember feeling tired. I was standing on the deck of a boat in an inky ocean, trying to read the stars, but every time I found one constellation, the stars began to blink and fade. I squinted at them, but the stars would not stay in place. Then my head snapped forward as the pickup careened off the shoulder.

The pickup landed in a ditch. Metal glittered in the headlights; the fields on this side of the highway were strung with barbed wire.

We got out by sacrificing our jackets, stuffing them under the rear tires until we had enough traction to slide back onto the pavement.

I insisted upon driving then. "I got my license," I lied. "And I'm not tired at all."

Duke settled into the passenger seat, his arms folded across his chest, his head tilted back, preparing to go to sleep again.

"D'ya think she'll be happy to see me?" he said out of the blue. "Sourdi sent me a Christmas card with a picture of the baby. Looks just like . . . But I didn't write back or nothing. She probably thought I was angry. She mad at me, you think?"

"Sourdi's never mad at anybody."

"She must be mad at her husband if she wants you to come get her."

"She doesn't know we're coming."

"What!"

"I didn't have time to explain to her."

"You're not running away from home, are you?" Duke's eyes narrowed and his voice grew slow as if he thought he was suddenly being clever.

"Yeah, Einstein. I'm running away to Des Moines."

Once upon a time, in another world, a place almost unimaginable to me sitting in the pickup with Madonna singing "Lucky Star" on the radio, Sourdi had walked across a minefield, carrying me on her back. She was nine and I was five. I could still see it all clearly: the startled faces of people who'd tripped a mine, their limbs in new arrangements, the bones peeking through the earth. Sourdi had said it was safest to step on the bodies; that way you knew a mine was no longer there.

This was nothing I would ever tell Duke. It was our own personal story, just for Sourdi and me to share. Nobody's business but ours.

I would walk on bones for my sister, I vowed. I would put my bare feet on rotting flesh. I would save Sourdi.

We found the house in West Des Moines after circling for nearly an hour through the identical streets with their neat lawns and boxy houses and chain link fences. I refused to allow Duke to ask for directions from any of the joggers or the van that sputtered by, delivering the *Register*. He figured people in the neighborhood would know, just ask where the Oriental family lived. I told him to go to hell. Then we didn't talk for a while.

But as soon as we found Locust Street, I recognized the house. I knew it was Sourdi's even though it had been painted a different color since the last set of pictures. The lace undercurtains before the cheerful flowered draperies, the flourishing plants in the windows next to little trinkets, figurines in glass that caught the light. Every space crammed with something sweet.

The heater in Duke's truck began to make a high-pitched sick-cat whine as we waited, parked across the street, staring at Sourdi's house

"So are we going to just sit here?"

"Shh," I said irritably. "Just wait a minute." Somehow I had imagined that Sourdi would sense our presence, the curtains would stir, and I'd only have to wait a moment for my sister to come running out the front door. But we sat patiently, shivering, staring at Sourdi's house. Nothing moved.

"Her husband's home," I said stupidly. "He hasn't gone to work yet."

"He wouldn't dare try anything. Not with the both of us here. We should just go and knock."

"They're probably still asleep."

"Nea, what's the matter with you? What are you afraid of all of a sudden?"

I'd had it with Duke. He just didn't understand anything. I hopped out of the truck and ran through the icy air, my arms wrapped around my body. The sidewalk was slick beneath my sneakers, still damp from the ditch, and I slid onto my knees on the driveway. My right hand broke the fall; a sharp jagged pain shot up to my elbow and stayed there, throbbing. I picked myself up and ran limping to the door and rang.

No one answered for a minute, and then it was *him.*

"What on earth? Nea!" Sourdi's husband was partially dressed for work, with his tie still hanging loose around his collar. He looked even older than I remembered, his thinning hair flat across his skull, his blood-shot eyes and swollen lids still heavy from sleep. He might have been handsome once, decades ago, but I saw no evidence of it now. He held the door open, and I slipped into the warmth without even removing my shoes first. "How did you get here? Did your mother come with you?"

My eyes started to water, the transition from cold to heat. Slowly the room came into focus. It was a mess. Baby toys on the carpet, shoes in a pile by the door, old newspapers scattered on an end table anchored by a bowl of peanut shells. The TV was blaring somewhere, and a baby was crying.

Sourdi emerged from the kitchen, dressed in a bright pink sweatsuit emblazoned with the head of Minnie Mouse, pink slippers over her feet, the baby on her hip. She had a bruise across her cheekbone and the purple remains of a black eye. Sourdi didn't say anything for a few seconds as she stared at me, blinking, her mouth falling open. "Where's Ma?"

"Home."

"Oh, no." Sourdi's face crumpled. "Is everything all right?"

I couldn't believe how dense my sister had become. We used to be able to communicate without words. "Everything's fine . . . *at home.* Of course." I tried to give her a look so that she'd understand that I had come to rescue her, but Sourdi stood rigidly in place in the doorway to the kitchen, her mouth twitching, puzzled.

"Please, Little Sister, sit down," her husband said. "Let me make you some tea."

Someone banged on the front door, three times. Before I could begin to feel annoyed that Duke couldn't even wait five minutes, that he just had to ruin everything, my sister's husband opened the door again. I didn't bother to turn; instead I watched Sourdi's eyes widen and her wide mouth pucker into an "O" as she gasped, "Duke!"

"What's goin' on?" Duke said.

Then everyone stared at me with such identical expressions of non-comprehension that I had to laugh. Then I couldn't stop, because I was tired and I hadn't slept and it was so cold and my nose was running and I didn't have any Kleenex.

"I said, what the hell is going on?" Duke repeated.

Sourdi's husband approached Duke. He smiled. "You must be Nea's—"

But by now, Duke had seen Sourdi's bruises. His mouth twisted into a sneer. "You bastard! I oughtta—" He punched Sourdi's husband in the nose. Sourdi screamed, her husband bent over double. Duke drew back his fist again, but Sourdi ran forward and grabbed him. She was punching him on the chest, "Out! Out! You! I'll call the police!" She tried to claw him with her nails, but Duke threw his arms up around his head.

Sourdi's husband stood up. Blood gushed from his nose all over his white shirt and tie.

"Come on!" I said stupidly. "Come on, Sourdi, let's go!" but it was pretty obvious that she didn't want to leave.

The baby began shrieking.

I started crying, too.

After everyone had calmed down, Duke went down the street to the 7-Eleven to get a bag of ice for Mr. Chhay, who kept saying, "I'm fine, don't worry," even though his nose had turned a deep scarlet and was starting to swell.

It turned out Sourdi's husband hadn't beaten her up. An economy-size box of baby wipes had fallen off the closet shelf and struck her full in the eye.

While Mr. Chhay went into the bedroom to change his clothes, I sat with Sourdi in the kitchen as she tried to get the squalling baby to eat its breakfast.

"Nea, what's wrong with you?"

"What's wrong with me? Don't you get it? I was trying to help you!"

Sourdi sighed as the baby spat a spoonful of the glop onto the table. "I'm a married woman. I'm not just some girl anymore. I have my own family. You understand that?"

"You were crying." I squinted at my sister. "I heard you."

"I'm gonna have another baby, you know. That's a big step. That's a big thing." She said this as though it explained everything.

"You sound like an old lady. You're not even nineteen, for Chrissake. You don't have to live like this. Ma is wrong. You can be anything, Sourdi."

Sourdi pinched her nose between two fingers. "Everything's gonna be fine. We just have a little argument, but it's O.K. He understands everything now. We had a good talk. I'm still gonna go to school. I haven't changed my mind. After the baby gets a little bigger. I mean, both babies. Maybe when they start preschool."

Just then her husband came back into the kitchen. He had to use the phone to call work, let them know he was going to be a little late. His face looked like a gargoyle's.

Sourdi looked at me then, so disappointed. I knew what she was thinking. She had grown up, and I had merely grown unworthy of her love.

After Duke got back with the ice, he and Sourdi's husband shook hands. Duke kept saying, "Gosh, I'm so sorry," and Mr. Chhay kept repeating, "No problem, don't worry."

Then Sourdi's husband had to go. We followed him to the driveway. My sister kissed him before he climbed into his Buick. He rolled down the window, and she leaned in and kissed him again.

I turned away. I watched Duke standing in the doorway, holding the baby in his arms, cooing at its face. In his tough wannabe clothes, the super-wide jeans and his fancy sneakers and the chain from his wallet to his belt loops, he looked surprisingly young.

Sourdi lent us some blankets and matching his-and-hers Donald and Daisy Duck sweatshirts for the trip back, since our coats were still wet and worthless.

"Don't tell Ma I was here, O.K.?" I begged Sourdi. "We'll be home by afternoon. She'll just think I'm with friends or something. She doesn't have to know, O.K.?"

Sourdi pressed her full lips together into a thin line and nodded in a way that seemed as though she were answering a different question. And I knew that I couldn't trust my sister to take my side anymore.

As we pulled away from Sourdi's house, the first icy snowflakes began to fall across the windshield.

Sourdi stood in the driveway with the baby on her hip. She waved to us as the snow swirled around her like ashes.

She had made her choice, and she hadn't chosen me.

CHAPTER 21

Super 8

We'd been driving for twenty minutes when I started to feel sick. Duke's music was pounding in my skull. The snow smeared against the windshield, making the world look dirty. I hated myself. I hated everything in the world. I was a failure. I couldn't do anything right. I wanted to kill Duke, then myself. I wanted to be a headline in a newspaper that Ma would read too late, after our bodies were discovered. Preferably, she'd have to identify me by my dental records. I clenched my teeth until my whole jaw ached.

The windshield wipers squawked and squeaked, the sound of something dying violently.

A truck passed and sent an ocean of slush across the windshield.

My heart pounded against my ribs. My bones throbbed.

Almost as soon as we found our way back onto the interstate, I told Duke we needed to pull over. My ears were buzzing. I didn't feel so good. I needed to get some sleep. The smell of the exhaust and the cold and the bumpy road. "I'm going to be sick," I said. "I need to lie down. We need to stop."

Duke pulled off at the first exit, which was marked by a tall metal water tower with the name of the town and a giant yellow smiley face painted on its side. We had just enough money between us for a room at the Super 8. The room was small and close and stuffy as a crypt. The deep purple paisley theme of the upholstery didn't help the atmosphere one bit. I pulled the drapes shut tight so we wouldn't have to see that bloated smiley face looming in the sky like a giant Hello Kitty mushroom cloud. Then without taking off my clothes, I crawled under the polyester bedspread, the spongy blanket and wilted sheet of the queen-sized bed.

Duke sat on the edge of the bed shyly. The bed bounced as he bent to untie his sneakers then sat up again to scoot back across the mattress. He lay atop the purple bedspread, arms crossed around his chest as he clicked the television remote, the channels flipping by so quickly the sound couldn't keep up.

I couldn't sleep. The TV sounded as though it were stuttering. Even with my head beneath the pillow, I could hear the heater fan whirring, water gushing in the walls as someone next door flushed the toilet, cars in the parking lot sliding on the ice. When I plugged my ears with my fingers, my heart roared in my ears like the ocean in a shell.

When I sat up, Duke didn't turn, didn't look my way, so I grabbed the remote and tossed it onto the floor. He bent his head and stared at his empty hands. But when I touched his shoulder, he rolled towards me immediately.

I peeled off the Donald Duck sweatshirt, then his Chicago Bulls T-shirt, exposing his smooth chest, pimpled with goose flesh. He tried to pull at my sweatshirt, Sourdi's sweatshirt, but I took his hands in mine and held them very tight while I kissed his throat, the trembling spot just to the left of his Adam's apple, where I could feel his heart beating beneath my tongue. I wondered if Sourdi had done this to him, too. If she had touched him here and there, if her lips had touched his cheek like this, like that. I could almost smell my sister's scent on his skin. But he didn't taste the same as Sourdi. When we were little, we'd licked melted popsicles, cake icing, satay sauce off each other's fingers. I'd recognize her taste the same as that of my own skin.

Now I pressed against Duke with my mouth closed while he struggled with my clothing. His hands ran across my stomach and my breasts; at first his skin felt cold and rough, then warmer, his palms moist. He fumbled with my jeans. His breathing had changed, he sounded like a horse, his breath wet and hot against my skin. I observed everything as though I were watching from a distance, as though this weren't me beneath him at all, but when he started pushing into me, it hurt and hurt, and I couldn't pretend that I was someone else.

"Ow," I said, pushing against his chest.

"Don't worry," he moaned. "It's okay, it's okay."

He was hard and pushing into me, as though I could be torn in two. Sex wasn't what I had imagined, not like a movie with good lighting and a refrain of romantic violins on the soundtrack. Duke's face was twisted into a grimace.

"Stop!" I grunted. "You don't have a condom!"

He pulled away, and I could breathe again. He wrapped my hand around his penis and had me pull on him until he came in a hot burst against my thigh. He collapsed then, his body a dead weight.

"Sourdi," Duke sighed, as he tried to nuzzle my cheek.

I turned away from him, pretended I was exhausted. I closed my eyes and watched my blood pulsing against the back of my eyelids. But he was the one who fell asleep.

I watched him for a while, his tousled hair standing straight up from his scalp, his face slack, the pale skin of his face almost blue, translucent.

The room was artificially dark. The curtains blocked most of the light, except for a thin band of gray where they didn't quite meet, but I could still see clearly how Duke lay with his mouth open and his arms thrown back, as if he'd been dropped onto the bed from a great height.

I shivered as I sat half-naked on top of the puffy bedspread, shiny in patches from wear. The heater was on automatic, and every time the temperature dropped to a certain level, it came whirring on with an annoying high-pitched whine. Now, however, the air was cool against my face, my arms, my goose flesh chest. My teeth chattered, but I couldn't bear to climb beneath the blankets to keep warm. I couldn't bear to lie under the covers next to Duke, his warm body, the helpless way he clutched at me in his sleep.

He sighed, a soft kitteny mew.

I got up to go to the bathroom and locked the door behind me. The fluorescent light flickered, turning my face in the mirror into a drowning girl's, her eyes ringed with shadow.

I wanted to cut myself.

I sat on the toilet. I stared at the dingy tiles on the wall, the greenish shower curtain, the dull floor. The base of the tub needed to be recaulked. The floor tiles had pulled away, revealing a dark crack the width of a finger. The fluorescent light hissed, flickered, then began to stutter. I switched it off and turned on the heat lamp instead. It hummed, ticking away on its timer, as I sat bathed in the red light. Tick tick tick tick.

I could kill myself now, I thought.

But how? Should I fill the tub with hot water then slash my wrists and jump in, waiting for my blood to leak out? But I didn't have a knife. I could hang myself. Maybe I could tie the sweatshirt around my neck, loop it around the shower rod. If I bent my knees, I could hang. I took hold of the rod in my hands to test its strength, and before I'd even put my whole weight on it, just tugged a little, the entire bar came off in my hands, clattering loudly against the tub.

Leaning my ear against the door, I listened for Duke. I tried to hold my breath, though my heart raced and I was panting. I could hear the TV, a war movie it sounded like, or maybe just some action film. Explosions and men groaning. I guessed if Duke could sleep through that, he could sleep through anything, and I relaxed a little.

Then I saw it. There was a complimentary toiletry kit on the side of the sink, by the deodorant soap. I pulled apart the cardboard box, and inside was a plastic comb, four Q-tips wrapped in cellophane, a toothbrush fit for a horse, and a Bic razor. I took the plastic guard off the razor and pressed my fingertip to the blade. I jerked back involuntarily, my body shuttering. It was sharp all right. It was perfect.

I decided to test the razor first, to find the proper pressure, the right angle. While sitting on the toilet, I extended my bare arm, then thinking better of it, decided to test my leg instead. Resting my ankle on the edge of the tub, I bore down with the razor. I had to bite my lips to keep from crying out. Sure enough, I drew blood, but the skin hadn't come off my calf evenly. Instead I had created an uneven strip of reddened skin, bleeding in patches.

My leg stung.

I thought it would probably be different across a wrist. Legs were thicker, more meaty than arms. But then I thought, what if I only managed to make a superficial wound? What if the razor was engineered to keep the blade from going too deep and all I could do was scrape up my skin? It'd just be like some corporation to think of this to keep from being sued.

My leg really, really stung.

I put the razor aside and grabbed some tissues to blot up the blood dotting my leg. Then I wet a washcloth with cold water from the tap and put it against my razor burn.

The girl in the mirror was staring at me, grimacing. She looked at me with disgust.

I turned my back to her and put my head against the door again. A war still raged on TV. Duke snored lightly. I tiptoed out into the room and found my underpants and jeans on the floor where we'd flung them. Then I found Duke's jeans. His keys were in the front pocket. I realized then I could leave. Just go. I'd take Duke's truck and drive as far and as fast as I could, out of Iowa, past Nebraska, all the way to the coast. I needed to get out of this flat cold land. I needed to find the source of the seagulls and watch the ocean pummel the earth.

On the TV, a Rambo-like action hero raised his machine gun and killed a row of people who looked just like me. Rat-a-tat-tat. Rat-a-tat. The extras didn't bother to act, they didn't writhe under the spray of bullets, they simply fell in a line, like marionettes whose strings had been cut. Rambo threw a grenade and a village went up in flames. WHOOSH. No children cried. No mothers wailed. Rambo pumped his fist in the air jubilantly as the hootches burned. A couple extras dressed in black ran through a field, their backs on fire, their faces impassive as they fell on the ground and waited for the stunt crew to come and put out the flames.

Sourdi had told me a story once about a magic serpent, the Naga, with a mouth so large, it could swallow people whole. Our ancestors carved Naga into the stones of Angkor Wat to scare away demons. Sourdi said people used to believe they could come alive in times of great evil and protect the temples. They could eat armies.

Watching Rambo in the Super 8, I wished I was a Naga. I would have swallowed the whole world in one gulp. But I didn't have any magic powers. None whatsoever.

I crouched on the floor, my back against the bed, the keys to Duke's pickup in my hand. If I ran away now, I still had nowhere to go. If I killed myself, I would be like those extras in the film, laughingstocks, throwing down their lives without a fight. There was nothing left for me to do but go home alone, without Sourdi, and face Ma.

I got dressed again, then sat on one of the paisley covered armchairs and waited for Duke to wake up.

CHAPTER 22

Giving in to the Ghost

After I got home, Ma didn't speak to me for nearly three weeks. Not a word. She sat opposite me at the breakfast table and at dinner, pretending I was not there. If she needed something, she asked my sisters or brother to pass the rice or the teapot or take the garbage out. When I passed the rice and the tea and took the trash out, she ignored me still.

At the Palace, I could tell customers thought this was strange, the way Ma would look right through me, but no one said anything outright. In Nebraska, people didn't pry into other people's business. They just stared a little more.

Finally, early one morning I walked into the kitchen and found Ma sitting at the table in her pajamas, her ashtray full as a crematorium, the air blue with smoke. She'd been up all night.

"Are you all right?" I asked, not really expecting a reply, as I filled the kettle with fresh water. "Are you coming down with something?"

"You!" Ma said. "You!"

And then she announced that I was every bad thing that a girl could be. I was disrespectful, disobedient, ungrateful, irresponsible, immoral. I ran off with a strange boy in the middle of the night. I was rude, arrogant, selfish, spoiled. I made my mother ashamed. I had no face. I was the worst kind of daughter.

She said if I ever ran away again, she would kill herself. She didn't care what happened to the rest of us anymore. She was tired, her bones ached, she was old now. She hadn't the strength to endure anymore. It was too much.

She grabbed a pair of scissors from the drawer where we kept the office supplies, the Scotch tape and twist ties and spare pens and pencils and Post-It notes, and she waved them in the air and said she was going to cut off all her hair. She was going to leave us all, her ungrateful children, and become a nun, see if she didn't. See if she didn't.

Then she put her head against her arm across the table top and cried.

I took the scissors then and cut off my own hair, right there in the kitchen, lopping off sections by the handful and tossing the strands onto the table, onto the floor at my mother's feet so that she could see.

When Sam and the twins came in that morning, they were shocked to find us fighting, Ma trying to grab the scissors out of my hands, me twisting and turning out of her reach, as I cut and cut, my long black hair writhing across the floor like so many snakeskins beneath our scuffling feet.

I had to wear a hat to school after that. I borrowed—all right—*stole* one of Sam's baseball caps. My homeroom teacher, Mr. Johannson, asked me after class if something was wrong, and I told him that I'd cut my hair off to honor the dead for Buddhist New Year. It was April after all. From then on, none of the teachers said anything to me about it, and they let me wear the hat in class.

Some of the popular girls laughed at me openly. There was a rumor that I had cancer and only had a few months to live. I know because I read about it on a stall in the girls' bathroom. Someone had written underneath, "Good!" And someone else added, "It's from eating dogs." Then another girl had written, "Jody Miller sucks Bobby Greene's cock!" and then the whole discussion went in another direction, ignoring me completely.

I thought I'd dodged the bullet then and would make it to the end of the semester without any more trouble at school—there was only one more month to go till summer vacation—when I received a note in homeroom from the school counselor, Mr. Ouellette. It said I was to go to his office in fifth period instead of Mrs. Krupp's Brit Lit class.

At least, he hadn't called Ma or written to her directly, I thought. She would have told me. Ma and I had finally reached a kind of détente. But now this threatened our truce. I was in more trouble.

I tried not to worry as I sat in the orange plastic molded chair in the guidance counselor's office, waiting for Mr. Ouellette to return from his Parenting class. All the pregnant girls in school had to take it, along with their boyfriends, but it was open to everyone else, including the couples who weren't planning on having any babies in school. Yet. Everyone thought that when they saw them walking down the halls carrying a flour baby. In Parenting, everyone was required to carry a five-pound sack of flour wrapped in a dishcloth diaper all day long for the semester. The idea was to make the kids realize what a burden a baby was. I kinda thought it was a little too late for the pregnant girls, but it was good for their boyfriends, since this might be the only Parenting they participated in. It was hard to guess who among them would be sticking around once the baby was actually born.

I would have thought the class carried a kind of stigma, a modern day Scarlet Letter, but it was supposed to be an easy A, so a lot of my classmates took it.

Me, I'd had enough of Parenting, what with the twins and Sam always having some kind of problem that Ma made me deal with. And I knew a five-pound sack of flour wouldn't have done a rat's tail bit of good with Sourdi.

The office was spare and overpacked at the same time. Mr. Ouellette's desk was piled with precarious towers of folders and handouts and random pieces of paper. There were books on psychology, career paths (I could read the title *What Color Is Your Parachute?* on one spine), drug use, and even hunting on the metal bookshelf and stacked on the floor.

I thought he might actually have forgotten about our meeting and was about to head to the library to get a start on my homework, when Mr. Ouellette came in, wiping flour off his hands onto his pant legs. Apparently somebody's baby was leaking.

He smiled to see me. "Don't look so glum. Nobody's in any trouble here."

"Mrs. Krupp said I had to come to see you?" I was missing Brit Lit for this meeting. I didn't care that much, we were still studying odes, but if my meeting ran over, I'd miss Advanced Algebra, and that would be hard to make up.

"It's not meant as a punishment . . . Nea."

Mr. Ouellette had an annoying habit of pausing dramatically before saying my name and then looking directly into my eyes without blinking. It made him seem oddly avian, like a seagull fixing on a piece of meat in the dumpster just before the dive. I imagined there was a class for counselors somewhere that taught them to behave this way. Maybe Uncle had brought home a library book with these type of instructions; they seemed vaguely familiar. How to project self-confidence. How to meet new people. Something like that. I couldn't remember anymore.

"Everything all right at home?"

"Yes."

"Good, good. You know, have you thought about college at all?"

"I'm only a sophomore."

"But that's when you should be thinking about college. Before it's too late. Your grades are good. Your teachers speak highly of you. You should think about college."

"I'm going to college," I said. "I'm not going to have a baby and get married, if that's what you think." I felt my cheeks burn, and knew I must be blushing. I wondered if he'd guessed about Duke. If there were rumors. If Ma had said anything. I felt as though I were covered in fine white particles, a permanent coating of flour. But no, that was crazy. I was just paranoid.

Unfortunately, I blushed more noticeably now that my hair was gone and I couldn't hide my face.

"I like your haircut . . . Nea," Mr. Ouellette said.

My god, I thought. *He's a mind reader!* I looked at my shoes. I wasn't going to make this easier for him.

"All you need is to keep up the good work . . . Nea. Now what about extracurricular activities?"

"I work after school."

"Every day?"

"And weekends."

"Maybe you could talk to your mother and say that you'd like some time for yourself. There are programs after school. I don't see how she could object to supervised school activities . . . Nea."

Obviously, he didn't know Ma. We girls weren't allowed to date, to stay after school, to go out alone with our friends. Sam, yes. Us girls? No. But I didn't feel this was any of Mr. Ouellette's business, my fights with Ma were our business, not his.

"You know, if you want a scholarship, you need extracurricular activities . . . Nea."

I looked up. Mr. Ouellette was leafing through sheets in a manila folder with my name on it. I didn't like that one bit.

"Mrs. Krupp says you're a good writer. Ever think of writing for the school paper?"

"No." The kids who wrote for the paper had to spend time covering sports events and band concerts and attend school plays. They gathered every Thursday night at the town newspaper's office for layout. I'd heard the spiel when they were recruiting new people at the beginning of the semester. There was no way I could take that much time off from work.

"Or what about yearbook committee? That could be a lot of fun . . . Nea. All the girls seem to enjoy it."

I knew those girls. They were popular. They weren't smart necessarily, but they had boyfriends who were good in sports and were popular. Things like that rubbed off. These girls dressed alike and did their hair in feathered waves, just so. Ways my hair would never go even when I still had hair. Other kids listened to them, were afraid of their opinions. I didn't understand it, but I could observe how they ruled in the lunchroom. It wasn't about grades, it wasn't really about looks, even. Sourdi had been more beautiful than any of them. Maybe it was merely confidence that got them where they were or some inherited position that their mothers had held in high school and that were passed down to them like family heirlooms. Or maybe it was merely their killer instincts. They got to decide whose picture appeared where and how in the yearbook. Upside down so you looked ridiculous. Embarrassing pictures with your eyes half closed, or your mouth open while you chewed your lunch in the cafeteria. They ran lists, like "Most Likely to Succeed," "Most Popular," "Biggest Dork," or "Worst Smile." They could brand you like a cow. It was a blessing that they ignored me, looked through me as though I were a ghost. Being invisible was better than being noticed sometimes.

If they'd been Cambodian, they'd definitely have joined the Communists. They would have enjoyed deciding who lived and who didn't, even if they were truly stupid and cruel and their reign lasted only four years.

"Mrs. Krupp is the yearbook advisor." Mr. Ouellette was leafing through the papers.

"I don't have time, Mr. Ouellette. I have to work." I looked at the large clock ticking on the cinderblock wall. "I have Advanced Algebra next. We have a test coming up."

"Think about yearbook . . . Nea. You could help out." He nodded in a deliberate manner that was meant to signal *confidence* but instead seemed

merely robotic. I could see his picture illustrating Uncle's old self-help
books. I wondered if Mr. Ouellette had read the same ones. There was
only one library in town after all.

I decided I had to end this play acting before I went mad. I looked
Mr. Ouellette in the eye. I spoke slowly and clearly. A confident voice that
said, *I am a success. I can win friends and influence people.* Only unlike the
practice dialogues in those books that showed you how to sell things like
cleaning products or life insurance, I spoke the truth. "Those girls don't
like me, Mr. Ouellette. We're not friends. We're not going to be friends. I
don't want to be on yearbook committee. I have real work to do. Running
a business can be my extracurricular activity."

I tried to say this with as much confidence as I could muster, but
frankly he'd spooked me. I'd wanted to go to college ever since I'd first
heard of it in Texas, when our sponsors had said the only job Ma could
get was as a maid since she didn't have a college education. I'd asked one
of my teachers what this meant in fourth grade when my English had improved, and she'd told me it was extra school, which hadn't sounded like
fun at the time. But then one night when she couldn't sleep, Ma had told
me about her plans to go to college, before the war changed everything.
She said it had been her dream. And she'd sighed then in such a heartsick
way, that I'd vowed at that moment that it would be my dream, too. I used
to want to please Ma so.

I hadn't imagined that the dream could be threatened because I
didn't have time to hang out with the popular kids after school in their
clubs. It didn't seem fair. I'd even taken a look at the college brochures
that Mr. Ouellette had put on display in the library for Career Day, glossy
sheets of pictures of tall stone buildings, students carrying books and
wearing college sweatshirts, lounging happily on manicured lawns. I tried
to make my face blank, a mask-face, like Ma's at work, so that Mr. Ouellette wouldn't see my disappointment.

"I understand how you feel . . . Nea."

Then you'd let me go to my class, I thought.

"But Mrs. Krupp—" Suddenly Mr. Ouellette stopped speaking mid-
sentence. He paused and looked behind me. I turned but there was only
the wall, covered with flyers for school events, bake sales and band try-
outs and signup sheets for counseling sessions and all the team sports
schedules.

Mr. Ouellette licked his lips. He put my folder down and ran his hand through his thinning brown hair.

"You're a smart girl, Nea. I'll level with you. Mrs. Krupp is the advisor, as I said. Some of the other girls are having trouble writing their copy. Mrs. Krupp is afraid they'll miss their deadline. In fact, there isn't much copy at all." Mr. Ouellette opened the folder and handed me some sheets of lined paper. I discovered the folder wasn't about me at all, but rather was filled with the "articles" for the yearbook. I recognized some of the looping handwriting. Only Kitty Carmichael drew actual smiley faces above all her "i's." One headline read, "Favorit Senior Activitees." Another, "Its' Been a Banner Year." All these years of translating for Ma had forced me to pay close attention to English. It was one of my best subjects now.

"We can't miss the deadline or the printer will charge more. It's not in the budget. And if we go over budget, we'll have to cancel the yearbook. Mrs. Krupp is going through a divorce, as you may have heard. If we don't have a yearbook, we don't need an advisor. You know about business. So you can see the dilemma. Mrs. Krupp said she thought the school could count on you."

I didn't really see why this was my dilemma: Mrs. Krupp losing her extra pay for advising the nonexistent yearbook's illiterate student committee. But Mr. Ouellette was right about one thing. I did know about business. "Will I get a free copy of the yearbook?"

"Of course. That could be arranged."

"How about two copies? And can I pick some of the pictures and write the captions?"

"Sure."

He answered too quickly. I knew then he was willing to compromise. "What if I write the copy at home and just bring it back and put it in Mrs. Krupp's box in the office when I'm done?"

"What a great idea, Nea!"

I almost rolled my eyes but refrained.

"And I can still list this as my extracurricular activity?" I looked Mr. Ouellette squarely in the eye.

"Of course. That's the whole point!"

That and Mrs. Krupp's job, I thought. I didn't know what Mr. Ouellette was so concerned about Mrs. Krupp for, but I could venture a guess, as gross a thought as that was. I tried not to think of my teachers' private lives.

"Tell Mrs. Krupp I'll do it." The bell rang. I had three minutes to get to Advanced Algebra. Grabbing my books, I tucked the manila folder into my binder. Then I remembered something Uncle had called "the Art of the Sell." I held out my hand and shook Mr. Ouellette's hand firmly. "Thank you, Mr. Ouellette, for this opportunity. I appreciate it. And I'll be sure to put it on my college applications."

"Glad to be of help ... Nea." He was back on his playbook, but when he shook my hand, I noticed his palms were sweaty. At least the flour absorbed most of the moisture, although it was caking a little.

As I walked out into the hall into the stream of students, I felt strangely lighthearted.

Until this point, I thought Americans born here, particularly adults, never felt uncertain of themselves, the way I felt most the time, but I had been wrong. I hadn't realized how some things might never change. How adults could still be like their younger selves, like us kids, still trying to figure out how to survive. Could the only difference be that they looked a lot older?

I wasn't sure what I could do with this insight, so for the time being I tucked it into a corner of my brain. It might be useful some day.

In the meantime, I began composing new headlines for the yearbook. Most Dramatic Laugh. Most Flamboyant Hair. Best-Dressed Flour Baby. Cheesiest Cheer. And I started making a mental list of all the kids I knew and liked, the ones who sat alone in the lunchroom, the ones who got written about on the bathroom walls, the Indians who spent one semester at our school and one semester on the reservation, the kids who'd never called me or Sourdi any names, all of whom I'd find some way to include.

Kitty Carmichael and her nasty, illiterate friends wouldn't know what hit them. Or their yearbook.

I might be a ghost to them, but ghosts were powerful. They hadn't learned that yet, but I knew.

CHAPTER 23

Duke

I saw Duke again one last time, in the summer.

He drove by the house one afternoon while everyone else was at work. Ma was forcing me to stay home on days when the Senior Express bus from Sioux Falls, South Dakota, stopped at the Palace on its way to the dog track in Iowa. She didn't want the seniors to think "a punk person" worked at the Palace now that my hair had grown out, unevenly, to a very awkward length. So Sam and the twins had to take over while I stayed at home and cleaned the house until my hair started to grow out a little more.

I hadn't seen Duke since Iowa.

Duke sat in the driveway for a long time. I recognized the sound of his truck idling, the angry garble of the souped-up engine. I peeped at him from behind the drapes. He was sitting in the cab, nodding to himself, as though he were rehearsing something, and the sudden thought came to me that he was going to propose. He'd finally realized there was no chance of his ever getting back together with Sourdi, and he was choosing me as consolation.

I took my baseball cap off and wiped my hand across my sweaty forehead, then set the hat back over my patchy hair. I watched from behind the curtains when at last Duke worked up his nerve, killed the engine and walked up the driveway, in his bowlegged way, the chain running from his wallet to his belt loop swinging with each step. It was a warm day for June, with just a slight breeze, but he was wearing his long, baggy jeans, his Public Enemy T-shirt, an orange ski cap pulled low over his forehead.

As he approached the door, I stepped away from the window quickly and leaned against the wall, holding my breath.

Finally, he knocked, very lightly. It was almost as though he hoped I wouldn't hear him.

I counted to five, then opened the door. He was facing the wrong way, as though he were leaving already.

"Duke!"

"Nea," he said softly, as though he were surprised to find me there. He looked at the ground.

I opened the door wider so that he could come inside.

"You want me take off my shoes?" he asked as he stepped into the hall. "I can, you know. It's no problem."

"Don't worry about it," I said. "Just come in."

He nodded, then licked his lips, starting over. "I wanted to talk to you about somethin' important. About the future. About some plans I have, is all."

Hearing him speak, I remembered how he'd been with Sourdi, which seemed so long ago now. The slow, awkward way sentences drifted in and out of his conversations. Maybe this was one of the reasons he and Sourdi had gotten along so well. For my sister, English was forever a net she had to weave anew in each conversation, something that trapped her real meaning, and sometimes something she could hide in, too. For Duke, expressing himself in general was a burden, English or otherwise.

"Want a Coke?" I asked, walking to the kitchen without waiting for an answer. Duke followed. I handed him a can from the fridge. He took it but didn't open it. Instead he turned the can around and around in his hands, as though he'd never seen a Coca-Cola before, as though he were newly arrived in a strange and foreign land, where even common, everyday things mystified him.

Finally, he began to speak. But he didn't ask me to marry him. Instead he said he'd come to let me know that he'd enlisted. He said he'd wanted to be the first to tell, he didn't want me to have to hear about it later after he'd gone. He wanted to say goodbye in person.

At first I didn't understand what he was talking about. The Army, basic training, moving away. And then it became very clear.

"Omigod, Duke! Are you crazy? You can't be a soldier! Not you! How could you? Don't you see? Don't you know anything?" I thought my heart was going to explode from my ribcage, trailing blood like a wounded pheasant in hunting season. It wasn't possible, not Duke.

I held my breath until I could speak again. And then everything tumbled out at once. I told him all the things that neither Sourdi nor I had ever mentioned to him, all the secrets we had kept, all the nightmares. I told him about the bombings of villages and burning of jungles, the destruction of cities, the shooting and the killing, the mines and the air raids, and how it didn't matter if you were a soldier or a civilian, a child or an adult, wars were all the same. I explained to him all the ways he was wrong for this line of work, and how he'd gotten himself tricked, he'd seen too many movies, it wasn't going to be like that. He didn't know, I said, but I did.

When I'd finished, I was sweating all over my body. I wanted to take my hat off and wipe my sweaty head, but I didn't want Duke to see my ugly, fuzzy skull, so I just stood there miserably, sweating from every pore.

Duke didn't say anything for a while. He didn't argue back, he only nodded to himself, chewing his lips.

"It won't be like your war," he said finally. "Those times are over. I'm not going to do any of those bad things. I'm just going to serve my country and then get me a real job. I'll get some training, and the Army can pay me to go to trade school. I can't just keep foolin' around. I'm not a kid anymore. It's time I did something with my life."

Duke bent over quickly and kissed me on the cheek, and then he was running out of the house, out the front door and down the driveway to his idling pickup.

As he drove away, he didn't turn around again to see me wave goodbye, my cheeks flushed, all the heat of my heart rising to my face, to the very top of my punky-haired head.

CHAPTER 24

Our Town

I wished I knew how to be a better older sister, a role model, a confidante. But I wasn't Sourdi. Just me. By the time I was seventeen and a senior, I felt my failure to be more than just me most acutely. Perhaps everyone feels this way, but if so, my classmates kept it to themselves. I was not responsible like Sourdi. I was moody, I ignored my siblings for weeks on end, I buried myself in books whose titles and plots I can barely recall today.

Sometimes when I watched my younger siblings, they seemed like strangers to me, and maybe I seemed that way to them, too.

At least the twins had each other; they could giggle together about boys and new clothes and complain about working in the Palace. They could fight with each other, too. Ferociously. More than once a week, I'd have to pull them apart before they inflicted real damage upon one another. It was hard to keep track of their squabbles, who borrowed which item of clothing without asking first, who gossiped to which friend about the other most. Normal junior high stuff. Perhaps that's what separated us the most. The fact that despite everything that had happened to our family, their lives were indeed incredibly *normal*.

It was harder for Sam.

About all that people had to break the monotony of winter in our town was drinking or watching high school wrestling. Sometimes both.

Wrestling was the one sport where our town could excel, where we could be proud, where our small-town ways didn't work against us. Boys in our town could never beat the quarterbacks from bigger schools with money and good coaches and a high-profile league; they'd never be able to compete against the black boys and Indians in basketball; they'd never heard of soccer; but wrestling was a sport where a farmer's son could hone himself down to the anger in his bones, and, one-on-one, take on the world that had forgotten places like our town even existed.

I wouldn't have cared much myself, I wasn't a sports fan in particular, but Sam was on the team, in the 103-pound category. I don't think they would have let him join, frankly, despite his record in middle school, but they were short of skinny players. In eighth grade, the Johnson twins, Tim and Jim, had been unstoppable in lightweight, but they'd both experienced growth spurts over the summer and started high school three inches taller and twenty pounds heavier. It was a disaster for the team. Or nearly was. Sam hadn't grown at all, which had made him moody and hard to be around, but Coach Passick saw the potential in this, and put him on the team his freshman year.

By the time, he was fifteen and a sophomore, he was already a varsity player, well on his way to lettering.

Ma wasn't that fond of sports either. I don't think she ever really understood the concept of wrestling; certainly she never figured out the point system or the terminology, the difference between a low single-leg takedown and a high-crotch one, the differences in break-downs whether spiral rides or tight-waist chops, or for that matter simple turks, power-half combinations, full- and half-nelsons. But she'd come to all the home meets, taking time off from work, and she'd cheer Sam on, clapping wildly, jumping to her feet, even shouting a little like the other parents— although she never quite mastered the ecstatic "whooo-eee!" that echoed from the stands when Sam pinned his opponent.

She wanted to be supportive, but she didn't understand that her presence made Sam nervous. Wrestling for Sam was about fitting in, and he couldn't do that if Ma was clapping at the wrong moments, smiling and occasionally cheering even when the other team scored points. The other teams never let Sam forget she was there. "That your Mama-san?" they'd call to him, as they lined up to shake hands before the meets. They pulled the skin back around their eyes to make them more slanted and bucked their teeth out. If they caught him alone in the parking lot, there were fights.

At least on away games, Sam could pretend he was an Indian. Not that the boys liked Indians any better, but when they called Sam a slur for Native Americans or made the fake whoo-aah-whoo-aah war cry by patting their hands over their howling mouths, it didn't hurt him as much. After all, it was a mistake. He wasn't a Native.

I understood these things, but Ma did not.

It was a shock to most people in our town when the high school principal announced that he was going to suspend the team, late in the season, just when it looked like they were headed to State, first time in five years. Turns out someone had hacked into the school computer system and changed the final grades for five of the team's star players.

I remember when the principal called the first time and wanted Ma to come to his office.

It had been an unusually busy Saturday. There was the crush of customers for the lunch buffet starting around eleven—on the weekends it was all-you-can-eat—but then just as things started to wind down around one-forty-five (word had got around that we stopped refilling the bins at one-thirty,) the Senior Express stopped by for lunch. I guess they'd added another run to their usual schedule.

I was the one who answered the phone. Ma was cooking, and my younger sisters were waiting tables. At first when I recognized Mr. Peaseman's voice, I thought he was ordering take-out, which surprised me because he'd never ordered anything from the Palace before. His wife had told Mrs. Johnson at the bank that she didn't like Chinese food. She said all the soy sauce gave her gas, and Mrs. Johnson, who could never resist passing along a bit of gossip when she went on her Mary Kay rounds, had told Ma.

But Mr. Peaseman wasn't calling for an order of General Tso's chicken. Instead he said in his official, principal voice, "I need to speak to the mother of Sam Chhim, please," formal like that. "It's urgent," he added. I got Ma out of the kitchen, and she wiped her hands on her apron, then patted her hair down—it grew unruly in the heat and steam—as though he could see her, as though she knew it would be important to make a good impression.

"Yes, this is me," she said, and then quickly her face changed, grew tight, as though invisible weights were pulling at her skin. Her voice grew louder, too, as she responded to him. "Mmm," she said, and "Mmm-hmm," and "I see," over and over. After a few minutes, it sounded as though she were talking to a deaf man, so loudly was she grunting into the receiver.

I was straining to hear what Mr. Peaseman was saying, but I could only make out the tinny contours of his voice, no individual words, except once, when I thought I heard him say Sam's name and Ma gasped.

The seniors were lining up to pay their checks, and I was supposed to be ringing them up, which was hard to do and eavesdrop at the same time; I kept making mistakes.

I was about to miscount a blue-haired harpy's change again, when Ma hung up the phone and said to me, "Come on. You go with me. Now."

Then she grabbed her coat off the rack by the front door and took off for the car. I waved at Maly to take my place then ran to catch up with Ma. Ma's English was pretty good by this point since she'd been forced to speak it at work every day of the week for years by now. Although kids at school claimed she had an accent, I couldn't hear it anymore; she just sounded the way she always did to me. Still, she always had me translate for her when matters were serious. Or when she wanted to pretend she couldn't understand something.

By the time we got to school, another set of parents had arrived before us, Brock Guterman's, so we had to wait outside Mr. Peaseman's office. I could hear Mr. Guterman shouting through Mr. Peaseman's door, something about "not while I have a breath left in my body," and "What do you think you're doing to the team?"

With each exclamation, Ma grew more nervous. She squeezed my hand, cutting off my circulation completely.

Finally Mr. Guterman came rushing out, his face flushed and sweaty. He was still wearing his down coat. He seemed startled to see Ma and me sitting there, and suddenly he stopped in his tracks, skidding a little on the slick floor. "They called you, too. Well, just remember, it's time to stick together. It's time for some solidarity." Then Mr. Guterman hurried off down the hall.

Mrs. Guterman, her eyes rimmed in red, pressing a tissue to her nose, stumbled out of the principal's office next. She teetered after her husband in her Sunday heels without stopping to speak to us.

Although Mr. Peaseman was waiting in his office, Ma hesitated for only a second then ran off after the Gutermans. They were headed for the gym. We followed them inside the double doors.

Coach Passick was nowhere to be seen, nor any of the wrestlers for that matter, though the wrestling mats were still out, and someone's headgear lay at the foot of the bleachers. The Gutermans went straight into the boys' locker room, and after another moment's hesitation, Ma and I followed them.

I'd never been in the boys' locker room before, but I was disappointed that everything looked almost the same as the girls' locker room, row after row of gray metal cages secured with padlocks, the wooden bins to deposit gym equipment and used towels in, the greenish lighting, the smell like old sneakers.

We found Sam sitting in the very back, still dressed in his singlet, along with the rest of the team, all sitting on the wooden changing benches. Coach Passick had his back to Ma and me, but Sam saw us as we came in. He looked shocked, his dark eyes widening, his bushy eyebrows leaping upwards, then embarrassed, and he quickly looked away.

Mr. Guterman was talking to the coach. "What's going on here? What the hell is Peaseman talking about? Canceling the season!"

"That's just what I was discussing with the team. Nothing's been fixed in stone yet—"

"We won't be railroaded! I won't let that happen!"

"As I was just telling my boys, innocent until proven guilty. No one can take that away—"

While Mr. Guterman was arguing with the coach, Ma sidled up to Sam. He was still studiously ignoring her, as though he couldn't take his eyes off his sneakers, they were that fascinating. Finally, one of the other boys, one of the Johnson twins, Tim or maybe it was Jim, had to tap Sam on the shoulder. "Hey, dude, your mom's here."

Sam looked up all surprised, like he'd just noticed.

"Sam," Ma said. Although Ma was standing next to him, and he was seated, their heads were practically level. Ma was tiny. "Sam," she repeated.

Sam looked up at Coach Passick, pleadingly, and I knew what he was thinking. He was thinking Ma was going to start talking in Khmer, in front of everyone. But then Coach Passick caught his eye, nodded. "Sam, you're excused for five minutes. You can go outside, see what your mother wants."

Sam nodded thankfully.

As all three of us walked away, I glanced back. Clint Miller, Brock Guterman, and the Johnsons were still watching Mr. Guterman and

Coach, but the other boys were watching us. I tried to read the expression in all those sets of unblinking eyes. Not exactly fear, not exactly contempt, but something in between. Something that could be swayed in either direction. I turned around quickly and hurried after Ma and Sam.

Ma gestured for Sam to follow her over to the bleachers, where she sat down, her hands folded in her lap. "Is it true? Is it true what the principal told me on the phone?" She looked him directly in the eyes, her face a mask, the face she wore to deal with unruly customers, with the health inspector, with the loan officer at the bank.

"I don't know what's going on, Mom." Sam had started calling Ma "Mom" now that he was in high school. It was another of the affectations he'd adopted this year, like the spiky haircut and gel in his bangs, the leather jacket that he'd saved up for all summer and bought at Wilson's from the mall in Sioux City. "I don't know anything."

"Don't you lie to me. I can tell." Ma narrowed her eyes.

"It's—"

"You lie to me, I'll take you to the police myself! I'll tell them lock you up, I don't know you, I don't have a son."

Sam looked stunned. His mouth fell open, and he took a step back, as though he'd been shoved. For a minute, I thought he was going to turn on his heel and run.

"We don't even have a computer at home. How could I hack into the school's system?"

Ma pressed her lips together tight. "The principal says they traced the day and time. They already know the house. But the family was away and someone breaks into their house, throws a big party for the team."

Sam shrugged. "I wasn't there."

"Don't lie to me. This is *your* team!"

"It was a Saturday," Sam said. "The ninth. We wrestled Creighton. I lost, but Clint and Brock and Tim and all the middleweights won."

"How come you didn't go to this party?"

"It was at night, and I had to work."

"I don't make you work. You don't have to work if someone has a party for your team. You can go with your friends."

"Mom! Are you kidding? You don't *make* us work at the Palace? Like, I just *want* to do that? I can go work at Hardees or Pamida if I want, or go to a party, is that what you're saying?" Sam's face twitched.

"But you were not there, at this party," Ma said, getting back to the subject. "Sam was not there," she repeated. "The ninth, Saturday night, you were working. In the restaurant."

"Don't you remember? Mom!" Sam's voice rose in anger. "There was that fire even."

I remembered the grease fire. It had filled the Palace with thick, black smoke, and we'd had to evacuate. While we were trying to clear the smoke out, opening the doors and windows, propping fans on folding chairs, several customers took the opportunity to go back to their cars and leave without paying. We'd all been worried the fire department would be called and, after our last disaster, we didn't want to seem fire-prone.

Sam had run to the Super 8 next door to borrow their fire extinguisher. The red one we'd kept on the wall all these years had inexplicably failed to operate when I'd pulled the pin. It had emitted a thin stream of foam along with a honk like a fart, and then nothing more.

I remembered all right. San had lost his match that afternoon, and he'd been depressed when he came to work that evening, refusing to talk to me or the twins, snarling at everyone, and then after the fire, he'd said, "This whole day's been nothing but shit," and Ma had heard him, and chewed him out for swearing in front of the customers.

Ma was smiling now so that all her teeth showed; she didn't bother to hide her smile behind her hand as usual.

"I can't believe you'd think I'd do something illegal like that," Sam said, pulling at the straps of his singlet. I noticed he had a rash on one tan shoulder.

"No," Ma said. "I was afraid because everyone else can say you did it. They can blame you. But we have an *alibi*." Ma pronounced the word carefully, and I wondered where she'd picked it up, maybe from some cop show. "A perfect alibi."

Then she hugged Sam to her, as though he were a little boy again, and Sam, surprising me, put his head against Ma's shoulder, closing his eyes, and hugged her back.

"Everything's gonna be all right now," Ma said. "Everything's A-okay."

Because of parents like Mr. Guterman, the team wasn't suspended after all. We heard the details from customers.

"Peaseman was trying to act without due process," the mailman said.

"Besides, there was no evidence our team was even at this so-called party," his wife pointed out. "Probably just some joker messing with the grades."

I filled her water glass without comment.

"Our wrestlers," said the mailman, "our boys wouldn't do a thing like that."

Ma didn't say anything when our customers talked like this; she merely nodded, her face blank, as though any sign of emotion—relief, fear, dread—might bring bad luck, might change everything.

By the beginning of February, everything looked like it would return to normal in our town. Because of the parental outcry, the season hadn't been suspended after all. The team didn't make State, but that was hardly surprising, people said, after all the stress they'd been through. It was a shame for the seniors, but next year, next year would be different.

The snow around the Palace turned color; it no longer seemed to be made of fresh milk but rather frozen exhaust. Ma smoked more than usual, and the air inside the Palace came to resemble the ashy snow banks. She also began to treat Sam differently, thanking him when he came to work and telling him frequently how happy she was to have him here, what a good job he was doing, how lucky she was to have a son to work with her. Ma didn't extend the same pleasantries to my sisters and me. She didn't thank us for showing up, but then again, we were girls. We were expected to work.

For my part, I had a knot in my stomach that wouldn't go away.

My little brother at fifteen spoke perfect American English, out of the corner of his mouth, like all the other boys in our town, like he'd been here his whole life. He moved like an athlete, with a wiry confidence, ready to fight. Sometimes he seemed like any other high school kid to me, when he wore the tough, blank look he'd been cultivating all year and seemed to sneer instead of smile, and sometimes he seemed like the little brother I remembered. The one who used to cry during thunderstorms in Texas when he had to hop in bed with Sourdi and me or he couldn't sleep.

I myself didn't ask Sam what he knew about the party and the changed grades, all for Spanish class. None of the teachers suspected

Sam. He was good in Spanish, straight As. Going to Head Start with Mexican kids in Texas had its advantages, and Sam spoke Spanish with a better accent than the teacher. He had no need to change his grade, and everyone knew the older boys on the team weren't friendly to him. He was above their suspicion.

But Ma's fear was contagious. No point inviting bad luck in through the front door, I figured, as she was prone to say. So I kept my mouth shut around Sam.

Then Mr. Peaseman announced that there was going to be an official school inquiry into the Incident, as it was now called. That meant he began to interview each of the wrestlers individually in his office, trying to get them to rat, to say who'd done what. People marveled, shaking their heads. The season was already ruined, what was the point? Who would have guessed Peaseman could be so stubborn? He didn't look like that kind of man, like somebody who hadn't grown up in our town, like somebody who didn't know to leave well enough alone. He looked ordinary.

Sam and I didn't mention any of this to Ma: the ongoing investigation, the grumblings of the other parents. I convinced myself we were doing it for her own good. No use worrying over nothing.

And the team stuck to its guns. No one knew anything about the alleged Incident. No one had heard a thing, not even a rumor. No one had anything to add.

Then just when it looked as though he'd have to give up, Mr. Peaseman showed up at the Palace with his wife and daughter in tow.

The Peasemans had never come to our restaurant before, and I was surprised to see them. It was well-known, Mrs. Peaseman's aversion to Chinese food. Yet they arrived in Sunday clothes one Friday evening and ordered three plates of the House Special. When Ma had taken their order, she felt it would be impolite to explain to them that they were supposed to order different dishes and then share them. Mr. Peaseman was the principal, after all, and Ma had been brought up to respect authority.

I was working in the kitchen that night, with Sam, as we were short handed. The flu had been raging through town, and we'd lost half the kitchen staff. I peered through the crack in the kitchen door.

"What are they doing?" Sam wanted to know.

"Just eating, I guess."

"That's weird," Sam said.

"I know." I told Sam to stay in the kitchen until Mr. Peaseman left, no matter what, and for once, Sam listened to me.

Then Mr. Peaseman showed up again. This time without his wife and daughter. For Saturday's all-you-can-eat brunch. Then again, on Sunday.

Mr. Peaseman ended up coming to the Palace to eat about three times a week throughout the rest of February.

Even Ma knew something funny was going on. She tried subtle Old World tricks to chase him away—oversalting his food, charring the vegetables, and undercooking the meat, which she served to him personally so that there would be no mistaking her intentions—but nothing worked. In fact, Mr. Peaseman seemed genuinely touched by her ministrations. "I admire your work ethic, Ma'am," I overheard him say to Ma. "The family values, the devotion I see here, it's a welcome addition to our community." He spoke slowly and loudly so that Ma wouldn't misunderstand.

She understood all right. She told Sam to stay in the kitchen. She put him on prep duty, even had him scrubbing the woks, just to keep him out of sight.

The next time Ma was called to Mr. Peaseman's office, he wanted Sam to come along as well. Mr. Peaseman was pleased to see us and smiled warmly as he told us to take a seat. It was a Saturday again, but he was wearing his usual school clothes, his Penney's suit and the safe, red-and-blue striped tie. He tried not to act too formal and sat on the corner of his paper-laden desk, folding his hands on top of his knees. And then he proceeded to tell us the story of his life.

Mr. Peaseman said that he understood what it was like to grow up without a father, Sam, because he himself had lost his dad in the Korean War when he was just a kid. He'd had a rough time. His mother had had to go out and get a job for the first time in her life at a time when women, especially mothers, weren't supposed to do that. Boys at school used to taunt him. Then he'd run home and hide. If he didn't run fast enough, they'd catch him and beat him up. Finally, one day his mother had had enough. She told him if he didn't start hitting those boys back, they were just going to continue picking on him for the rest of his life. So the next time the boys came after him, he fought back, and got hurt worse than ever before. A group of five boys attacked him, and he ended up with broken ribs and a broken arm. But the next time, he fought smarter. He learned to pick his fights, so that the odds were better, so that it wasn't always five against one.

Mr. Peaseman took his handkerchief from his pants pocket and wiped his flushed face, his moist neck, his damp palms. His glasses had fogged up from the exertion of recounting his memories, and even the top of his balding head was sweaty and pink.

"I understand what it's like to be different," Mr. Peaseman said. "I just want you to know that."

I don't know how much Ma had understood of Mr. Peaseman's story, but she stared straight ahead now, a fake smile frozen on her face, and nodded, up and down, up and down. "Thank you," she said. "Thank you."

But Sam had understood all right. During Mr. Peaseman's speech, Sam had sat staring at his feet. I could tell he was deeply embarrassed to have Mr. Peaseman confide in him. But now when Sam looked up, I could tell he was angry, too.

Sam was smaller than the other boys his age, it was true, but he was fast. He could anticipate a punch and dodge it, then strike before these lumbering farm boys could pull back for another hit. He was quick, he was strong, and when he was angry, he was ruthless. The coach had understood this, and that's why Sam was on the team when other boys, whose fathers and older brothers had wrestled before them, were not. Mr. Peaseman may have thought Sam was the weakest link, the one who would talk, breaking the team's wall of silence, thus breaking the team, but Sam hadn't fought this hard to fit in to give that up now.

"I'm not worried," Sam told the principal, and he pulled back his lips as if to smile, as if to say everything was okay, but I recognized the look. Sam was baring his teeth.

It was the second week of March when Mr. Peaseman called Sam into his office again. He talked to Sam almost casually about doing the right thing, standing up to bullies, as though he were talking to an old friend instead of a student. He talked about the all-American values of honesty and fair play, hard work and studying, as Sam would tell me later.

"It's not fair," Mr. Peaseman said, shaking his pink head, and Sam could tell that Mr. Peaseman might just as well have been talking about himself as a boy, thinking about his own hard, unfair life, his dead father, his overworked mother, his broken ribs. "We've got to do the right thing," Mr. Peaseman said, and he looked at Sam with his pale gray eyes, full of trust, as though he knew that Sam would agree.

Then Sam told Mr. Peaseman again that he didn't know anything about what had happened at the party or the grade changing scheme. He said he didn't have anything to say about it nor would he in the future. Then he turned on his heel and left Mr. Peaseman's office without waiting to be dismissed.

That night after work, Sam told me all about his encounter with Mr. Peaseman. It was late, past midnight, when we got done talking. We were headed to bed when we discovered that Ma had fallen asleep in the family room in front of the television. She was stretched out on the couch, slumped against the cushions, her mouth open, snoring slightly, while QVC played in the background.

"Ma looks old, doesn't she?" Sam said.

"I don't know. She looks like she always does," I said loyally.

"No, she's gotten old," he insisted. He scowled. "Someday I'm going to take care of her. She shouldn't have to work like this. She can stay at home, all day. She won't have to do anything."

"Ma likes to work," I pointed out. "She likes to be in charge." It was true.

But Sam shook his head. "When I graduate, I'm gonna get a real job, and she won't have to do anything," he repeated. "I've been acting like a kid. Like a baby."

Then he punched the air, jabbing right, left, right, kicking too, felling an invisible opponent. He grunted a little, panting.

"Hey, you *are* a kid," I said, trying to lighten his mood. "You're just a squirt."

Sam didn't smile or even get angry. He merely shook his head and looked at Ma sadly.

Back in Texas, what seemed like lifetimes ago, Sourdi used to tell us stories about what Ma was like before the war, how pretty she'd been, a woman who liked to sing love songs along with the radio, a woman who'd turned men's heads. But neither Sam nor I nor our younger sisters remembered that mother, only this mother with missing teeth, who spoke broken English and who smelled like smoke, not perfume.

It's hard to say if Mr. Peaseman would have come back to the Palace again, or if he would have finally given up on his own. As things turned out, we'll never know.

At the end of March, just as the spring winds had returned, finally melting the snow so that the fields turned to lakes and the roads to mud, and we all grumbled about how much prettier the snow had been when in fact all winter long we'd complained about how sick we were of looking at nothing but white fields, Mr. Peaseman announced his resignation. Rumors among our customers were that if he hadn't resigned, the school board would have fired him. Rumor in school was that he was leaving to go back to being a history teacher in Minnesota, although someone said her mother had overhead at the beauty parlor that Mr. Peaseman was moving to Omaha to sell cars at his father-in-law's Ford dealership.

The Methodist Church held a good-bye party/potluck for the Peasemans. Ma insisted we go, since "he was such a good customer." It was after Sunday service, and the Pastor in his sermon had quoted from the Book of Job and gone on and on about the trials of a good man as a test of his faith to God. I'd never fully understood the Book of Job, back when we went to church with our sponsors in Texas. Suffering was never rewarded in my experience, it simply happened. You endured or you didn't. That was all.

After the service, Sam and I didn't follow Ma and the twins down into the church basement for the reception, where the Ladies Auxiliary were serving sandwiches and Jell-O salads—and the tray of spring rolls Ma brought from the Palace. It was too hot in the church, the air close and stale. Everyone had been sweating, packed together for hours. The air smelled like the boys' locker room.

Instead we slipped out a side door and went walking down the alley beside the church. I'd lifted Ma's pack of cigarettes from her purse and offered one to Sam. He shook his head, but I lit one for myself.

We walked for some time. We had to watch our step to avoid stumbling into the pools of water that had collected in the ruts of the road. The gray sky, heavy with clouds, with spring storms, was reflected in the puddles, as though the alley had been littered with broken shards of mirror. When the wind blew, the water rippled and the sky dissolved. It was a kind of beauty, I guess.

When we reached the end of the alley, we turned east onto First

Street, walking faster, our heads down against the wind, not speaking until we had reached the limits of our town—as I've said before, it was a *small* town—and we looked out at the fields that surrounded us on the prairie, now filled with muddy water, giant lakes that reflected the entire sky from one end of the horizon all the way to Iowa.

Finally, Sam began to speak.

He told me about the party, the one he said he'd never attended. It had all happened very quickly, that afternoon after the meet, before work. It was just supposed to be a joke at first. Someone had gotten the idea to break into the Obermeyers' house while they were away. They had a stash of beer in the fridge, and some of the seniors managed to bring a keg. Sam didn't get invited to many parties. He thought it would be fun. Then some of the seniors took him upstairs to the master bedroom, said they wanted to show him something. It was the Obermeyers' pet dog, a schnauzer-dachsund mix. Pathetic. They had it tied up in a bag, and they wanted Sam to kill it and cook it "gook-style" so no one would know and then serve it to everyone. It would be funny, they said. It would be his way of showing the team he was one of them.

That's when Sam said he'd show them something ever better. He'd seen the computer in the corner. Then he showed them all the porn sites that he'd managed to find on the computer in the school library, right under the librarian's nose. He said he knew how to hack past her security codes, the ones that were supposed to keep such sites off school PC's.

One of the boys suggested if he knew so much about computers, if he was so effin' smart and proud of himself, he should hack into the school's computer and check on their grades. Wouldn't be good for the team if the best players got kicked off just because they couldn't speak some foreign language. This was America, after all.

Which side was Sam on? America's or not?

They'd all known about it, the whole team, everything: the break-in, the underage drinking, the hacking of the school's computer system, every single one of them knew, and they'd all kept quiet. That's what it meant to belong to a team of winners. Nobody could break that kind of team spirit. Sam said this last bit with pride.

I tossed Ma's cigarette into one of the puddles in the ditch. It floated on the surface of the water, which glistened with oil. Old herbicide in the runoff, I figured. Roundup or Guardian. The fields around our town were filled with poisons.

I stared at the water so that I wouldn't have to look at my brother.

"I didn't think anyone would notice. Not for a while anyway. Not till way after the season. I didn't think anyone would get so upset. Or Mr. Peaseman would lose his job," he said and for a moment, Sam looked younger than his fifteen-year-old self; he looked like my round-faced little brother, the one who used to douse us with the hose when we came back from school to our trailer in Texas, the one who had the bottomless stomach, the one who once put tacks in all four of One Arm's tires. I'd forgotten all about that, how angry One Arm had become, and how we'd laughed, all five of us kids, while hiding behind the sheets on a neighbor's clothes line.

The wind grew colder even as the sun burned a hole through the clouds just above the horizon and its flames were reflected in the watery fields, the whole world turning red as an open wound.

"Are you sure no one else on the team told on you? Do you think Mr. Peaseman suspected you all along? I didn't think he was being sneaky. I think he actually liked you, but maybe he really knew and just needed proof or a confession to exonerate you, to say it wasn't your fault. Maybe those seniors set you up," I said. The enormity of the betrayal was just beginning to dawn on me. I forced myself to look directly into Sam's wide, black eyes.

"No. Of course not. No one said anything. Peaseman had no idea." Sam glared at me. I'd insulted him to his core. "They wouldn't tell on me. Everyone on the team *likes* me." And then suddenly, he knelt down onto the muddy ground and hid his face into the arm of his leather jacket. He was crying, his shoulders shaking, a strange strangled sound emerging from his throat. I immediately knelt down beside him, wrapping my arms around him, and to my surprise he threw his arms around my neck, put his wet, hot, tear-streaked face against my left shoulder and wept as though he would never stop.

"It's okay, it's okay, Sam. I believe you. Don't worry, it's okay."

"No, it's not okay!" he shouted suddenly and pushed me away. He wiped his eyes on his fists and his nose on the sleeve of his prized leather jacket. Then he tore off his jacket and bunched it up and threw it into the

ditch full of filthy water. "I'm so stupid!" he shouted. "I'm stupid! Stupid!"
And in his good dress shirt, the cotton one that buttoned up to the collar,
pale blue with thin white stripes, he boxed at the air, battling an invisible foe, maybe his own self, until he popped some of the buttons off and
they rolled away into the weeds. I couldn't find any of them although I
searched on my hands and knees.

At last he was calm. His face was red and sweaty but he was no longer crying. He watched me dig around in the weeds. "Forget it," he said.
"We should go back now. Mom will notice we're gone." When I looked
up at him again, I saw that the tough mask had fallen back over his eyes.
I climbed out of the ditch and scraped the mud on my shoes onto the
sidewalk.

"If we say anything, Mom's going to feel bad. She'll feel responsible,"
Sam said, his voice suddenly calculating, sly even, and I realized that my
brother could become someone I didn't recognize. "You know how she
is."

"She's so proud of you," I said. I turned away from him then, looking
out at the wide, vast fields. "It would break her heart."

We didn't say anything more to each other, Sam and I, but walked
back in silence to the church, the wind blowing colder than I'd imagined
possible this late in the season.

CHAPTER 25

Ang Kor Wat of Des Moines

The summer after I graduated from high school, before I left our small town and moved to the city and began my own life apart from my family, Ma rose early one Saturday morning and disappeared with my brother. That evening, she returned alone.

She then announced to my sisters and me that she had taken Sam to Des Moines to become a monk.

"A monk!" my younger sisters giggled. "What's a monk?"

Ma then explained to them that their brother was going to spend the summer in the temple, making merit for their father's soul, who had died, after all, without any prayers recited over his bones. What if his soul were still wandering, still trapped by an unlucky death in the realm between the living and the dead? What then? she asked. What if a secret sin from a past life were keeping him from being reborn? What if all these years he had been suffering, forgotten by his living family, lost in the cycle of death and rebirth, unable to find the peace he deserved?

After Ma finished talking like this, my sisters were crying. Their father, our father, whom they barely remembered, wandering like a ghost on the earth, like a Halloween tale they'd been told in school. They'd never imagined such a thing, and it frightened them now.

I could tell their fear pleased Ma. They were in junior high now, that dangerous giddy age for girls in Ma's eyes, the age where they might stray and fall and never get up again. Maly and Navy went by the names Marie and Jennifer now. They permed their hair and bared their bellies in the summer, walked in short shorts with their girlfriends, giggled on the phone late at night. She didn't want them following in Sourdi's footsteps, or mine for that matter, certainly not my tainted, disobedient, American steps. My sisters were growing up but they were still young enough to believe in her ghost stories. Ma was not going to miss this opportunity, she was not going to be caught by surprise as she'd been with Sourdi and me, when we'd started to grow up without giving notice first.

She waved her cigarette in the air now for emphasis. "I only hope three months in the temple is enough. Your poor father," she shook her head, "your poor father."

I didn't say anything, but I had to hand it to Ma. She always knew more than she ever let on.

The Ang Kor Wat temple in Des Moines was not like the temples in books, not like a grand palace with eaves arching towards the sky, with spires on the yellow-tiled roof, with silver and gold on the facade, not like the ancient temples with stone faces peering from the jungle, dancing girls and magic snakes writhing across the lintels, armies carved into the walls. Nor was it like the temples at home that had been forgotten too long, turned into granaries during the war, the monks beaten to death before the doorways, soldiers' bullets lodged in the stonework, statues carted off and sold to buy more guns.

A monk had been found and the house bought and now it was a temple, and good Cambodian boys, and even not so good Cambodian boys, could come as acolytes. At home before the war, a young man should have a spent a year in the temple to gain merit for his family, but here, summer vacation would do.

I was never sure about Ma's views on religion. Uncle told us all a story once shortly after we'd started working in the Palace. He said he'd had a religious vision once. But it wasn't Buddhist. Uncle had gone to the French Catholic schools in Phnom Penh, as was fitting for a rich boy, Chinese school on the weekend. His grandmother was a devout Buddhist although his father had converted to Catholicism. Better for business in those days, his father figured.

One day during the Civil War, when independence-minded revolutionaries were trying to expel the French, Uncle was on his way to lycée, riding in the backseat of a cyclo cart. Normally he might have walked, but it was raining and he was about to be late to classes. The nuns could beat you in those days, with long hard wooden yardsticks for any manner of transgressions, so Uncle had bribed the cyclo driver to peddle particularly fast. The bell tower of the Catholic cathedral was just coming into view as they rounded the corner, when the wind picked up. The rain fell horizontally, dousing Uncle in his good school uniform and his satchel, melting his notebooks of the fussy, neat handwriting that the nuns so approved of. So much for Uncle's homework and any chance of escaping punishment.

"I prayed to the Holy Mother then," Uncle said. "I was terrified of being beaten. 'Protect me, blessed Mother, and I will do your bidding for the rest of my life,' I prayed. And that's when my miracle occurred."

The wind turned over peddlers' carts, soup noodle stands lost their awnings, farmers chased the produce flying off the markets as the wind took hold of cucumbers and papayas, mangosteens and durians, cilantro and scallions, aubergine and tangerines, and juggled them just out of reach. The bells of the Cathedral were ringing loud as thunder, when Uncle looked up and happened to see a flock of black crows circling above the flame trees. In fact, the wind had picked up the priest and nuns, sending them tumbling towards Heaven. As Uncle watched in amazement, he saw the priest, Father Dominic-Sébastion, lifted higher and higher, his black robe billowing up around his waist, revealing two spindly black-clad legs, until Father managed to grab hold of the Cathedral's cross. He held tight even as the wind seemed determined to drag the man into the clouds. He hung there for a day and a half until a crew of seven men was assembled to build special ladders from the longest bamboo poles they could find, so that they could climb up onto the roof and rescue the priest. Most of the sisters ended up perched atop trees, nestled in the arms of baobabs or dangling from palms, where trained monkeys were sent up to lead them down. But one poor nun was carried away altogether by the wind. No one ever saw her again although a mob of cyclo boys chased after her, weaving through the streets as she sailed like a great black kite through the sky.

"And that was my very teacher, the one who would surely have beaten me for being late and getting my homework wet," Uncle concluded, triumphantly. "That is why I know that prayer works!"

"What nonsense!" Auntie said then, rubbing her temples.

But Ma had remained silent, turning her head slightly, so that I could see the faint smile on her face whereas Auntie could not.

Later when we were alone, I'd confronted my mother. "You don't really believe Uncle's story, do you?" I accused. I was that age; everything I said was an accusation.

"Don't be rude," Ma said. "It's not for me to say what anyone's God chooses to do or whose prayers he will answer."

Before we left our first town in Texas, to pay back our sponsors for their kindness, for their trailer, for the visas, Ma had allowed my sisters and brother and me to be baptized. I had thought you had to decide for yourself if you were born again, but apparently the Pastor was willing to take Ma's word for it.

He'd been applying pressure for months, coming to the trailer at odd times, he and his thin, nervous wife, peering in the screen door at us, like pandas they had purchased for a zoo.

Ma used to worry about the Pastor and his wife, as she paced in the kitchen, trailing one hand over the Formica-top table, the Corningware nonbreakable dishes, the AM/FM radio, the folding chairs, the dish-towels. As she paced, Ma said over and over, "The Baptists are such good people. I have no face, I have no face." She meant that they had given us a lot of things, they had brought us to America, they had saved our lives. She meant that she was in their debt. "I'll never be able to repay them," she sighed.

The week before we left our sponsors' town and moved to East Dallas, Ma insisted that my sisters and brother and I be baptized. She'd decided she knew how to repay our sponsors. She could not give them her soul, because our father might be looking for it in his next life, but she could give them ours. She waited to tell us of her decision after we were all packed together in the car, headed towards the church.

"I don't want to!" I cried out then. "I won't do it!"

I'd seen baptisms before, the parade of people who stood before the altar and announced the moment they were born again. The stories of heartbreak and despair, the thoughts of suicide, the divorces, the bank-ruptcies and the addictions that the congregants had shared before the world, admitting, "I was an alcoholic," "I beat my wife," "I had an affair," "I led a shameful life," over and over, story after story of lives derailed, and then Jesus's healing hand upon their hearts, cleansing everyone, a fresh start for a failed life.

I didn't want to join the parade.

Ma pulled the car over to the shoulder, our tires squealing. She turned around to glare at me. "What's wrong with you?" she demanded, and then before I could reply, she listed my sins herself: I wanted to be an American, I talked back to my mother, I never obeyed, I thought of myself before my family, I sang *their* songs, I danced around just like *them*. She'd heard me with her own ears, she'd seen with her own eyes, and now here she was giving me the opportunity to be baptized like a real American, and yet I still complained.

Ma turned away from me then and stared out the windshield as rabbits startled by our headlights hopped frantically through the weeds in the ditches on the side of the road.

"The problem is," Ma said, "you don't love your mother." Then she started to cry.

My little sisters started to cry then, and Sam, too. They cried whenever Ma cried. The sound of her tears was like glass breaking in their hearts. Nothing they could bear.

"We'll do it, Ma," Sourdi said, finally, from beside me in the backseat. She squeezed my hand in hers, hard. "We want to be baptized."

"No, nobody makes you do anything," Ma said, crying.

"I want to," I said then. "We all want to."

Ma searched in her purse then for a pack of Kleenex and handed them out to the little kids, then she blew her own nose, once, twice, dabbed away the mascara running from her eyes. She checked her face in the rearview mirror and then pulled the car back onto the road.

The Pastor's wife helped us to dress in white robes, the color of death, of mourning, of ghosts. She lined us up before the altar and took a picture, her husband in the middle smiling with all those long white teeth of his. She herself did not smile, she did not blink, until the ceremony was over, until we'd each been dunked three times in the cold, dark baptismal on the side of the altar, the Pastor's large heavy hand on the top of our heads. One, two, three, and up we came, water dripping from our nostrils, the world a blur of clapping hands and shining teeth.

The Pastor's wife allowed herself a smile. For the first time since we'd met, her face did not appear to hurt from the effort. She went up to Ma and put her bony arms around Ma's narrow shoulders. "I just knew it was the right thing to do, bringing y'all here to America," the Pastor's wife said. "Now the little ones have accepted the Lord." Then she smiled some more, so that all her pointy, little teeth snapped at the air.

"You're welcome," said Ma in English. "You're welcome very much." And then Ma squeezed my hand so tightly, I had to bite my lips to keep from calling out.

I asked Ma that summer I turned eighteen, how it was possible that Sam could become an apprentice monk, that he could make merit for his family, if his soul was already pledged to the Christians. I asked this question maliciously, because by this time I had already grown quite cynical about all things religious, and I only wanted to make Ma feel guilty about making us become Born Agains all those years ago.

But Ma only smiled at me. "I asked the monk this, and he said it's okay. Of course it's polite to do as our sponsors say, but the *dhamma* of Buddha remains the same."

For the rest of the summer, Ma was fond of announcing all the miracles that she had observed since sending Sam to the temple. The double rainbow that appeared after a storm, the lightning bolt that hit the Super 8 but for once missed the Palace sign, the increasing bus loads of seniors stopping en route to the dog tracks in Iowa.

And then Ma's Big Miracle, as she put it, occurred.

I wasn't there for the arrival, as I'd gone to Sioux City for the day to pick up some supplies we needed before our distributor passed through town again at the end of the month—several fifty pound bags of rice, more soy sauce, the usual industrial-size cans of fruit cocktail. I dawdled, too, stopping by the Mayfaire Mall to buy some clothes for college in the fall while the summer sales were still on. Then I stopped by the Palace to drop off the groceries.

By the time I drove up to our house, it was close to midnight. It was a warm night for August, with just a hint of fall in the wind, and I sat in my car on the street for a while, just watching, with the engine off and the windows down. I'd cut my hair short again, this time because I liked the lightness, the sun against the back of my neck, and now the wind tickled my ears. It was a pleasant feeling. I could hear crickets hidden in the lawn, and somewhere a radio played, a man singing nasally about love gone wrong, and in the distance, I could hear the hush-hush-hush of the cornstalks swaying in the wind.

Our house was small but tidy, not the huge show house Uncle had rented for us all when we'd first moved to Nebraska, but a house Ma had bought herself a year ago. A real mortgage this time. No loan sharks. No sponsors. The real, bona-fide American dream. Ma said she wanted to paint it yellow, but it was still white, even though this was not a lucky color. The top layer of paint was peeling in places.

Blue lights danced behind the curtains in the front room, and I figured Ma and my sisters must be watching television.

I grabbed my purse, slinging the strap over my shoulder, and climbed out of the car, my limbs stiff and awkward after my long drive.

I could smell the coriander and mint floating lightly on the wind, the heavy scent of garlic and onions and anise growing stronger as I approached the front door. I was surprised that Ma would be cooking so late, but we would be going to Des Moines soon to pick up Sam from the temple, and she had started cooking her offerings for the monks in advance. I figured there was something she'd forgotten to make and remembered all at once.

Walking up the three brick steps to the entrance, I could hear my sisters' music, the drumbeats throbbing in the air. I could imagine them sitting together in the kitchen, a bowl of chives and shrimp between them as they stuffed wontons or springrolls, and I realized how much I would miss them all when I left in a few weeks. It was funny how I'd longed to leave this town, my family, for years and years, and now when I was going, I began to feel regret.

I let myself in.

The TV was on in the living room, loud. Explosions and screams. Why my sisters and Ma would want to watch *Platoon* was beyond me. There was someone slouched on the corner of the sofa. It was too dark to see which of my sisters was sleeping there. I flipped the overhead light on and then jumped through the doorway.

"Boo!" I said.

The old man sitting on the sofa shook himself awake. "Hmm—whaa?"

For a minute, I had the horrible feeling that I'd made a mistake and broken into a complete stranger's house.

The old man blinked and rubbed his face on his shoulder.

"Excuse me—" I began, and then the old man rose from the sofa and stepped towards me, smiling, revealing a full mouth of perfect, white, movie-star teeth.

I recognized the smile immediately. It was One Arm's.

"Nea, my daughter!" he cried out excitedly. "So good to see you!"

I couldn't believe it, after all these years. Except for his teeth, he looked much worse for wear. He had, in fact, withered. His head was mostly bald except for a few strands of white hair; his rheumy eyes watered; his veins protruded like worms along his skull; even his arm was broken. It hung limply from a sling around his neck. I hadn't noticed it at first because in a typical gesture, he'd made sure the fabric matched his shirt, as though he were wearing a scarf draped around his neck and not a sling. The same vain man, only old now.

"Oh, Mom!" One Arm called towards the kitchen in English. "Nea's home."

I was too furious to speak. I left him standing there, smiling like a monkey, and stormed into the kitchen.

My sisters were seated around the table, their hands deep into plastic bowls of chopped vegetables, chives by the smell, as Ma stood with her back to me in front of a boiling pot at the stove, a ladle in one hand.

"Ma," I said.

My sisters jumped.

"Oh, you're back!" Ma smiled.

"Ma, what's *he* doing here?"

Ma looked at me, her face a mask of innocence. "Are you hungry? Have some tea."

"Ma, don't you remember what happened?"

But then One Arm shuffled into the kitchen.

"The family reunited!" he proclaimed. "What a happy night!" He smiled, nodding at me benevolently, as though I were an honored guest in *his* house. "Let's have tea for everyone," he said.

"Ma!" I cried, but she wouldn't let me continue.

"Now, now," she said, wiping her hands on a dishrag. "Why don't you put on an apron?"

Then Ma pretended she didn't understand my pointed looks, my frowns and sighs. Instead she turned up the radio and set me to work wrapping spring rolls, while she warmed up a bowl of noodles for me in the microwave and One Arm told me about his miraculous journey back to Ma.

One Arm had arrived that afternoon on the Greyhound bus. He'd tried to find Ma again, years ago, after his luck had turned cold. He'd gone back to Texas, all the way to our old town, looking for her, and was disappointed to discover that we'd moved. He'd managed to track Ma down to the last restaurant she'd worked at in East Dallas when the trail ran cold. The owner remembered that we'd moved someplace far away, some state he'd never heard of before, some place in the South, he thought.

For a time, One Arm had given up.

He'd had a lot of problems in Texas. He was old, he was tired, no one was his friend anymore now that he didn't have his good government job that could provide people with favors. There were his financial problems, too. He'd left the first time owing a lot of people money, money that he'd fully intended to repay, he now claimed. He wasn't a thief, he wasn't that kind of low-class person, but it was a question of starting over, and no one wanted to give him the time he needed. The gangs got involved. He was beaten by the Angkor Tigers and the Dragon Sons. That's when he'd decided he needed a change of scenery, a place where he'd be given the benefit of a doubt. An old pai gow-playing friend of his was opening a business in Omaha. One Arm decided this could be the change in luck he'd been looking for.

To buy the bus ticket, he'd pawned his watch, his suit, and his good silver locket, the one he'd carried with his wife's picture in it all these years, since before the war, not that it had mattered one bit to her once they were reunited. Sure, she'd acted happy to see him at first, but in truth she'd fallen in love with another man, a younger man, a man with all his limbs intact, and she demanded he grant her a divorce. Not that there was any point to talk of this bitterness now.

But then things in Omaha hadn't turned out as he'd hoped. His friend's business never materialized, there was a problem with money, there were always problems with money. His friend moved north to South Dakota, and One Arm followed, trying to get the wages that were owed him, but then his friend disappeared one night, and One Arm found himself alone in Sioux Falls, without a friend in the world and nothing left to pawn. He tried to get a job as a cook in a couple stir-fry joints, but they hadn't wanted him on account of his having only one arm. Finally, he'd managed to find a job as a mechanic. Lube and oil jobs at first, but then the shop discovered he had a knack with the customers. He could sell them anything, brake jobs, engine rehauls, timing belt replacements. He was a natural salesman. He talked openly about escaping

the war, he told his exciting shark attack story, he gladly shared all the
wisdom that he'd gained from being a refugee, how disasters loomed just
over the horizon, ones you couldn't foresee. Then he explained why it was
so important to try to prevent the little disasters, the ones we could control, the balding brake pads, the skittish alignment, the rust guard and the
protective coating of sealant. He'd nod happily, pleased that his customer
had seen the light, had chosen to protect his family while he still could.
Why quibble over a few dollars when you were buying the future itself,
ensuring the safety of your loved ones? If only he could turn back time,
One Arm would say then, if only he could do the same.

And that's how he'd run into Ma again. He'd heard from his customers about the bus trips to the dog track in Council Bluffs, the Senior
Express, the bus that stopped at the Chinese restaurant with the all-you-
can-eat buffet, and One Arm had had a sudden flash of intuition. His
luck had returned.

He bought himself a bus ticket the next day.

When he came into the Palace, he'd recognized Ma immediately,
even after all these years. Her face was lined, her hair streaked with white,
her girls no longer children but young women. Ma had aged in the nine
years that had passed since they'd last seen each other, but One Arm said
he would have recognized her anywhere.

"Oh, Ma!" I exclaimed, turning to her at the end of his story, I didn't
care who was listening, I didn't care what One Arm would think. "Don't
you see? He was going gambling again!"

But One Arm shook his head. No, he said, he had no interest in bet-
ting on dumb animals running around in circles. It was the bus ticket that
was the gamble, and he'd hit the jackpot. Then he smiled in his movie-star
way, and Ma laughed like a young girl.

That night after everyone else had gone to bed—One Arm was safely ensconced on the couch, I was pleased to see—we sat in the kitchen,
just Ma and me, with the light off, only the moon spilling blue through
the curtains. I drank hot water and Ma smoked, just like old times, just
as we had when I was a child.

"How can you forget what he was like?" I pushed my empty teacup
around on the table top, tracing circle after circle.

"He's not the same man. He's really suffered."

"Ma!" I rolled my eyes.

"Besides, he can't hurt me now. What can he steal? Where can he go? He's an old man. He has no family. His wife didn't want him. I'm all he has left."

"There may be a good reason nobody else wants him around."

To my surprise, Ma laughed. With each explosive "Ha!" a ring of blue smoke emerged from her mouth and rose gently in the moonlight, settling above her head like a crooked halo.

I sighed. "How long is he staying?"

Ma shrugged a little. "He still has his job in the city. He's just here for a little visit. He's leaving tomorrow on the bus."

I nodded. I'd given up arguing with my mother. It was too late, and I was too tired. Nothing I said to her ever made a difference anyway. "I'm going to bed," I said. "I need to sleep."

"Ha! You're getting old. When did you ever need to sleep?" Then she laughed once more, coughing up a final, perfect ring of smoke. "He gave me my money back." She nodded at my shocked face. "All of it."

"With interest?"

"He's a friend. I don't charge interest," Ma said, drawing her shoulders back as though I'd offended her. "It's a miracle."

"That's for sure."

"So we can all go now."

"Go where?"

"To the temple," Ma said it as though I were being thick. "To pick your brother up. We can shut the Palace for a day and take a vacation. All of us. I want to see my grandchildren."

The next morning, One Arm left on the Greyhound—promising to return, I noted, my stomach clenching as Ma smiled and waved goodbye. The rest of us loaded up the van with the food we'd prepared for the monks and headed east to Iowa. I managed to get us to Des Moines in just over four and a half hours. We had a tail wind, and most importantly, no cops on the highway. It occurred to me as the twins chattered excitedly in the backseat, that we'd never taken a vacation together as a family. The last time we'd driven like this we were fleeing Texas, ready to embark on our new life in Nebraska.

"When are we going to get there?" Maly/Marie asked.

"Can we go to the fair? New Kids on the Block are singing!" Navy/Jennifer cajoled.

"Are we getting closer?" they asked.

"Be quiet. You're giving your poor mother a headache," Ma said.

I wished the minivan could spring wings. My foot pushed harder on the gas pedal, and it was all I could do to restrain myself from flooring it. I was going to see Sourdi again. My heart beat against the confines of my ribcage, a hummingbird trapped.

But first, we would stop at the Temple.

When we arrived at the Des Moines exit, I asked Ma which street.

"Downtown somewhere," she said.

"You don't remember the address?"

"I know what it looks like. Don't worry. I don't need an address."

The streets in Des Moines ran from 1st to 115th in several directions, east and west, which we seemed to traverse back and forth, again and again, as I hoped something would strike a chord with Ma.

"Does anything look familiar?" I asked hopefully.

Ma squinted. "Keep driving."

Finally after we passed the gold-capped capital building, and the skyscrapers of the business district (for the third time,) Ma's memory improved and she recalled that the temple was on an odd-numbered street, under twenty. "I am remembering," she said, her eyes closed, a hand to her forehead, like Carnac the Magnificent.

And then, after all, we were able to find the temple, on 7th.

"You see, I told you," Ma cried out happily.

There were cars parked up and down the street, red good-luck amulets and stone rosaries hanging from rear-view mirrors, license plates from as far away as Texas and Minnesota and Illinois, all paths leading to the temple.

I didn't expect it to mean anything to me, visiting the temple, but as we walked down the street, carrying the grocery bags filled with our offerings to the monks, I found my heart beating faster, although this neighborhood looked like any other, this house like any other, modest, a little rundown even. Maybe it was the scent of incense on the wind, or the smell of all the food Ma had cooked, combined with my hunger, I began to feel lightheaded and the world took on a new cast, the clouds sped overhead, the sun grew brighter, and I had to squint, shielding my eyes with a hand above my forehead. The house seemed to change as we approached, to grow taller, wider, its walls pulsing in the wind, its windows mirroring the street. As we walked up the driveway, I could see my family reflected in the glass. We were growing larger, too, as we approached the temple, like giants rising from a dark lake.

Shoes were piled like offerings before the door, down the front steps, spilling onto the lawn, sandals and sneakers, cowboy boots, Doc Martens, flip flops, a pair of pointy pink stilettos.

There was a series of folding tables on the lawn covered with food, casseroles and Tupperware, covered plates and metal trays. A teenage boy dressed like a monk, his head shaved, an orange robe thrown over his thin brown shoulders, jumped up from a folding chair under a tree. He raised his palms together in greeting and gestured for us to leave our brown bags on the table. "You look like a boy," he said, and I started.

Then Sam appeared from around the corner of the house, carrying a bag of ice over one shoulder. He waved to us cheerfully and broke into a run.

"That your sister?" the first acolyte called to Sam. "She doesn't look like her picture."

Sam came running up and hugged me tightly. His back was cold and damp from the ice. Then he pulled back suddenly.

"I don't know if I'm supposed to touch you. You're a girl."

"Don't be stupid. I'm your sister."

"You shouldn't have cut your hair," Sam remarked, squinting at me. "What did you do this time?"

"Hey, maybe she wants to be a monk, too," the first boy said. "With hair like that, you can always tell the monks, you didn't know she was a girl!"

They laughed uproariously at that. But for their orange robes and shaved heads, they could have been two boys anywhere, on any street corner.

Then Sam waved over my shoulder, to Ma and the girls, but before they could speak, an old monk appeared in the door of the house and called the boys back inside with a wave of his hand, palm downward. Sam sighed but ran off quickly.

"See you," he called happily over his shoulder.

We put the bags of food on the folding tables on the lawn, slipped our shoes off into the piles by the door, and went inside the temple.

I couldn't understand a word of the monks' prayers as we sat in the living room of the house, on a patch of towel. The entire carpet had been covered with bath towels and beach towels, in all colors and patterns, stripes and flowers, improvised prayer mats. There were two monks, one quite elderly, with large folds of skin that drooped around his eyes, jowls that sagged from his chin to his adam's apple, his wrinkles so deep, his skin so dry and stiff, he seemed to have been carved from wood. He barely moved at all as he stood to the side of a younger monk, who was also quite an old man, but who seemed centuries younger next to the tree monk. He had long curved eyes and a wide flat nose and lips that appeared always to smile, and he led the chanting, his voice rising and falling, the syllables blurring together the way the waters of a single river are lost in the ocean. I could not distinguish a word that he said, although Ma seemed to have no problem and soon she joined in with the man, her smoky voice rising above the rest of the crowd. I closed my eyes to help me to concentrate.

I didn't know how to pray, I didn't know the words. I put my head in my hands, all the things I didn't know, all the things I had forgotten, throbbing in my brain. I wasn't even sure to whom I should be praying.

Then all at once, a sound like a rock splitting, like a tree growing, like the earth moving. I opened my eyes and saw that the old monk, as still as ever, only his lips moving slightly, had begun to chant. The sound that emerged seemed to hang in the air, and then all at once, the old monk's voice seeped into my skin, rushed into my blood. I could feel his voice in my veins, pulsing in my heart, and then it entered my bones, and I realized his voice was the sound of bones if they could speak, bones that were left exposed in barren fields, bleached in the sun, dragged by feral dogs, gnawed by animals with sharp teeth, broken, abandoned, forgotten.

I opened my mouth, but my voice would not come out. Instead, the old monk's voice emerged from the bones of my body, vibrating in the air, like molecules, the sound of his chant moved through the room, through each person, until it seemed as though a hundred voices were speaking, but it was only one, the old monk, speaking for us all.

Then suddenly he stopped chanting. The silence that followed buzzed in my head, growing louder, until I had to throw my hands over my ears. I winced, the pain in my head increasing, as the silence grew stronger, pricking my skin, pressing upon the back of my head, pushing me forward to the ground. I could barely breathe, and then finally, the younger monk resumed his chant, and I was released.

I continued to cradle my head in my hands. I closed my eyes and tried to relax, letting the sound of the chant move through me as it had with the old monk, but this time, the voice remained outside of me. But it didn't matter; I wasn't really concentrating on his chant. Instead, I was startled to discover that I could clearly see in my mind's eye the face of my father, his thick black hair, his bushy eyebrows, his long, sloping eyes, his high sharp cheekbones, and his laugh, explosive and startled, shaking his entire body when it emerged. He didn't look the way I remembered him in the village prison camp, like a thin man about to die, but rather he now appeared in my memories looking like a university student, a handsome man, a young man with prospects, a man Ma could fall in love with.

And I knew then that I didn't need to pray for his soul, but instead I prayed for Sam and me, for my little sisters, for Sourdi, Ma, and all of us who were still living, who could use all the help we could get in this life not just the next one, all of our struggling souls.

After the ceremony ended, many of the families gathered on the lawn talking with each other, planning a picnic with the extra food they had prepared, but Ma had no desire to linger. Her business at the temple done, she was ready to move on, to visit Sourdi, to see her grandchildren, to enjoy life in the big city before we had to drive home again.

Ma was in a good mood, almost giddy. "Hurry up, slowpoke," she called to me as she hurried down the sidewalk, Sam and my sisters following. Sam had changed back into his blue jeans and a T-shirt; now that he was freed from his obligations at the temple, he was just an ordinary boy again, no longer an acolyte. "Race ya!" he shoved the twins and took off toward our car.

Still, I stood rooted on the sidewalk, halfway between the minivan and the temple, staring at the house behind us. I wanted to look at the temple and really see so that I would remember it always. I wanted the temple to look the way I had felt inside while the old monk chanted, but from the outside it was still a small house in a poor neighborhood. The only thing distinguishing it from all the other houses was not a sense of holiness or grandeur but the families scattered across the lawn and the two monks walking down the driveway, their orange robes blowing in the wind.

CHAPTER 26

Sourdi's Story

"This one's going to be a boy," Sourdi said, her hand across her enormous belly.

"How can you tell? Did you have some kind of dream?" I asked.

"You sound like Ma now," Sourdi said, laughing at me. "We could see on the ultrasound, silly." She dug around in her enormous purse and pulled out a grainy black and white copy. "Look," she said, pointing with her little finger, and sure enough, I could see it, a tiny penis like a sixth finger floating between the fetus's frog-like legs.

I laced my arm through hers as we walked together through the fairgrounds. The Iowa State Fair was wrapping up this weekend. Ma was pleased we hadn't missed it.

Mr. Chhay was watching the children, their two daughters, holding the youngest on his lap as they rode wooden carousel horses, round and round, the music tinkling across the fairways.

Ma and the twins had gone off by themselves as well; they had wanted to see the Butter Cow, a life-size sculpture of a Holstein, but there was a long line before the refrigerated hall where it was stored, so Sourdi and I had left them to walk the sawdust-covered grounds, watching all the people milling about, the state senator waving from a soybean oil-powered car, the Iowa hogs that had been cross-bred with Chinese sows, the little children running about, gnawing on cotton candy and caramel apples and turkey legs the size of their own forearms.

Sam disappeared with a group of boys. They were dressed well, in leather jackets and fancy jeans, designer sunglasses that hadn't been purchased at Sunglass Hut in the mall. At first I thought they must be Indians, it'd been so long since I'd seen Asians other than us. They might have been Chinese, they might have been Cambodian, they might have been any number of things. Sam didn't bother to introduce his friends but sauntered off with them quickly, to try his hand at the games of chance.

I wasn't interested in the rides or the games. It was enough to walk with Sourdi again, just the two of us, well, the three of us.

"I thought I could remember Pa today," I told her. "It was strange. I could see his face perfectly. He looked healthy. Not like I used to remember."

Sourdi nodded. "In the beginning when I had nightmares, Pa was always sick, he couldn't breathe. But now I don't dream of him like that anymore. I only think of him from before the war. When he used to take me for rides on his motorbike."

"That's good," I said.

"I don't know," said Sourdi. "I think it means I'm forgetting."

She rubbed her eyes against the back of her hand, quickly.

"Anyway, you're going to be a college girl soon. Isn't that exciting? Aren't you happy? You're going to get away from here. You can forget about all of us and go see the world." Sourdi squeezed my arm tight, then tighter. My skin hurt beneath her hands.

We didn't say anything more for a while as we walked together, arm in arm, past the whirling tilt-o-whirl, the octopus, the spinning two-armed Ferris wheel.

"I'm so hot. I just wish I could have this baby right now. I'm just so hot!" Sourdi said, finally. She fanned herself furiously. I could smell her sweat on each puff of air, the same salty-sweet smell that I had loved as a little girl. I wanted to wrap my arms around her neck, I wanted to press my nose to her skin, as I had as a child, but I wasn't a child anymore and instead I looked away, watching the faces of the people as they shot past on the tilt-o-whirl, their red mouths wide-open screaming, their eyes squeezed tight.

That night, Mr. Chhay insisted upon making dinner for us all, Sourdi and the girls had bought him a barbecue from Sears for Father's Day, and he said he never had time to use it, so he grilled us burgers and chicken legs, dressed in his *Field of Dreams* apron and the Cornhuskers baseball cap that we'd sent to him for Christmas the year before.

We sat in the backyard at their redwood picnic table, watching my sisters and Sam push Sourdi's older daughter on the swing set while the baby slept in its bouncer on the grass. As the sun dipped in the horizon, the sky turned a pale and lovely pink, like the inside of a shell, and light-ning bugs glittered like diamonds above the thick green grass.

After a while, when everyone had had a little too much to drink, Mr. Chhay began to make speeches. Standing up, he raised his can of Miller Lite to the sky. "Seeing our family together again, I feel as though I have traveled across a distant sea only to return home at last. I have battled the despair of the sailor who is lost, I have tasted the bitterness of exile, I have felt the heat of the sun and the cold of the moon. And now, at last, my ship returns to the harbor, I see a light burning in the window, my heart is released."

I looked over at Sourdi, but it was too dark to see her features clearly. She would have grown used to her husband's poetic ways by now. She reached out and took his hand in hers, and Mr. Chhay brought it to his lips. I had to admit he no longer looked as bad as I'd remembered. Mar-ried life seemed to suit him. He'd stopped combing his hair over his bald spot, and he smiled easily now. He didn't look exactly handsome, but he did look happy, and he gazed upon my sister with adoration.

And then before I could wonder at these changes, Ma stood up, ready to make her own toast now. "I have lived and loved. I have loved and lost," Ma said. Her voice was only a little slurred. "But I have no regrets. I have never been afraid to follow my heart. Not everyone can say that." She raised her cup to Mr. Chhay and they both drank.

Mr. Chhay cleared his throat, and I could tell he was preparing to launch into another speech, so I rose quickly and gathered up the dirty dishes and brought them inside the house.

I set the dirty plates in the sink. Sourdi's kitchen looked almost the same as it had when I'd last visited, with Duke, the flowered wallpaper, the lacy curtains held back with pink ties, except now the refrigerator was covered with photos of the children, held in place with magnets shaped like Disney characters, and the walls were decorated with crayon draw-ings of flowers and houses and girls in rainbow-colored dresses.

I was filling one side of the sink with soapy water, when Sourdi came in behind me and put a hand on my shoulder. Then without speaking, she took her place beside me, and we stood at the sink just as we had as girls, me washing, Sourdi drying, and it seemed we might be able to talk easily, about anything that popped into our heads, and I might be able to admit to Sourdi that I was afraid, now that I would be leaving home in a few weeks, as I'd always wished, as I'd always wanted. How I felt unsettled instead of pleased, as though I would be losing a limb, as though I would never come back again. But before I could say any of these things, Sourdi told me about the baby clothes she was buying, and the way she'd decided to fix up the nursery, how she'd even had her husband paint the walls blue, and what her daughter was doing in preschool. Then her oldest daughter came running inside, chattering about a fall from the swings, and then Mr. Chhay came in, too, with the toddler, who was also crying, and he put his hand on Sourdi's shoulder, pulling her from me, and Sourdi took the girls to their bedroom with her husband, her voice light and airy, like a song, promising a bedtime story, and I was left alone.

And I realized then that my sister was happy. The idea startled me so much, I had to lean against the sink, but it was true. Sourdi had a stable home for herself and her children, she had a calm husband who adored her, she did not have to worry about money.

I'd been wrong about Sourdi. She was no fool. She was no pushover. She was her mother's daughter, all right. It was me, I wondered about. How I could have been so blind.

As I was finishing drying the dishes, Sourdi surprised me, coming in so quietly that I hadn't noticed until her cool hand touched the back of my neck.

"Oh!" I startled. Then abashed, I apologized. "I hope I didn't wake the girls."

"No, they're sound asleep. I'm going to make us some tea. You're going away soon. This will be our last time to talk as sisters."

"It's not like I'm moving to another country. I'm just going to college."

"College," Sourdi sighed. "That's a big change. A big deal. You should be proud." She filled the kettle with water and set it upon the stove, adjusting the blue flames.

A quell of laughter burst through the open windows. Ma and Mr. Chhay and the kids. Someone was telling jokes.

"You know, Nea, I've always considered you my best friend. My very best." Sourdi sat down next to me at her table. She set a cup before me and held hers between her long fingers. "I'll always think of you that way. Even if you hate me."

"Hate you? Why would I hate you?"

"Ssh. Not so loud. I need to tell you something."

"I'm sorry. I forgot about the babies."

"No, it's not that." She glanced anxiously over her shoulder, as though she expected to find a ghost or Ma scowling or something, but there was nothing behind her but the curtains blowing in the wind over the sink.

"Ma didn't want to say. Uncle didn't either. Auntie—I think Auntie wanted to tell you, but she wasn't well, you know."

"Tell me what?"

"Auntie was sick before the war, too. Not this bad. Not like she was here. But her health wasn't ever very good. She had many miscarriages. Sometimes she grew depressed. She couldn't care for all her children. She hired wet nurses for the boys, but she let Ma take care of her daughter. Uncle paid Ma. We needed the money. And she knew I liked playing with you so much."

"So we played with Auntie's daughter? The one that died in the war?"

"She didn't die."

"What happened to her?"

"She—she looked so much like us. She didn't inherit Auntie's pale skin. She was darker, like Ma and me. Auntie thought it would be better if she stayed with us. And she didn't think she could take care of four children by herself. Uncle was already gone. When the soldiers came and made everybody leave the city, she kept the boys, but she let the girl live with us. She didn't know Pa would die so soon."

"She just gave away her daughter?" I was shocked. The way Auntie had bragged about the girl, it seemed as though she thought she'd given birth to a princess.

"Don't say that. It's not like that. She wanted to protect you. She gave you to us to protect you. She didn't just give you away."

"Me? What you mean 'me'?"

"Oh, Nea. I didn't want to tell you. I never wanted you to find out. When I was younger, I was so afraid Auntie would try to take you back. I was so selfish. I made Ma promise me not to tell you. I told Ma that I would run away if she said anything. That I would run away with you and we'd never come back. And I think she believed me. But I know that Ma didn't want to give you back either. And besides, Auntie wasn't well.

You saw her. You know how she was. She couldn't take care of you. Even Uncle agreed."

I couldn't speak. My stomach lurched, as though a fist had socked me in the guts. I could taste steak and corn on the cob coming back up sour-like. My tongue felt swollen in my mouth.

"I'm Auntie's daughter?"

"You never guessed? You really never remembered anything?"

I jumped up from my seat, spilling my tea onto the floor, as I rushed to the sink and vomited. The air was too hot this evening. I wretched until I choked.

Sourdi patted me on my back. "I'm sorry. I'm so sorry," she wept. "I shouldn't have told you. It was wrong of me."

I leaned my forehead against the edge of the sink, turned the faucet on, splashed cool water on my face. The smell of my vomit was overpowering. I thought I might retch again. Quickly, I gathered up some paper towels and sopped up my mess.

"Can you forgive me? Nea, say something. Please say something."

I put the vomit-covered towels into the trash bin under the sink. Splashed cold water on my hot cheeks. Dipping my head, I drank from the faucet, trying to wash the terrible bile taste from my mouth.

"Nea? Are you all right?"

"Sssh!" I turned, glaring at Sourdi. "That's not even my name, is it? You changed it. Or Ma did. You all wanted me to forget."

"It was Ma's nickname for you. And Channary seemed too fancy. A city name. A dangerous name. The soldiers wouldn't like a name like that." Sourdi was still crying. I wanted to slap her. I wanted to slap some sense into my sister.

No. Not my sister. My cousin.

I almost got sick again.

But then I didn't.

"I need another beer. Do you have one?"

Sourdi hurriedly rummaged through her fridge and handed me a bottle of Bud. I opened it on the edge of the counter and took a long drink.

"Why did you tell me? Why did you have to tell me, Sourdi?"

"You should know."

"No, no. It's too late. That was a different life. You shouldn't have told me."

"You're going away. I wanted you to know. I didn't want you to hate me—"

"Sourdi, I would never hate you. I would never even have found out. Quit lying."

"I'm not—"

"You didn't tell me because I'm going to college. You told me because you're afraid you're going to be reborn as an insect."

Sourdi stared at me with her mouth open, her mascara running down her cheeks, her hair plastered against her tear-stained cheeks. "That's stupid," she said.

My sister. My Sourdi. My everything.

My lying cousin.

My savior. My ally. My betrayer.

Sourdi, my sweet sweet once-upon-a-time sister, who had planted this knife in my heart.

Why couldn't she have just kept lying? Why couldn't Sourdi be more like Ma?

I couldn't speak.

Sourdi continued to sob, but I didn't try to console her.

Then it was time to head back home to Nebraska. It was a long drive and we all had to work the next day.

CHAPTER 27

The Belly of the Prairie

By the time we arrived home, it was well into the middle of the night. Maly and Navy shuffled off to their rooms. Even Sam was too sleepy to talk. The windshield of the van was smeared with insect eviscera, even the windshield wipers on high had done little to clear the mess, and my face was twisted into a permanent squint from trying to see through the smeared glass.

Ma was irritable, too, from the long ride, and perhaps the buzz from the alcohol wearing off at last, and we argued the moment we stepped in the house.

"I don't know why you did that to your hair," she said, coming up behind me as I put Mr. Chhay's barbecue leftovers into the refrigerator.

"My hair?"

"Yeah. Why make it ugly like that?" Ma pursed her lips as though sucking on limes.

"Gee, I don't know. Maybe I just like to look ugly. I must be perverse."

"I'm just trying to help you."

"What does it matter what I do to my hair?"

"It makes you look tired. And it's so uneven. Short and long. You should try to look more pretty."

"Oh, my god. I can't believe this! Can't you ever stop?"

"I didn't want to say anything in front of the others," Ma began, eyeing me carefully, as though I were a fish in a tank she was contemplating preparing for dinner. "But you don't look so good. I'm worried, that's all. I can't help worrying. You're going to be leaving soon. You'll be going away to school, and I won't be there to tell you things. Other people won't care the way I do. You'll be sorry then that you didn't listen to me."

"Well, you shouldn't trouble yourself, Ma. I can take care of myself. When have you ever cared about me really?" I ran out of the kitchen and down the hall. I slipped my feet into my shoes without stopping, without bothering to tie up the laces of my sneakers, and escaped out the front door. I had made it to our old car and was about to jump in and drive off, when I remembered that I'd left my purse inside on the kitchen table with my keys in it.

Ma was standing in the front door, shouting out at me, "Look how you treat me! I'm your mother! I'm your mother!" over and over. With as much dignity as I could muster, I pretended I couldn't hear her, the liar, the terrible liar, and I continued running down the sidewalk, away from my mother's house, my *fake* mother's house, as fast as I could. I wanted to escape, flee this nightmare world, where nothing was what it seemed. Where everyone had been lying to me, my whole family. This world where I was not the person I had imagined. I wanted to run like a girl in a fairy tale fleeing an enchanted forest filled with witches and spells and poison apples. Where was the real world? Where was the world where my real life was taking place and not this crazy carnival mirror version of a life?

I cried so hard I couldn't see as I passed all the familiar wooden houses with the chainlink fences, the ceramic gnomes set along garden paths amidst the marigolds and the morning glories, the cheerfully painted mailboxes and windsocks, and kept running until I'd reached the main street that went downtown. All the stores were closed, of course, even the bars, but I continued walking, past the newsstand and the funeral parlor and the store that used to be a five-and-dime which had been bought out by a national chain, until I'd walked right through the middle of town to the other side and I knew there would be a few streets of houses and churches and then I'd find myself face to face with the corn and the soybeans and perhaps the field of sunflowers that a farmer had started planting that spring.

What I remembered was the way the yellow sunflowers stood out against the dense green corn, how their heads raised towards the sun, and then bowed again at night as though in prayer. They would seem to change color over the course of the day, appearing bright yellow in the morning and then deeper orange-red as the sun set.

But of course in the middle of the night, the sunflowers would have bowed their heads towards the earth, their yellow petals hidden, and there'd be nothing to see. So I turned around without trying to make it all the way to that field of flowers.

By the time I had walked back home, my heart was racing, I was panting heavily, and my back was drenched in sweat. I vowed then and there that when I got to college, I would get in shape and I'd quit smoking. I'd be serious and concentrate and not be distracted by memories or nightmares or dreams or the crazy lies of my family, their stories, their thousand and one emotions that coursed through my heart every moment of the day. I'd said this all before, many times, but this time I had real motivation.

Ma was waiting for me in the kitchen. She wasn't smoking, or drinking tea, or reading a magazine, she was just sitting at the table, as though she'd been expecting me.

"You want to go for a drive?" she asked.

"Sure," I said. She's going to tell me, I thought. Just like Sourdi. Maybe they even planned it. My going-away-to-college present. I braced myself, but I didn't have any idea what I'd say to Ma when the moment of truth came.

I grabbed my purse off the table, and she followed me out to the car.

The moon was bright enough for me to see quite well. We rolled the windows down all the way, so that the wind blew in along with the moonlight, the sound of the cornfields like the waves of the sea. And then I started to drive.

With the headlights off so that we wouldn't have to deal with the bugs hitting the windshield, I drove past the fallow fields that were on off rotation this season to replenish the soil, and the sunflower field, where indeed all the flowers had their heads tucked down, like birds nesting for the night, past the Olsons' soybean fields, and the Johnsons' cattle pasture, and on and on, until there was nothing but fields of seed corn, no matter where we looked. I knew what I wanted to find, I just didn't remember exactly where it was anymore. There was a road that rose like a swell in the ocean, the only hill in our part of Nebraska from which we could see our whole town. Duke had shown Sourdi and me once, years ago, when we used to ride together in his pickup. Life back then was so much simpler. I just had no idea then how lucky I was.

I drove on and on, past abandoned barns and dead cottonwoods that had long ago been felled by lightning, where the farmhouses were set far back from the road behind scrims of evergreens. I raced past fields where giant metal irrigation machines stretched above the corn like highway overpasses, their spiky metal appendages like the vertebra of a dinosaur's spine, silhouetted against the starry sky. Sometimes the road rose for a while but then it dipped again, never high enough. I must have driven halfway to South Dakota, when I found what I was looking for: the road that rose and rose, high enough to see above the corn. I drove to the very top of the hill and then parked, so that Ma could see.

"Look, that's our town," I said, pointing to the string of lights twinkling like a galaxy at the far end of the ocean of corn. "If you left the sign on, I bet we could even see the Palace."

"Where? Show me." Ma craned her neck this way and that, squinting through the windshield.

I indicated a dark spot south by southeast, on the far edge of the spill of lights, and Ma nodded solemnly, circling the area on the glass with her index finger. "So there it is," she whispered. "There."

We sat quietly for a while, just looking at our town shining in the distance.

Then Ma put her fists over her eyes.

I thought she was crying, the way she had when I was a child, as though she were ashamed. But when a moment later she brought her fists back down to her sides, her eyes were dry. This is it, I thought. She said, "The problem is we're both too stubborn. We're too proud."

"Who?"

"Me and you."

Then she placed her fists against her temples and pressed as though she wished she could push into the bone. She closed her eyes tight.

I needed a smoke. I reached into my purse and pulled out my Camels, turned the pack on its side and tapped out a cigarette. I put it between my lips, flipped my Zippo open and lit the end. Then I handed the cigarette to Ma.

Ma's nostrils flared. Her eyelids snapped open. "When did you start smoking?" she asked.

I shrugged. "I dunno. When I was thirteen maybe."

She took the cigarette from me and brought it to her mouth, inhaling deeply. I lit another one for myself, the last one. I crumpled the pack up and tossed it into the back seat of the car.

"You shouldn't smoke," she said. "It's a bad habit."

"I know."

"When you go to college, you promise me you'll stop. I don't want people thinking I'm a bad mother."

"Okay, Ma. I promise. This will be my last one." I waited for her to continue.

We sat together in the dark, smoking, without talking. Ma blew three perfect smoke rings out the car window, and I watched them float over the hood and disappear. In the far distance, at the very edge of the world, heat lightning flashed across the sky like the glow from a bomb or a Fourth of July fireworks display. The stars remained steady.

"My life has been a true miracle," Ma said. "I have two beautiful granddaughters. Soon I will have a grandson. I am a businesswoman. I own a palace." She smiled at her own joke.

I waited for my mother to add, *And I need to tell you that you're not my real daughter. I've lied to you all these years. I'm sorry. But you need to know the truth.* But Ma didn't say it.

Crickets chirped in the dark. Fireflies sparked in the ditches.

And I realized then that Ma would never tell, which is why Sourdi had, when my sister had felt it was finally safe to say so. Sourdi had told me because I was no longer a child. I was an adult. She recognized that. The truth was her gift to me. And I had thrown it back into her face.

Me, the once-upon-a-time rich girl, still acting like a spoiled child. I almost laughed. Despite Ma's best efforts, maybe a part of me would always be Auntie's spoiled daughter.

And suddenly my anger left, like sweat drying from my skin, my body cleansed as though by fire. Ma was my mother, my true mother, the only mother I remembered. And Auntie, poor Auntie, was my birth mother, also my true mother. And someday I would go to California and I would find Uncle and tell him that I knew. I couldn't imagine what would follow, what he would say, if he'd even want to see me now that Auntie was dead. Maybe I'd only make him sadder. But I knew that I would go find him anyway.

Someday.

But tonight, I knew what I wanted to do. What I could do.

"There's one more thing I want to show you while we're out here," I said at last. "Put your seatbelt on, Ma. Then close your eyes."

Ma looked at me suspiciously for a second, her eyebrows rising, but then she did as I asked. "Okay," she said, her hands clasped in her lap. "I'm ready."

I turned the engine back on and inched forward, then I put the car in neutral and we sailed down the hill, faster and faster and faster, and my stomach rose up to my throat, just as it had when I was girl, discovering gravity for the first time on our improvised roller-coaster, and the wind grabbed our hair as we fell and I wanted to throw my arms up, but before I could, Ma reached out and grabbed my hand in hers and squeezed, hard.

"Aaaiieee!" she shouted.

And then we were at the bottom of the hill, the cornfields rising up around the car as though we had just dropped into the ocean from a great height, splashing the ink-black seawater up around us in walls. The sky was a circle above our heads, the stars like distant eyes, blinking, the road before us too shadowed to see.

We sat like this, in the belly of the prairie, for quite some time.

ACKNOWLEDGMENTS

Dragon Chica was first inspired by my experiences living in the Midwest from 1979–1989. During this time, the American Heartland witnessed a vast number of cultural changes, including the economic devastation of family farms which affected businesses both small and large throughout the region. The Midwest also confronted social change. For the first time in decades, new immigrants began to make their way inland, searching for their own American dream. Many of these newcomers were Southeast Asians who had survived the wars in Vietnam, Cambodia, and Laos. My own family moved to the Midwest from the East Coast in 1979. I remember a profound sense of culture shock upon moving to a rural town after having lived in the New York metropolitan area. Unfortunately, I also remember the violence my family encountered as we tried to fit into our new surroundings. As a mixed-race family—my father is Chinese, my mother Caucasian—we were seen as harbingers of change, both racial and cultural, that many people feared.

When I was fifteen and writing for our town newspaper, a Sino-Cambodian family moved to our town to open a Chinese restaurant. The movie *The Killing Fields* had just opened. I interviewed the mother about her experiences under the Khmer Rouge, and she told me how three of her children had died before she could escape to a refugee camp in Thailand. However, her family received so many threats that she moved the family away from our town before I could finish writing my article. My inability to tell her story has haunted me for years.

In college, I co-founded a student group to mentor the children of 70 Southeast Asian refugee families who'd been relocated to Grinnell, Iowa. Later, as an Associated Press reporter, I made sure to include the Cambodian community in my articles, especially as they rebuilt Buddhist temples in America. My first short story about Cambodians in America was published in *Seventeen* in 1994. When I created Nea, she became the protagonist who could best narrate the experiences of so many Cambodians and Cambodian Americans whom I had met over the years. She cannot, of course, represent everyone, but she embodies the fighting spirit, the loyalty, the pain, and the promise of a new generation.

I would like to acknowledge many people and organizations for their assistance: Joe Bargmann, the former fiction editor of *Seventeen* magazine for his encouragement as I first began to tell this story; the Cambodian Buddhist Society of Des Moines, Iowa, and the Venerable Vannak Troeng; the erstwhile Cambodian Student Association of the University of Colorado-Boulder (1993); the Chhin family; Daophahat Khanakhounkhong for long ago telling me about his experiences as a Buddhist acolyte; the Grinnell College A.S.I.A. Club; Howard Junker, editor of *Zyzzyva*; Dennis and Karla Lappe for their hospitality in Des Moines and Clive, Iowa; the New Mandarin Restaurant of Laramie, Wyoming, and especially its generous owners, the Huang family; Lorraine Saulino-Klein; my students from Amherst College who participated in our Special Topics course "Hidden Histories: Gender and War" for asking tough questions and seeking answers—Justine Chae, Francis Lee, Patty Limaco, Sharon Lin, and Eugenia Tsai; and cover model Lotus Tai. I owe a special debt of gratitude to Winberg Chai for reading multiple versions of this story over the years; the National Endowment for the Arts whose generous support made it possible for me to write this novel; Penn Whaling for her unflagging enthusiasm; and my most gracious and judicious editor, Trish O'Hare.

Portions of *Dragon Chica* first appeared in *The Compact Bedford Introduction to Literature*, *The Jakarta Post Weekender Magazine*, my short story collection *Glamorous Asians*, *Seventeen* and *Zyzzyva*, in somewhat different form.

MAY-LEE CHAI

May-lee Chai is the author of six internationally acclaimed books, including the award-winning memoir *Hapa Girl* and *The Girl from Purple Mountain*, written with her father, Winberg Chai, which was nominated for the National Book Award. She is the recipient of an NEA Grant in Literature: Fellowship in Prose. Her short stories and essays have appeared in publications in the U.S. and abroad, including *Seventeen*, *Missouri Review*, *North American Review* and *Zyzzyva*. A former reporter for the Associated Press, she currently writes for *The Jakarta Post Weekender Magazine* and is a Chinese translator for PEN American Center. She is the recipient of an Award for Creative Excellence in Screenwriting from ABC Entertainment Television Group.

May-lee Chai lives in San Francisco.